Here are fifteen of Isaac Asimov's expertly contrived stories of imagination. They vary from an absorbing tale of the frightening possibilities of a machine that views the past, to a chilling vignette about the first super-slow-motion film of an atomic explosion during which the unmistakable outline of – but that would be revealing too much.

Each story contains the ingredient that is vital to convincing science-fiction: an impeccable set of facts which only a distinguised, real-life biochemist like Isaac Asimov would have.

Also by Isaac Asimov

*Foundation*
*Foundation and Empire*
*Second Foundation*

*The Stars Like Dust*
*The Martian Way*
*The Currents of Space*
*The End of Eternity*
*The Naked Sun*
*The Caves of Steel*
*Asimov's Mysteries*
*The Gods Themselves*
*Nightfall One*
*Nightfall Two*

*I. Robot*
*The Rest of the Robots*

*The Early Asimov : Volume I*
*The Early Asimov : Volume II*
*The Early Asimov : Volume III*

*Nebula Award Stories* 8 (ed)
*The Stars in their Courses* (non-fiction)
*Tales of the Black Widowers* (detection stories)

Isaac Asimov

# Earth Is Room Enough

Panther

Granada Publishing Limited
Published in 1960 by Panther Books Ltd
Frogmore, St Albans, Herts AL2 2NF
Reprinted 1962, 1967 (twice), 1969, 1971, 1972 (twice),
1973, 1975, 1977

First published in the U.S.A. by
Doubleday & Co Inc 1957
Copyright © Isaac Asimov 1957
Made and printed in Great Britain by
Hunt Barnard Printing Ltd
Aylesbury, Bucks
Set in Monotype Plantin

# DEDICATION

# Contents

# The Dead Past

ARNOLD POTTERLEY, Ph.D., was a Professor of Ancient History. That, in itself, was not dangerous. What changed the world beyond all dreams was the fact that he *looked* like a Professor of Ancient History.

Thaddeus Araman, Department Head of the Division of Chronoscopy, might have taken proper action if Dr. Potterley had been owner of a large, square chin, flashing eyes, aquiline nose and broad shoulders.

As it was, Thaddeus Araman found himself staring over his desk at a mild-mannered individual, whose faded blue eyes looked at him wistfully from either side of a low-bridged button nose; whose small, neatly dressed figure seemed stamped "milk-and-water" from thinning brown hair to the neatly brushed shoes that completed a conservative middle-class costume.

Araman said pleasantly, "And now what can I do for you, Dr. Potterley?"

Dr. Potterley said in a soft voice that went well with the rest of him, "Mr. Araman, I came to you because you're top man in chronoscopy."

Araman smiled. "Not exactly. Above me is the World Commissioner of Research and above him is the Secretary-General of the United Nations. And above both of them, of course, are the sovereign peoples of Earth."

Dr. Potterley shook his head. "They're not interested in chronoscopy. I've come to you, sir, because for two years I have been trying to obtain permission to do some time viewing—chronoscopy, that is—in connection with my researches on ancient Carthage. I can't obtain such permission. My research grants are all proper. There is no irregularity in any of my intellectual endeavors and yet——"

"I'm sure there is no question of irregularity," said Araman soothingly. He flipped the thin reproduction sheets in the folder to which Potterley's name had been attached. They had been produced by Multivac, whose vast analogical mind kept all the department records. When this was over, the sheets could be destroyed, then reproduced on demand in a matter of minutes.

And while Araman turned the pages, Dr. Potterley's voice continued in a soft monotone.

9

The historian was saying, "I must explain that my problem is quite an important one. Carthage was ancient commercialism brought to its zenith. Pre-Roman Carthage was the nearest ancient analogue to pre-atomic America, at least insofar as its attachment to trade, commerce and business in general was concerned. They were the most daring seamen and explorers before the Vikings; much better at it than the overrated Greeks.

"To know Carthage would be very rewarding, yet the only knowledge we have of it is derived from the writings of its bitter enemies, the Greeks and Romans. Carthage itself never wrote in its own defense or, if it did, the books did not survive. As a result, the Carthaginians have been one of the favorite sets of villains of history and perhaps unjustly so. Time viewing may set the record straight."

He said much more.

Araman said, still turning the reproduction sheets before him, "You must realize, Dr. Potterley, that chronoscopy, or time viewing, if you prefer, is a difficult process."

Dr. Potterley, who had been interrupted, frowned and said, "I am asking for only certain selected views at times and places I would indicate."

Araman sighed. "Even a few views, even one . . . It is an unbelievably delicate art. There is the question of focus, getting the proper scene in view and holding it. There is the synchronization of sound, which calls for completely independent circuits."

"Surely my problem is important enough to justify considerable effort."

"Yes, sir. Undoubtedly," said Araman at once. To deny the importance of someone's research problem would be unforgivably bad manners. "But you must understand how long-drawn-out even the simplest view is. And there is a long waiting line for the chronoscope and an even longer waiting line for the use of Multivac which guides us in our use of the controls."

Potterley stirred unhappily. "But can nothing be done? For two years——"

"A matter of priority, sir. I'm sorry. . . . Cigarette?"

The historian started back at the suggestion, eyes suddenly widening as he stared at the pack thrust out toward him. Araman looked surprised, withdrew the pack, made a motion as though to take a cigarette for himself and thought better of it.

Potterley drew a sigh of unfeigned relief as the pack was put out of sight. He said, "Is there any way of reviewing matters, putting me as far forward as possible. I don't know how to explain——"

Araman smiled. Some had offered money under similar circumstances which, of course, had gotten them nowhere, either.

He said, "The decisions on priority are computer-processed. I could in no way alter those decisions arbitrarily."

Potterley rose stiffly to his feet. He stood five and a half feet tall. "Then, good day, sir."

"Good day, Dr. Potterley. And my sincerest regrets."

He offered his hand and Potterley touched it briefly.

The historian left, and a touch of the buzzer brought Araman's secretary into the room. He handed her the folder.

"These," he said, "may be disposed of."

Alone again, he smiled bitterly. Another item in his quarter-century's service to the human race. Service through negation.

At least this fellow had been easy to dispose of. Sometimes academic pressure had to be applied and even withdrawal of grants.

Five minutes later, he had forgotten Dr. Potterley. Nor, thinking back on it later, could he remember feeling any premonition of danger.


During the first year of his frustration, Arnold Potterley had experienced only that—frustration. During the second year, though, his frustration gave birth to an idea that first frightened and then fascinated him. Two things stopped him from trying to translate the idea into action, and neither barrier was the undoubted fact that his notion was a grossly unethical one.

The first was merely the continuing hope that the government would finally give its permission and make it unnecessary for him to do anything more. That hope had perished finally in the interview with Araman just completed.

The second barrier had been not a hope at all but a dreary realization of his own incapacity. He was not a physicist and he knew no physicists from whom he might obtain help. The Department of Physics at the university consisted of men well stocked with grants and well immersed in specialty. At best, they would not listen to him. At worst, they would report him for intellectual anarchy and even his basic Carthaginian grant might easily be withdrawn.

That he could not risk. And yet chronoscopy was the only way to carry on his work. Without it, he would be no worse off if his grant were lost.

The first hint that the second barrier might be overcome had come a week earlier than his interview with Araman, and it had gone unrecognized at the time. It had been at one of the faculty teas. Potterley attended these sessions unfailingly because he conceived attendance to be a duty, and he took his duties seriously. Once there, however, he conceived it to be no responsibility of his to make light conversation or new friends. He sipped abstemiously at a drink or two, exchanging a polite word with the dean or such department heads as happened to be present, bestowed a narrow smile on others and finally left early.

Ordinarily, he would have paid no attention, at that most recent tea, to a young man standing quietly, even diffidently, in one corner. He would never have dreamed of speaking to him. Yet a tangle of circumstance persuaded him this once to behave in a way contrary to his nature.

That morning at breakfast, Mrs. Potterley had announced somberly that once again she had dreamed of Laurel, but this time a Laurel grown up, yet retaining the three-year-old face that stamped her as their child. Potterley had let her talk. There had been a time when he fought her too frequent preoccupation with the past and death. Laurel would not come back to them, either through dreams or through talk. Yet if it appeased Caroline Potterley—let her dream and talk.

But when Potterley went to school that morning, he found himself for once affected by Caroline's inanities. Laurel grown up! She had died nearly twenty years ago; their only child, then and ever. In all that time, when he thought of her, it was as a three-year-old.

Now he thought: But if she were alive now, she wouldn't be three, she'd be nearly twenty-three.

Helplessly, he found himself trying to think of Laurel as growing progressively older; as finally becoming twenty-three. He did not quite succeed.

Yet he tried. Laurel using make-up. Laurel going out with boys. Laurel—getting married!

So it was that when he saw the young man hovering at the outskirts of the coldly circulating group of faculty men, it occurred to him quixotically that, for all he knew, a youngster just such as this might have married Laurel. That youngster himself, perhaps. . . .

Laurel might have met him, here at the university, or some evening when he might be invited to dinner at the Potterleys'. They might grow interested in one another. Laurel would surely have been pretty and this youngster looked well. He was dark in coloring, with a lean intent face and an easy carriage.

The tenuous daydream snapped, yet Potterley found himself staring foolishly at the young man, not as a strange face but as a possible son-in-law in the might-have-been. He found himself threading his way toward the man. It was almost a form of autohypnotism.

He put out his hand. "I am Arnold Potterley of the History Department. You're new here, I think?"

The youngster looked faintly astonished and fumbled with his drink, shifting it to his left hand in order to shake with his right. "Jonas Foster is my name, sir. I'm a new instructor in physics. I'm just starting this semester."

Potterley nodded. "I wish you a happy stay here and great success."

That was the end of it, then. Potterley had come uneasily to his senses, found himself embarrassed and moved off. He stared back over his shoulder once, but the illusion of relationship had gone. Reality was quite real once more and he was angry with himself for having fallen prey to his wife's foolish talk about Laurel.

But a week later, even while Araman was talking, the thought of that young man had come back to him. An instructor in physics. A new instructor. Had he been deaf at the time? Was there a short circuit between ear and brain? Or was it an automatic self-censorship because of the impending interview with the Head of Chronoscopy?

But the interview failed, and it was the thought of the young man with whom he had exchanged two sentences that prevented Potterley from elaborating his pleas for consideration. He was almost anxious to get away.

And in the autogiro express back to the university, he could almost wish he were superstitious. He could then console himself with the thought that the casual meaningless meeting had really been directed by a knowing and purposeful Fate.

Jonas Foster was not new to academic life. The long and rickety struggle for the doctorate would make anyone a veteran. Additional work as a postdoctorate teaching fellow acted as a booster shot.

But now he was Instructor Jonas Foster. Professorial dignity lay ahead. And he now found himself in a new sort of relationship toward other professors.

For one thing, they would be voting on future promotions. For another, he was in no position to tell so early in the game which particular member of the faculty might or might not have the ear of the dean or even of the university president. He did not fancy himself as a campus politican and was sure he would make a poor one, yet there was no point in kicking his own rear into blisters just to prove that to himself.

So Foster listened to this mild-mannered historian who, in some vague way, seemed nevertheless to radiate tension, and did not shut him up abruptly and toss him out. Certainly that was his first impulse.

He remembered Potterley well enough. Potterley had approached him at that tea (which had been a grizzly affair). The fellow had spoken two sentences to him stiffly, somehow glassy-eyed, had then come to himself with a visible start and hurried off.

It had amused Foster at the time, but now . . .

Potterley might have been deliberately trying to make his acquaintance, or, rather, to impress his own personality on Foster as that of a queer sort of duck, eccentric but harmless. He might now be probing Foster's views, searching for unsettling opinions. Surely, they ought to have done so before granting him his appointment. Still . . .

Potterley might be serious, might honestly not realize what he was doing. Or he might realize quite well what he was doing; he might be nothing more or less than a dangerous rascal.

Foster mumbled, "Well, now——" to gain time, and fished out a package of cigarettes, intending to offer one to Potterley and to light it and one for himself very slowly.

But Potterley said at once, "Please, Dr. Foster. No cigarettes."

Foster looked startled. "I'm sorry, sir."

"No. The regrets are mine. I cannot stand the odour. An idiosyncrasy, I'm sorry."

He was positively pale. Foster put away the cigarettes.

Foster, feeling the absence of the cigarette, took the easy way out. "I'm flattered that you ask my advice and all that, Dr. Potterley, but I'm not a neutrinics man. I can't very well do anything professional in that direction. Even stating an opinion would be out of line, and, frankly, I'd prefer that you didn't go into any particulars."

The historian's prim face set hard. "What do you mean, you're not a neutrinics man? You're not anything yet. You haven't received any grant, have you?"

"This is only my first semester."

"I know that. I imagine you haven't even applied for any grant yet."

Foster half-smiled. In three months at the university, he had not succeeded in putting his initial requests for research grants into good enough shape to pass on to a professional science writer, let alone to the Research Commission.

(His Department Head, fortunately, took it quite well. "Take your time now, Foster," he said, "and get your thoughts well organized. Make sure you know your path and where it will lead, for, once you receive a grant, your specialization will be formally recognized and, for better or for worse, it will be yours for the rest of your career." The advice was trite enough, but triteness has often the merit of truth, and Foster recognized that.)

Foster said, "By education and inclination, Dr. Potterley, I'm a hyperoptics man with a gravitics minor. It's how I described myself in applying for this position. It may not be my official specialization yet, but it's going to be. It can't be anything else. As for neutrinics, I never even studied the subject."

"Why not!" demanded Potterley at once.

Foster stared. It was the kind of rude curiosity about another man's professional status that was always irritating. He said, with the edge of his own politeness just a trifle blunted, "A course in neutrinics wasn't given at my university."

"Good Lord, where did you go?"

"M.I.T.," said Foster quietly.

"And they don't teach neutrinics?"

"No, they don't." Foster felt himself flush and was moved to a defense. "It's a highly specialized subject with no great value. Chronoscopy, perhaps, has some value, but it is the only practical application and that's a dead end."

The historian stared at him earnestly. "Tell me this. Do you know where I can find a neutrinics man?"

"No, I don't," said Foster bluntly.

"Well, then, do you know a school which teaches neutrinics?"

"No, I don't."

Potterley smiled tightly and without humour.

Foster resented that smile, found he detected insult in it and grew sufficiently annoyed to say, "I would like to point out, sir, that you're stepping out of line."

"What?"

"I'm saying that, as a historian, your interest in any sort of physics, your *professional* interest, is——" He paused, unable to bring himself quite to say the word.

"Unethical?"

"That's the word, Dr. Potterley."

"My researches have driven me to it," said Potterley in an intense whisper.

"The Research Commission is the place to go. If they permit——"

"I have gone to them and have received no satisfaction."

"Then obviously you must abandon this." Foster knew he was sounding stuffily virtuous, but he wasn't going to let this man lure him into an expression of intellectual anarchy. It was too early in his career to take stupid risks.

Apparently, though, the remark had its effect on Potterley. Without any warning, the man exploded into a rapid-fire verbal storm of irresponsibility.

Scholars, he said, could be free only if they could freely follow their own free-swinging curiosity. Research, he said, forced into a predesigned pattern by the powers that held the purse strings became slavish and had to stagnate. No man, he said, had the right to dictate the intellectual interests of another.

Foster listened to all of it with disbelief. None of it was strange to him. He had heard college boys talk so in order to shock their professors and he had once or twice amused himself in that fashion, too. Anyone who studied the history of science knew that many men had once thought so.

Yet it seemed strange to Foster, almost against nature, that a modern man of science could advance such nonsense. No one would advocate running a factory by allowing each individual worker to do whatever pleased him at the moment, or of running a ship according to the casual and conflicting notions of each individual crewman. It would be taken for granted that some sort of centralized supervisory agency must exist in each case. Why should direction and order benefit a factory and a ship but not scientific research?

People might say that the human mind was somehow qualitatively different from a ship or factory but the history of intellectual endeavor proved the opposite.

When science was young and the intricacies of all or most of the known was within the grasp of an individual mind, there was no need for direction, perhaps. Blind wandering over the uncharted tracts of ignorance could lead to wonderful finds by accident.

But as knowledge grew, more and more data had to be absorbed before worthwhile journeys into ignorance could be organized. Men had to specialize. The researcher needed the resources of a library he himself could not gather, then of instruments he himself could not afford. More and more, the individual researcher gave way to the research team and the research institution.

The funds necessary for research grew greater as tools grew more numerous. What college was so small today as not to require at least one nuclear micro-reactor and at least one three-stage computer?

Centuries before, private individuals could no longer subsidize research. By 1940, only the government, large industries and large universities or research institutions could properly subsidize basic research.

By 1960, even the largest universities depended entirely upon government grants, while research institutions could not exist without tax concessions and public subscriptions. By 2000, the industrial combines had become a branch of the world government and, thereafter, the financing of research and therefore its direction naturally became centralized under a department of the government.

It all worked itself out naturally and well. Every branch of science was fitted neatly to the needs of the public, and the various branches of science were co-ordinated decently. The material advance of the last half-century was argument enough for the fact that science was not falling into stagnation.

Foster tried to say a very little of this and was waved aside impatiently by Potterley who said, "You are parroting official propaganda. You're sitting in the middle of an example that's squarely against the official view. Can you believe that?"

"Frankly, no."

"Well, why do you say time viewing is a dead end? Why is neutrinics unimportant? You say it is. You say it categorically. Yet you've never studied it. You claim complete ignorance of the subject. It's not even given in your school——"

"Isn't the mere fact that it isn't given proof enough?"

"Oh, I see. It's not given because it's unimportant. And it's unimportant because it's not given. Are you satisfied with that reasoning?"

Foster felt a growing confusion. "It's in the books."

"That's all. The books say neutrinics is unimportant. Your professors tell you so because they read it in the books. The books say so because professors write them. Who says it from personal experience and knowledge? Who does research in it? Do you know of anyone?"

Foster said, "I don't see that we're getting anywhere, Dr. Potterley. I have work to do——"

"One minute. I just want you to try this on. See how it sounds to you. I say the government is actively suppressing basic research in neutrinics and chronoscopy. They're suppressing application of chronoscopy."

"Oh, no."

"Why not? They could do it. There's your centrally directed research. If they refuse grants for research in any portion of science, that portion dies. They've killed neutrinics. They can do it and have done it."

"But why?"

"I don't know why. I want you to find out. I'd do it myself if I knew enough. I came to you because you're a young fellow with a brand-new education. Have your intellectual arteries hardened already? Is there no curiosity in you? Don't you want to *know*? Don't you want *answers*?"

The historian was peering intently into Foster's face. Their noses were only inches apart, and Foster was so lost that he did not think to draw back.

He should, by rights, have ordered Potterley out. If necessary, he should have thrown Potterley out.

It was not respect for age and position that stopped him. It was certainly not that Potterley's arguments had convinced him. Rather, it was a small point of college pride.

Why didn't M.I.T. give a course in neutrinics? For that matter, now that he came to think of it, he doubted that there was a single book on neutrinics in the library. He could never recall having seen one.

He stopped to think about that.

And that was ruin.


Caroline Potterley had once been an attractive woman. There were occasions, such as dinners or university functions, when, by considerable effort, remnants of the attraction could be salvaged.

On ordinary occasions, she sagged. It was the word she applied to herself in moments of self-abhorrence. She had grown plumper with the years, but the flaccidity about her was not a matter of fat entirely. It was as though her muscles had given up and grown limp so that she shuffled when she walked while her eyes grew baggy and her cheeks jowly. Even her graying hair seemed tired rather than merely stringy. Its straightness seemed to be the result of a supine surrender to gravity, nothing else.

Caroline Potterley looked at herself in the mirror and admitted this was one of her bad days. She knew the reason, too.

It had been the dream of Laurel. The strange one, with Laurel grown up. She had been wretched ever since.

Still, she was sorry she had mentioned it to Arnold. He didn't say anything; he never did any more; but it was bad for him. He was particularly withdrawn for days afterward. It might have been that he was getting ready for that important conference with the big government official (he kept saying he expected no success), but it might also have been her dream.

It was better in the old days when he would cry sharply at her, "Let the dead past *go*, Caroline! Talk won't bring her back, and dreams won't either."

It had been bad for both of them. Horribly bad. She had been away from home and had lived in guilt ever since. If she had stayed at home, if she had not gone on an unnecessary shopping expedition, there would have been two of them available. One would have succeeded in saving Laurel.

Poor Arnold had not managed. Heaven knew he tried. He had nearly died himself. He had come out of the burning house, staggering in agony, blistered, choking, half-blinded, with the dead Laurel in his arms.

The nightmare of that lived on, never lifting entirely.

Arnold slowly grew a shell about himself afterward. He cultivated a low-voiced mildness through which nothing broke, no lightning struck. He grew puritanical and even abandoned his minor vices, his cigarettes, his penchant for an occasional profane exclamation. He obtained his grant for the preparation of a new history of Carthage and subordinated everything to that.

She tried to help him. She hunted up his references, typed his notes and microfilmed them. Then that ended suddenly.

She ran from the desk suddenly one evening, reaching the bathroom in bare time and retching abominably. Her husband followed her in confusion and concern.

"Caroline, what's wrong?"

It took a drop of brandy to bring her around. She said, "Is it true? What they did?"

"Who did?"

"The Carthaginians."

He stared at her and she got it out by indirection. She couldn't say it right out.

The Carthaginians, it seemed, worshiped Moloch, in the form of a hollow, brazen idol with a furnace in its belly. At times of national crisis, the priests and the people gathered, and infants, after the proper ceremonies and invocations, were dextrously hurled, alive, into the flames.

They were given sweetmeats just before the crucial moment, in order that the efficacy of the sacrifice not be ruined by displeasing cries of panic. The drums rolled just after the moment, to drown out the few seconds of infant shrieking. The parents were present, presumably gratified, for the sacrifice was pleasing to the gods. . . .

Arnold Potterley frowned darkly. Vicious lies, he told her, on the part of Carthage's enemies. He should have warned her. After all, such propagandistic lies were not uncommon. According to the Greeks, the ancient Hebrews worshiped an ass's head in their Holy of Holies. According to the Romans, the primitive Christians were haters of all men who sacrificed pagan children in the catacombs.

"Then they didn't do it?" asked Caroline.

"I'm sure they didn't. The primitive Phoenicians may have. Human sacrifice is commonplace in primitive cultures. But Carthage in her great days was not a primitive culture. Human sacrifice often gives way to symbolic actions such as circumcision. The Greeks and Romans might have mistaken some Carthaginian symbolism for the original full rite, either out of ignorance or out of malice."

"Are you sure?"

"I can't be sure yet, Caroline, but when I've got enough evidence, I'll apply for permission to use chronoscopy, which will settle the matter once and for all."

"Chronoscopy?"

"Time viewing. We can focus on ancient Carthage at some time of crisis, the landing of Scipio Africanus in 202 B.C., for instance, and see with our own eyes exactly what happens. And you'll see, I'll be right."

He patted her and smiled encouragingly, but she dreamed of Laurel every night for two weeks thereafter and she never helped him with his Carthage project again. Nor did he ever ask her to.

But now she was bracing herself for his coming. He had called her after arriving back in town, told her he had seen the government man and that it had gone as expected. That meant failure, and yet the little telltale sign of depression had been absent from his voice and his features had appeared quite composed in the teleview. He had another errand to take care of, he said, before coming home.

It meant he would be late, but that didn't matter. Neither one of them was particular about eating hours or cared when packages were taken out of the freezer or even which packages or when the self-warming mechanism was activated.

When he did arrive, he surprised her. There was nothing untoward about him in any obvious way. He kissed her dutifully and smiled, took off his hat and asked if all had been well while he was gone. It was all almost perfectly normal. Almost.

She had learned to detect small things, though, and his pace in all this was a trifle hurried. Enough to show her accustomed eye that he was under tension.

She said, "Has something happened?"

He said, "We're going to have a dinner guest night after next, Caroline. You don't mind?"

"Well, no. Is it anyone I know?"

"No. A young instructor. A newcomer. I've spoken to him." He suddenly whirled toward her and seized her arms at the elbow, held them a moment, then dropped them in confusion as though disconcerted at having shown emotion.

He said, "I almost didn't get through to him. Imagine that. Terrible, *terrible*, the way we have all bent to the yoke; the affection we have for the harness about us."

Mrs. Potterley wasn't sure she understood, but for a year she had been watching him grow quietly more rebellious; little by little more daring in his criticism of the government. She said, "You haven't spoken foolishly to him, have you?"

"What do you mean, foolishly? He'll be doing some neutrinics for me."

"Neutrinics" was trisyllabic nonsense to Mrs. Potterley, but she knew it had nothing to do with history. She said faintly, "Arnold, I don't like you to do that. You'll lose your position. It's——"

"It's intellectual anarchy, my dear," he said. "That's the phrase you want. Very well. I am an anarchist. If the government will not allow me to push my researches, I will push them on my own. And when I show the way, others will follow. . . . And if they don't, it makes no difference. It's Carthage that counts and human knowledge, not you and I."

"But you don't know this young man. What if he is an agent for the Commissioner of Research."

"Not likely and I'll take that chance." He made a fist of his right hand and rubbed it gently against the palm of his left. "He's on my side now. I'm sure of it. He can't help but be. I can recognize intellectual curiosity when I see it in a man's eyes and face and attitude, and it's a fatal disease for a tame scientist. Even today it takes time to beat it out of a man and the young ones are vulnerable. . . . Oh, why stop at anything? Why not build our own chronoscope and tell the government to go to——"

He stopped abruptly, shook his head and turned away.

"I hope everything will be all right," said Mrs. Potterley, feeling helplessly certain that everything would not be, and frightened, in advance, for her husband's professorial status and the security of their old age.

It was she alone, of them all, who had a violent presentiment of trouble. Quite the wrong trouble, of course.

Jonas Foster was nearly half an hour late in arriving at the Potterleys' off-campus house. Up to that very evening, he had not quite decided he would go. Then, at the last moment, he found he could not bring himself to commit the social enormity of breaking a dinner appointment an hour before the appointed time. That, and the nagging of curiosity.

The dinner itself passed interminably. Foster ate without appetite. Mrs. Potterley sat in distant absent-mindedness, emerging out of it only once to ask if he were married and to make a deprecating sound at the news that he was not. Dr. Potterley himself asked neutrally after his professional history and nodded his head primly.

It was as staid, stodgy—boring, actually—as anything could be. Foster thought: He seems so harmless.

Foster had spent the last two days reading up on Dr. Potterley. Very casually, of course, almost sneakily. He wasn't particularly anxious to be seen in the Social Science Library. To be sure, history was one of those borderline affairs and historical works were frequently read for amusement or edification by the general public.

Still, a physicist wasn't quite the "general public." Let Foster take to reading histories and he would be considered queer, sure as relativity, and after a while the Head of the Department would wonder if his new instructor were really "the man for the job."

So he had been cautious. He sat in the more secluded alcoves and kept his head bent when he slipped in and out at odd hours.

Dr. Potterley, it turned out, had written three books and some dozen articles on the ancient Mediterranean worlds, and the later articles (all in "Historical Reviews") had all dealt with pre-Roman Carthage from a sympathetic viewpoint.

That, at least, checked with Potterley's story and had soothed Foster's suspicions somewhat. . . . And yet Foster felt that it would have been much wiser, much safer, to have scotched the matter at the beginning.

A scientist shouldn't be too curious, he thought in bitter dissatisfaction with himself. It's a dangerous trait.

After dinner, he was ushered into Potterley's study and he was brought up sharply at the threshold. The walls were simply lined with books.

Not merely films. There were films, of course, but these were far outnumbered by the books—print on paper. He wouldn't have thought so many books would exist in usable condition.

That bothered Foster. Why should anyone want to keep so many books at home? Surely all were available in the university library, or, at the very worst, at the Library of Congress, if one wished to take the minor trouble of checking out a microfilm.

There was an element of secrecy involved in a home library. It breathed of intellectual anarchy. That last thought, oddly, calmed Foster. He would rather Potterley be an authentic anarchist than a play-acting *agent provocateur*.

And now the hours began to pass quickly and astonishingly.

"You see," Potterley said, in a clear, unflurried voice, "it was a matter of finding, if possible, anyone who had ever used chronoscopy in his work. Naturally, I couldn't ask baldly, since that would be unauthorized research."

"Yes," said Foster dryly. He was a little surprised such a small consideration would stop the man.

"I used indirect methods——"

He had. Foster was amazed at the volume of correspondence dealing with small disputed points of ancient Mediterranean culture which somehow managed to elicit the casual remark over and over again: "Of course, having never made use of chronoscopy——" or, "Pending approval of my request for chronoscopic data, which appears unlikely at the moment——"

"Now these aren't blind questionings," said Potterley. "There's a monthly booklet put out by the Institute for Chronoscopy in which items concerning the past as determined by time viewing are printed. Just one or two items.

"What impressed me first was the triviality of most of the items, their insipidity. Why should such researches get priority over my work? So I wrote to people who would be most likely to do research in the directions described in the booklet. Uniformly, as I have shown you, they did *not* make use of the chronoscope. Now let's go over it point by point."

At last Foster, his head swimming with Potterley's meticulously gathered details, asked, "But why?"

"I don't know why," said Potterley, "but I have a theory. The original invention of the chronoscope was by Sterbinski—you see, I know that much—and it was well publicized. But then the government took over the instrument and decided to suppress further research in the matter or any use of the machine. But then, people might be curious as to why it wasn't being used. Curiosity is such a vice, Dr. Foster."

Yes, agreed the physicist to himself.

"Imagine the effectiveness, then," Potterley went on, "of pretending that the chronoscope *was* being used. It would then be not a mystery, but a commonplace. It would no longer be a fitting object for legitimate curiosity or an attractive one for illicit curiosity."

"*You* were curious," pointed out Foster.

Potterley looked a trifle restless. "It was different in my case," he said angrily. "I have something that *must* be done, and I wouldn't submit to the ridiculous way in which they kept putting me off."

A bit paranoid, too, thought Foster gloomily.

Yet he had ended up with something, paranoid or not. Foster could no longer deny that something peculiar was going on in the matter of neutrinics.

But what was Potterley after? That still bothered Foster. If Potterley didn't intend this as a test of Foster's ethics, what *did* he want?

Foster put it to himself logically. If an intellectual anarchist with a touch of paranoia wanted to use a chronoscope and was convinced that the powers-that-be were deliberately standing in his way, what would he do?

Supposing it were I, he thought. What would I do?

He said slowly, "Maybe the chronoscope doesn't exist at all?"

Potterley started. There was almost a crack in his general

calmness. For an instant, Foster found himself catching a glimpse of something not at all calm.

But the historian kept his balance and said, "Oh, no, there *must* be a chronoscope."

"Why? Have you seen it? Have I? Maybe that's the explanation of everything. Maybe they're not deliberately holding out on a chronoscope they've got. Maybe they haven't got it in the first place."

"But Sterbinski lived. He built a chronoscope. That much is a fact."

"The books say so," said Foster coldly.

"Now listen." Potterley actually reached over and snatched at Foster's jacket sleeve. "I need the chronoscope. I must have it. Don't tell me it doesn't exist. What we're going to do is find out enough about neutrinics to be able to——"

Potterley drew himself up short.

Foster drew his sleeve away. He needed no ending to that sentence. He supplied it himself. He said, "Build one of our own?"

Potterley looked sour as though he would rather not have said it point-blank. Nevertheless, he said, "Why not?"

"Because that's out of the question," said Foster. "If what I've read is correct, then it took Sterbinski twenty years to build his machine and several millions in composite grants. Do you think you and I can duplicate that illegally? Suppose we had the time, which we haven't, and suppose I could learn enough out of books, which I doubt, where would we get the money and equipment? The chronoscope is supposed to fill a five-story building, for Heaven's sake."

"Then you won't help me?"

"Well, I'll tell you what. I have one way in which I may be able to find out something——"

"What is that?" asked Potterley at once.

"Never mind. That's not important. But I may be able to find out enough to tell you whether the government is deliberately suppressing research by chronoscope. I may confirm the evidence you already have or I may be able to prove that your evidence is misleading. I don't know what good it will do you in either case, but it's as far as I can go. It's my limit."

Potterley watched the young man go finally. He was angry with himself. Why had he allowed himself to grow so careless as to permit the fellow to guess that he was thinking in terms of a chronoscope of his own. That was premature.

But then why did the young fool have to suppose that a chronoscope might not exist at all?

It *had* to exist. It *had* to. What was the use of saying it didn't?

And why couldn't a second one be built? Science had advanced in the fifty years since Sterbinski. All that was needed was knowledge.

Let the youngster gather knowledge. Let him think a small gathering would be his limit. Having taken the path to anarchy, there would be no limit. If the boy were not driven onward by something in himself, the first steps would be error enough to force the rest. Potterley was quite certain he would not hesitate to use blackmail.

Potterley waved a last good-bye and looked up. It was beginning to rain.

Certainly! Blackmail if necessary, but he would not be stopped.

Foster steered his car across the bleak outskirts of town and scarcely noticed the rain.

He *was* a fool, he told himself, but he couldn't leave things as they were. He had to know. He damned his streak of undisciplined curiosity, but he had to know.

But he would go no further than Uncle Ralph. He swore mightily to himself that it would stop there. In that way, there would be no evidence against him, no real evidence. Uncle Ralph would be discreet.

In a way, he was secretly ashamed of Uncle Ralph. He hadn't mentioned him to Potterley partly out of caution and partly because he did not wish to witness the lifted eyebrow, the inevitable half-smile. Professional science writers, however useful, were a little outside the pale, fit only for patronizing contempt. The fact that, as a class, they made more money than did research scientists only made matters worse, of course.

Still, there were times when a science writer in the family could be a convenience. Not being really educated, they did not have to specialize. Consequently, a good science writer knew practically everything. . . . And Uncle Ralph was one of the best.

Ralph Nimmo had no college degree and was rather proud of it. "A degree," he once said to Jonas Foster, when both were considerably younger, 'is a first step down a ruinous highway. You don't want to waste it so you go on to graduate work and doctoral research. You end up a thoroughgoing ignoramus on everything in the world except for one subdivisional sliver of nothing.

"On the other hand, if you guard your mind carefully and keep it blank of any clutter of information till maturity is reached, filling it only with intelligence and training it only in clear thinking, you then have a powerful instrument at your disposal and you can become a science writer."

Nimmo received his first assignment at the age of twenty-five, after he had completed his apprenticeship and been out in the field for less than three months. It came in the shape of a clotted manuscript whose language would impart no glimmering of understanding to any reader, however qualified, without careful study and some inspired guesswork. Nimmo took it apart and put it together again (after five long and exasperating interviews with the authors, who were biophysicists), making the language taut and meaningful and smoothing the style to a pleasant gloss.

"Why not?" he would say tolerantly to his nephew, who countered his strictures on degrees by berating him with his readiness to hang on the fringes of science. "The fringe is important. Your scientists can't write. Why should they be expected to? They aren't expected to be grand masters at chess or virtuosos at the violin, so why expect them to know how to put words together? Why not leave that for specialists, too?

"Good Lord, Jonas, read your literature of a hundred years ago. Discount the fact that the science is out of date and that some of the expressions are out of date. Just try to read it and make sense out of it. It's just jaw-cracking, amateurish. Pages are published uselessly; whole articles which are either non-comprehensible or both."

"But you don't get recognition, Uncle Ralph," protested young Foster, who was getting ready to start his college career and was rather starry-eyed about it. "You could be a terrific researcher."

"I get recognition," said Nimmo. "Don't think for a minute I don't. Sure, a biochemist or a strato-meteorologist won't give me the time of day, but they pay me well enough. Just find out what happens when some first-class chemist finds the Commission has cut his year's allowance for science writing. He'll fight harder for enough funds to afford me, or someone like me, than to get a recording ionograph."

He grinned broadly and Foster grinned back. Actually, he was proud of his paunchy, round-faced, stub-fingered uncle, whose vanity made him brush his fringe of hair futilely over the desert on his pate and made him dress like an unmade haystack because such negligence was his trademark. Ashamed, but proud, too.

And now Foster entered his uncle's cluttered apartment in no mood at all for grinning. He was nine years older now and so was Uncle Ralph. For nine more years, papers in every branch of science had come to him for polishing and a little of each had crept into his capacious mind.

Nimmo was eating seedless grapes, popping them into his mouth one at a time. He tossed a bunch to Foster who caught them by a hair, then bent to retrieve individual grapes that had torn loose and fallen to the floor.

"Let them be. Don't bother," said Nimmo carelessly. "Someone comes in here to clean once a week. What's up? Having trouble with your grant application write-up?"

"I haven't really got into that yet."

"You haven't? Get a move on, boy. Are you waiting for me to offer to do the final arrangement?"

"I couldn't afford you, Uncle."

"Aw, come on. It's all in the family. Grant me all popular publication rights and no cash need change hands."

Foster nodded. "If you're serious, it's a deal."

"It's a deal."

It was a gamble, of course, but Foster knew enough of Nimmo's science writing to realize it could pay off. Some dramatic discovery of public interest on primitive man or on a new surgical technique, or on any branch of spationautics could mean a very cash-attracting article in any of the mass media of communication.

It was Nimmo, for instance, who had written up, for scientific consumption, the series of papers by Bryce and co-workers that elucidated the fine structure of two cancer viruses, for which job he asked the picayune payment of fifteen hundred dollars, provided popular publication rights were included. He then wrote up, exclusively, the same work in semidramatic form for use in trimensional video for a twenty-thousand-dollar advance plus rental royalties that were still coming in after five years.

Foster said bluntly, "What do you know about neutrinics, Uncle?"

"Neutrinics?" Nimmo's small eyes looked surprised. "Are you working in that? I thought it was pseudo-gravitic optics."

"It is p.g.o. I just happen to be asking about neutrinics."

"That's a devil of a thing to be doing. You're stepping out of line. You know that, don't you?"

"I don't expect you to call the Commission because I'm a little curious about things."

"Maybe I should before you get into trouble. Curiosity is an occupational danger with scientists. I've watched it work. One of them will be moving quietly along on a problem, then curiosity leads him up a strange creek. Next thing you know they've done so little on their proper problem, they can't justify for a project renewal. I've seen more——"

"All I want to know," said Foster patiently, "is what's been passing through your hands lately on neutrinics."

Nimmo leaned back, chewing at a grape thoughtfully. "Nothing. Nothing ever. I don't recall ever getting a paper on neutrinics."

"What!" Foster was openly astonished. "Then who does get the work?"

"Now that you ask," said Nimmo, "I don't know. Don't recall anyone talking about it at the annual conventions. I don't think much work is being done there."

"Why not?"

"Hey, there, don't bark. I'm not doing anything. My guess would be——"

Foster was exasperated. "Don't you know?"

"Hmp. I'll tell you what I know about neutrinics. It concerns the applications of neutrino movements and the forces involved——"

"Sure. Sure. Just as electronics deals with the applications of electron movements and the forces involved, and pseudo-gravitics deals with the applications of artificial gravitational fields. I didn't come to you for that. Is that all you know?"

"And," said Nimmo with equanimity, "neutrinics is the basis of time viewing and that *is* all I know."

Foster slouched back in his chair and massaged one lean cheek with great intensity. He felt angrily dissatisfied. Without formulating it explicitly in his own mind, he had felt sure, somehow, that Nimmo would come up with some late reports, bring up interesting facets of modern neutrinics, send him back to Potterley able to say that the elderly historian was mistaken, that his data was misleading, his deductions mistaken.

Then he could have returned to his proper work.

But now...

He told himself angrily: So they're not doing much work in the field. Does that make it deliberate suppression? What if neutrinics is a sterile discipline? Maybe it is. I don't know. Potterley doesn't. Why waste the intellectual resources of humanity on nothing? Or the work might be secret for some legitimate reason. It might be . . .

The trouble was, he had to know. He couldn't leave things as they were now. *He couldn't!*

He said, "Is there a text on neutrinics, Uncle Ralph? I mean a clear and simple one. An elementary one."

Nimmo thought, his plump cheeks puffing out with a series of sighs. "You ask the damnedest questions. The only one I ever heard of was Sterbinski and somebody. I've never seen it, but I viewed something about it once. . . . Sterbinski and LaMarr, that's it."

"Is that the Sterbinski who invented the chronoscope?"

"I think so. Proves the book ought to be good."

"Is there a recent edition? Sterbinski died thirty years ago."
Nimmo shrugged and said nothing.

"Can you find out?"

They sat in silence for a moment, while Nimmo shifted his bulk to the creaking tune of the chair he sat on. Then the science writer said, "Are you going to tell me what this is all about?"

"I can't. Will you help me anyway, Uncle Ralph? Will you get me a copy of the text?"

"Well, you've taught me all I know on pseudo-gravitics. I should be grateful. Tell you what—I'll help you on one condition."

"Which is?"

The older man was suddenly very grave. "That you be careful, Jonas. You're obviously way out of line whatever you're doing. Don't blow up your career just because you're curious about something you haven't been assigned to and which is none of your business. Understand?"

Foster nodded, but he hardly heard. He was thinking furiously.

A full week later, Ralph Nimmo eased his rotund figure into Jonas Foster's on-campus two-room combination and said, in a hoarse whisper, "I've got something."

"What?" Foster was immediately eager.

"A copy of Sterbinski and LaMarr." He produced it, or rather a corner of it, from his ample topcoat.

Foster almost automatically eyed door and windows to make sure they were closed and shaded respectively, then held out his hand.

The film case was flaking with age, and when he cracked it the film was faded and growing brittle. He said sharply, "Is this all?"

"Gratitude, my boy, gratitude!" Nimmo sat down with a grunt, and reached into a pocket for an apple.

"Oh, I'm grateful, but it's so old."

"And lucky to get it at that. I tried to get a film run from the Congressional Library. No go. The book was restricted."

"Then how did you get this?"

"Stole it." He was biting crunchingly around the core. "New York Public."

"What?"

"Simple enough. I had access to the stacks, naturally. So I stepped over a chained railing when no one was around, dug this up, and walked out with it. They're very trusting out there. Meanwhile, they won't miss it in years. . . . Only you'd better not let anyone see it on you, nephew."

Foster stared at the film as though it were literally hot.

Nimmo discarded the core and reached for a second apple. "Funny thing, now. There's nothing more recent in the whole field of neutrinics. Not a monograph, not a paper, not a progress note. Nothing since the chronoscope."

"Uh-huh," said Foster absently.

Foster worked evenings in the Potterley home. He could not trust his own on-campus rooms for the purpose. The evening work grew more real to him than his own grant applications. Sometimes he worried about it but then that stopped, too.

His work consisted, at first, simply in viewing and reviewing the text film. Later it consisted in thinking (sometimes while a section of the book ran itself off through the pocket projector, disregarded).

Sometimes Potterley would come down to watch, to sit with prim, eager eyes, as though he expected thought processes to solidify and become visible in all their convolutions. He interfered in only two ways. He did not allow Foster to smoke and sometimes he talked.

It wasn't conversation talk, never that. Rather it was a low-voiced monologue with which, it seemed, he scarcely expected to command attention. It was much more as though he were relieving a pressure within himself.

Carthage! Always Carthage!

Carthage, the New York of the ancient Mediterranean. Carthage, commercial empire and queen of the seas. Carthage, all that Syracuse and Alexandria pretended to be. Carthage, maligned by her enemies and inarticulate in her own defense.

She had been defeated once by Rome and then driven out of Sicily and Sardinia, but came back to more than recoup her losses by new dominions in Spain, and raised up Hannibal to give the Romans sixteen years of terror.

In the end, she lost again a second time, reconciled herself to fate and built again with broken tools a limping life in shrunken territory, succeeding so well that jealous Rome deliberately forced a third war. And then Carthage, with nothing but bare hands and tenacity, built weapons and forced Rome into a two-year war that ended only with complete destruction of the city, the inhabitants throwing themselves into their flaming houses rather than surrender.

"Could people fight so for a city and a way of life as bad as the ancient writers painted it? Hannibal was a better general than any Roman and his soldiers were absolutely faithful to him. Even his bitterest enemies praised him. There was a Carthaginian. It is fashionable to say that he was an atypical Carthaginian, better than the others, a diamond placed in garbage. But then why was

he so faithful to Carthage, even to his death after years of exile ?
They talk of Moloch——"

Foster didn't always listen but sometimes he couldn't help
himself and he shuddered and turned sick at the bloody tale of
child sacrifice.

But Potterley went on earnestly, "Just the same, it isn't true.
It's a twenty-five-hundred-year-old canard started by the Greeks
and Romans. They had their own slaves, their crucifixions and
torture, their gladiatorial contests. They weren't holy. The
Moloch story is what later ages would have called war propaganda, the big lie. I can prove it was a lie. I can prove it and, by
Heaven, I will—I will——"

He would mumble that promise over and over again in his
earnestness.

Mrs. Potterley visited him also, but less frequently, usually on
Tuesdays and Thursdays when Dr. Potterley himself had an
evening course to take care of and was not present.

She would sit quietly, scarcely talking, face slack and doughy,
eyes blank, her whole attitude distant and withdrawn.

The first time, Foster tried, uneasily, to suggest that she leave.
She said tonelessly, "Do I disturb you ?"

"No, of course not," lied Foster restlessly. "It's just that—
that——" He couldn't complete the sentence.

She nodded, as though accepting an invitation to stay. Then
she opened a cloth bag she had brought with her and took out a
quire of vitron sheets which she proceeded to weave together by
rapid, delicate movements of a pair of slender, tetra-faceted
depolarizers, whose battery-fed wires made her look as though
she were holding a large spider.

One evening, she said softly, "My daughter, Laurel, is your
age."

Foster started, as much at the sudden unexpected sound of
speech as at the words. He said, "I didn't know you had a
daughter, Mrs. Potterley."

"She died. Years ago."

The vitron grew under the deft manipulations into the uneven
shape of some garment Foster could not yet identify. There was
nothing left for him to do but mutter inanely, "I'm sorry."

Mrs. Potterley sighed. "I dream about her often." She raised
her blue, distant eyes to him.

Foster winced and looked away.

Another evening she asked, pulling at one of the vitron sheets
to loosen its gentle clinging to her dress, "What is time viewing
anyway ?"

That remark broke into a particularly involved chain of

thought, and Foster said snappishly, "Dr. Potterley can explain."

"He's tried to. Oh, my, yes. But I think he's a little impatient with me. He calls it chronoscopy most of the time. Do you actually see things in the past, like the trimensionals? Or does it just make little dot patterns like the computer you use?"

Foster stared at his hand computer with distaste. It worked well enough, but every operation had to be manually controlled and the answers were obtained in code. Now if he could use the school computer . . . Well, why dream, he felt conspicuous enough, as it was, carrying a hand computer under his arm every evening as he left his office.

He said, "I've never seen the chronoscope myself, but I'm under the impression that you actually see pictures and hear sound."

"You can hear people talk, too?"

"I think so." Then, half in desperation, "Look here, Mrs. Potterley, this must be awfully dull for you. I realize you don't like to leave a guest all to himself, but really, Mrs. Potterley, you mustn't feel compelled——"

"I don't feel compelled," she said. "I'm sitting here, waiting."

"Waiting? For what?"

She said composedly, "I listened to you that first evening. The time you first spoke to Arnold. I listened at the door."

He said, "You did?"

"I know I shouldn't have, but I was awfully worried about Arnold. I had a notion he was going to do something he oughtn't and I wanted to hear what. And then when I heard——" She paused, bending close over the vitron and peering at it.

"Heard what, Mrs. Potterley?"

"That you wouldn't build a chronoscope."

"Well, of course not."

"I thought maybe you might change your mind."

Foster glared at her. "Do you mean you're coming down here hoping I'll build a chronoscope, waiting for me to build one?"

"I hope you do, Dr. Foster. Oh, I hope you do."

It was as though, all at once, a fuzzy veil had fallen off her face, leaving all her features clear and sharp, putting color into her cheeks, life into her eyes, the vibrations of something approaching excitement into her voice.

"Wouldn't it be wonderful," she whispered, "to have one? People of the past could live again. Pharoahs and kings and—just people. I hope you build one, Dr. Foster. I really—hope——"

She choked, it seemed, on the intensity of her own words and let the vitron sheets slip off her lap. She rose and ran up the basement stairs, while Foster's eyes followed her awkwardly fleeing body with astonishment and distress.

It cut deeper into Foster's nights and left him sleepless and painfully stiff with thought. It was almost a mental indigestion.

His grant requests went limping in, finally, to Ralph Nimmo. He scarcely had any hope for them. He thought numbly: They won't be approved.

If they weren't, of course, it would create a scandal in the department and probably mean his appointment at the university would not be renewed, come the end of the academic year.

He scarcely worried. It was the neutrino, the neutrino, only the neutrino. Its trail curved and veered sharply and led him breathlessly along uncharted pathways that even Sterbinski and LaMarr did not follow.

He called Nimmo. "Uncle Ralph, I need a few things. I'm calling from off the campus."

Nimmo's face in the video plate was jovial, but his voice was sharp. He said, "What you need is a course in communication. I'm having a hell of a time pulling your application into one intelligible piece. If that's what you're calling about——"

Foster shook his head impatiently. "That's *not* what I'm calling about. I need these." He scribbled quickly on a piece of paper and held it up before the receiver.

Nimmo yiped. "Hey, how many tricks do you think I can wangle?"

"You can get them, Uncle. You know you can."

Nimmo reread the list of items with silent motions of his plump lips and looked grave.

"What happens when you put those things together?" he asked. Foster shook his head. "You'll have exclusive popular publication rights to whatever turns up, the way it's always been. But please don't ask any questions now."

"I can't do miracles, you know."

"Do this one. You've got to. You're a science writer, not a research man. You don't have to account for anything. You've got friends and connections. They can look the other way, can't they, to get a break from you next publication time?"

"Your faith, nephew, is touching. I'll try."

Nimmo succeeded. The material and equipment were brought over late one evening in a private touring car. Nimmo and Foster lugged it in with the grunting of men unused to manual labour.

Potterley stood at the entrance of the basement after Nimmo had left. He asked softly, "What's this for?"

Foster brushed the hair off his forehead and gently massaged a sprained wrist. He said, "I want to conduct a few simple experiments."

"Really?" The historian's eyes glittered with excitement.

Foster felt exploited. He felt as though he were being led along a dangerous highway by the pull of pinching fingers on his nose; as though he could see the ruin clearly that lay in wait at the end of the path, yet walked eagerly and determinedly. Worst of all, he felt the compelling grip on his nose to be his own.

It was Potterley who began it, Potterley who stood there now, gloating; but the compulsion was his own.

Foster said sourly, "I'll be wanting privacy now, Potterley. I can't have you and your wife running down here and annoying me."

He thought: If that offends him, let him kick me out. Let him put an end to this.

In his heart, though, he did not think being evicted would stop anything.

But it did not come to that. Potterley was showing no signs of offense. His mild gaze was unchanged. He said, "Of course, Dr. Foster, of course. All the privacy you wish."

Foster watched him go. He was left still marching along the highway, perversely glad of it and hating himself for being glad.

He took to sleeping over on a cot in Potterley's basement and spending his weekends there entirely.

During that period, preliminary word came through that his grants (as doctored by Nimmo) had been approved. The Department Head brought the word and congratulated him.

Foster stared back distantly and mumbled, "Good. I'm glad," with so little conviction that the other frowned and turned away without another word.

Foster gave the matter no further thought. It was a minor point, worth no notice. He was planning something that really counted, a climactic test for that evening.

One evening, a second and third and then, haggard and half beside himself with excitement, he called in Potterley.

Potterley came down the stairs and looked about at the home-made gadgetry. He said, in his soft voice, "The electric bills are quite high. I don't mind the expense, but the City may ask questions. Can anything be done?"

It was a warm evening, but Potterley wore a tight collar and a semi-jacket. Foster, who was in his undershirt, lifted bleary eyes and said shakily, "It won't be for much longer, Dr. Potterley. I've called you down to tell you something. A chronoscope can be built. A small one, of course, but it can be built."

Potterley seized the railing. His body sagged. He managed a whisper. "Can it be built here?"

"Here in the basement," said Foster wearily.

"Good Lord. You said——"

"I know what I said," cried Foster impatiently. "I said it couldn't be done. I didn't know anything then. Even Sterbinski didn't know anything."

Potterley shook his head. "Are you sure? You're not mistaken, Dr. Foster? I couldn't endure it if——"

Foster said, "I'm not mistaken. Damn it, sir, if just theory had been enough, we could have had a time viewer over a hundred years ago, when the neutrino was first postulated. The trouble was, the original investigators considered it only a mysterious particle without mass or charge that could not be detected. It was just something to even up the bookkeeping and save the law of conservation of mass energy."

He wasn't sure Potterley knew what he was talking about. He didn't care. He needed a breather. He had to get some of this out of his clotting thoughts. . . . And he needed background for what he would have to tell Potterley next.

He went on. "It was Sterbinski who first discovered that the neutrino broke through the space-time cross-sectional barrier, that it traveled through time as well as through space. It was Sterbinski who first devised a method for stopping neutrinos. He invented a neutrino recorder and learned how to interpret the pattern of the neutrino stream. Naturally, the stream had been affected and deflected by all the matter it had passed through in its passage through time, and the deflections could be analyzed and converted into the images of the matter that had done the deflecting. Time viewing was possible. Even air vibrations could be detected in this way and converted into sound."

Potterley was definitely not listening. He said, "Yes. Yes. But when can you build a chronoscope?"

Foster said urgently, "Let me finish. Everything depends on the method used to detect and analyze the neutrino stream. Sterbinski's method was difficult and roundabout. It required mountains of energy. But I've studied pseudo-gravities, Dr. Potterley, the science of artificial gravitational fields. I've specialized in the behavior of light in such fields. It's a new science. Sterbinski knew nothing of it. If he had, he would have seen—anyone would have—a much better and more efficient method of detecting neutrinos using a pseudo-gravitic field. If I had known more neutrinics to begin with, I would have seen it at once."

Potterley brightened a bit. "I knew it," he said. "Even if they stop research in neutrinics there is no way the government can be sure that discoveries in other segments of science won't reflect knowledge on neutrinics. So much for the value of centralized direction of science. I thought this long ago, Dr. Foster, before you ever came to work here."

"I congratulate you on that," said Foster, "but there's one thing——"

"Oh, never mind all this. Answer me. Please. When can you build a chronoscope?"

"I'm trying to tell you something, Dr. Potterley. A chronoscope won't do you any good." (This is it, Foster thought.)

Slowly, Potterley descended the stairs. He stood facing Foster. "What do you mean? Why won't it help me?"

"You won't see Carthage. It's what I've got to tell you. It's what I've been leading up to. You can never see Carthage."

Potterley shook his head slightly. "Oh, no, you're wrong. If you have the chronoscope, just focus it properly——"

"No, Dr. Potterley. It's not a question of focus. There are random factors affecting the neutrino stream, as they affect all subatomic particles. What we call the uncertainty principle. When the stream is recorded and interpreted, the random factor comes out as fuzziness, or 'noise' as the communications boys speak of it. The further back in time you penetrate, the more pronounced the fuzziness, the greater the noise. After a while, the noise drowns out the picture. Do you understand?"

"More power," said Potterley in a dead kind of voice.

"That won't help. When the noise blurs out detail, magnifying detail magnifies the noise, too. You can't see anything in a sun-burned film by enlarging it, can you? Get this through your head, now. The physical nature of the universe sets limits. The random thermal motions of air molecules set limits to how weak a sound can be detected by any instrument. The length of a light wave or of an electron wave sets limits to the size of objects that can be seen by any instrument. It works that way in chronoscopy, too. You can only time view so far."

"How far? How far?"

Foster took a deep breath. "A century and a quarter. That's the most."

"But the monthly bulletin the Commission puts out deals with ancient history almost entirely." The historian laughed shakily. "You must be wrong. The government has data as far back as 3000 B.C."

"When did you switch to believing them?" demanded Foster, scornfully. "You began this business by proving they were lying; that no historian had made use of the chronoscope. Don't you see why now? No historian, except one interested in contemporary history, could. No chronoscope can possibly see back in time further than 1920 under any conditions."

"You're wrong. You don't know everything," said Potterley.

"The truth won't bend itself to your convenience either. Face it. The government's part in this is to perpetuate a hoax."

"Why?"

"I don't know why."

Potterley's snubby nose was twitching. His eyes were bulging. He pleaded, "It's only theory, Dr. Foster. Build a chronoscope. Build one and try."

Foster caught Potterley's shoulders in a sudden, fierce grip. "Do you think I haven't? Do you think I would tell you this before I had checked it every way I knew? I *have* built one. It's all around you. Look!"

He ran to the switches at the power leads. He flicked them on, one by one. He turned a resistor, adjusted other knobs, put out the cellar lights. "Wait. Let it warm up."

There was a small glow near the centre of one wall. Potterley was gibbering incoherently, but Foster only cried again, "Look!"

The light sharpened and brightened, broke up into a light-and-dark pattern. Men and women! Fuzzy. Features blurred. Arms and legs mere streaks. An old-fashioned ground car, un-clear but recognizable as one of the kind that had once used gasoline-powered internal-combustion engines, sped by.

Foster said, "Mid-twentieth century, somewhere. I can't hook up an audio yet so this is soundless. Eventually, we can add sound. Anyway, mid-twentieth is almost as far back as you can go. Believe me, that's the best focusing that can be done."

Potterley said, "Build a larger machine, a stronger one. Improve your circuits."

"You can't lick the Uncertainty Principle, man, any more than you can live on the sun. There are physical limits to what can be done."

"You're lying. I won't believe you. I——"

A new voice sounded, raised shrilly to make itself heard.

"Arnold! Dr. Foster!"

The young physicist turned at once. Dr. Potterley froze for a long moment, then said, without turning, "What is it, Caroline? Leave us."

"No!" Mrs. Potterley descended the stairs. "I heard. I couldn't help hearing. Do you have a time viewer here, Dr. Foster? Here in the basement?"

"Yes, I do, Mrs. Potterley. A kind of time viewer. Not a good one. I can't get sound yet and the picture is darned blurry, but it works."

Mrs. Potterley clasped her hands and held them tightly against her breast. "How wonderful. How wonderful."

"It's not at all wonderful," snapped Potterley. "The young fool can't reach further back than——"

"Now, look," began Foster in exasperation. . . .

"Please!" cried Mrs. Potterley. "Listen to me. Arnold, don't you see that as long as we can use it for twenty years back, we can see Laurel once again? What do we care about Carthage and ancient times? It's Laurel we can see. She'll be alive for us again. Leave the machine here, Dr. Foster. Show us how to work it."

Foster stared at her then at her husband. Dr. Potterley's face had gone white. Though his voice stayed low and even, its calmness was somehow gone. He said, "You're a fool!"

Caroline said weakly, "Arnold!"

"You're a fool, I say. What will you see? The past. The dead past. Will Laurel do one thing she did not do? Will you see one thing you haven't seen? Will you live three years over and over again, watching a baby who'll never grow up no matter how you watch?"

His voice came near to cracking, but held. He stepped closer to her, seized her shoulder and shook her roughly. "Do you know what will happen to you if you do that? They'll come to take you away because you'll go mad. Yes, mad. Do you want mental treatment? Do you want to be shut up, to undergo the psychic probe?"

Mrs. Potterley tore away. There was no trace of softness or vagueness about her. She had twisted into a virago. "I want to see my child, Arnold. She's in that machine and I want her."

"She's *not* in the machine. An image is. Can't you understand? An image! Something that's not real!"

"I want my child. Do you hear me?" She flew at him, screaming, fists beating. "*I want my child.*"

The historian retreated at the fury of the assault, crying out. Foster moved to step between, when Mrs. Potterley dropped, sobbing wildly, to the floor.

Potterley turned, eyes desperately seeking. With a sudden heave, he snatched at a Lando-rod, tearing it from its support, and whirling away before Foster, numbed by all that was taking place, could move to stop him.

"Stand back!" gasped Potterley, "or I'll kill you. I swear it." He swung with force, and Foster jumped back.

Potterley turned with fury on every part of the structure in the cellar, and Foster, after the first crash of glass, watched dazedly.

Potterley spent his rage and then he was standing quietly amid shards and splinters, with a broken Lando-rod in his hand. He said to Foster in a whisper, "Now get out of here! Never come back! If any of this cost you anything, send me a bill and I'll pay for it. I'll pay double."

Foster shrugged, picked up his shirt and moved up the basement stairs. He could hear Mrs. Potterley sobbing loudly, and, as he turned at the head of the stairs for a last look, he saw Dr. Potterley bending over her, his face convulsed with sorrow.

Two days later, with the school day drawing to a close, and Foster looking wearily about to see if there were any data on his newly approved projects that he wished to take home, Dr. Potterley appeared once more. He was standing at the open door of Foster's office.

The historian was neatly dressed as ever. He lifted his hand in a gesture that was too vague to be a greeting, too abortive to be a plea. Foster stared stonily.

Potterley said, "I waited till five, till you were . . . May I come in?"

Foster nodded.

Potterley said, "I suppose I ought to apologize for my behavior. I was dreadfully disappointed; not quite master of myself. Still, it was inexcusable."

"I accept your apology," said Foster. "Is that all?"

"My wife called you, I think."

"Yes, she has."

"She has been quite hysterical. She told me she had but I couldn't be quite sure——"

"She has called me."

"Could you tell me—would you be so kind as to tell me what she wanted?"

"She wanted a chronoscope. She said she had some money of her own. She was willing to pay."

"Did you—make any commitments?"

"I said I wasn't in the manufacturing business."

'Good," breathed Potterley, his chest expanding with a sigh of relief. "Please don't take any calls from her. She's not—quite——"

"Look, Dr. Potterley," said Foster, "I'm not getting into any domestic quarrels, but you'd better be prepared for something. Chronoscopes can be built by anybody. Given a few simple parts that can be bought through some etherics sales centre, it can be built in the home workshop. The video part, anyway."

"But no one else will think of it beside you, will they? No one has."

"I don't intend to keep it secret."

"But you can't publish. It's illegal research."

"That doesn't matter any more, Dr. Potterley. If I lose my grants, I lose them. If the university is displeased, I'll resign. It just doesn't matter."

"But you can't do that!"

"Till now," said Foster, "you didn't mind my risking loss of grants and position. Why do you turn so tender about it now? Now let me explain something to you. When you first came to me, I believed in organized and directed research; the situation as it existed, in other words. I considered you an intellectual anarchist, Dr. Potterley, and dangerous. But, for one reason or another, I've been an anarchist myself for months now and I have achieved great things.

"Those things have been achieved not because I am a brilliant scientist. Not at all. It was just that scientific research had been directed from above and holes were left that could be filled in by anyone who looked in the right direction. And anyone might have if the government hadn't actively tried to prevent it.

"Now understand me. I still believe directed research can be useful. I'm not in favor of a retreat to total anarchy. But there must be a middle ground. Directed research can retain flexibility. A scientist must be allowed to follow his curiosity, at least in his spare time."

Potterley sat down. He said ingratiatingly, "Let's discuss this, Foster. I appreciate your idealism. You're young. You want the moon. But you can't destroy yourself through fancy notions of what research must consist of. I got you into this. I am responsible and I blame myself bitterly. I was acting emotionally. My interest in Carthage blinded me and I was a damned fool."

Foster broke in. "You mean you've changed completely in two days? Carthage is nothing? Government suppression of research is nothing?"

"Even a damned fool like myself can learn, Foster. My wife taught me something. I understand the reason for government suppression of neutrinics now. I didn't two days ago. And, understanding, I approve. You saw the way my wife reacted to the news of a chronoscope in the basement. I had envisioned a chronoscope used for research purposes. All *she* could see was the personal pleasure of returning neurotically to a personal past, a dead past. The pure researcher, Foster, is in the minority. People like my wife would outweigh us.

"For the government to encourage chronoscopy would have meant that everyone's past would be visible. The government officers would be subjected to blackmail and improper pressure, since who on Earth has a past that is absolutely clean? Organized government might become impossible."

Foster licked his lips. "Maybe. Maybe the government has

some justification in its own eyes. Still, there's an important principle involved here. Who knows what other scientific advances are being stymied because scientists are being stifled into walking a narrow path ? If the chronoscope becomes the terror of a few politicians, it's a price that must be paid. The public must realize that science must be free and there is no more dramatic way of doing it than to publish my discovery, one way or another, legally or illegally."

Potterley's brow was damp with perspiration, but his voice remained even. "Oh, not just a few politicians, Dr. Foster. Don't think that. It would be my terror, too. My wife would spend her time living with our dead daughter. She would retreat further from reality. She would go mad living the same scenes over and over. And not just my terror. There would be others like her. Children searching for their dead parents or their own youth. We'll have a whole world living in the past. Midsummer madness."

Foster said, "Moral judgments can't stand in the way. There isn't one advance at any time in history that mankind hasn't had the ingenuity to pervert. Mankind must also have the ingenuity to prevent. As for the chronoscope, your delvers into the dead past will get tired soon enough. They'll catch their loved parents in some of the things their loved parents did and they'll lose their enthusiasm for it all. But all this is trivial. With me, it's a matter of important principle."

Potterley said, "Hang your principle. Can't you understand men and women as well as principle ? Don't you understand that my wife will live through the fire that killed our baby ? She won't be able to help herself. I know her. She'll follow through each step, trying to prevent it. She'll live it over and over again, hoping each time that it won't happen. How many times do you want to kill Laurel ?" A huskiness had crept into his voice.

A thought crossed Foster's mind. "What are you really afraid she'll find out, Dr. Potterley ? What happened the night of the fire ?"

The historian's hands went up quickly to cover his face and they shook with his dry sobs. Foster turned away and stared uncomfortably out of the window.

Potterley said after a while, "It's a long time since I've had to think of it. Caroline was away. I was baby-sitting. I went into the baby's bedroom midevening to see if she had kicked off the bedclothes. I had my cigarette with me . . . I smoked in those days. I must have stubbed it out before putting it in the ashtray on the chest of drawers. I was always careful. The baby was all right. I returned to the living room and fell asleep before the video. I awoke, choking, surrounded by fire. I don't know how it started."

"But you think it may have been the cigarette, is that it?" said Foster. "A cigarette which, for once, you forgot to stub out?"

"I don't know. I tried to save her, but she was dead in my arms when I got out."

"You never told your wife about the cigarette, I suppose."

Potterley shook his head. "But I've lived with it."

"Only now, with a chronoscope, she'll find out. Maybe it wasn't the cigarette. Maybe you did stub it out. Isn't that possible?"

The scant tears had dried on Potterley's face. The redness had subsided. He said, "I can't take the chance. . . . But it's not just myself, Foster. The past has its terrors for most people. Don't loose those terrors on the human race."

Foster paced the floor. Somehow, this explained the reason for Potterley's rabid, irrational desire to boost the Carthaginians, deify them, most of all disprove the story of their fiery sacrifices to Moloch. By freeing them of the guilt of infanticide by fire, he symbolically freed himself of the same guilt.

So the same fire that had driven him on to causing the construction of a chronoscope was now driving him on to the destruction.

Foster looked sadly at the older man. "I see your position, Dr. Potterley, but this goes above personal feelings. I've got to smash this throttling hold on the throat of science."

Potterley said, savagely, "You mean you want the fame and wealth that goes with such a discovery."

"I don't know about the wealth, but that, too, I suppose. I'm no more than human."

"You won't suppress your knowledge?"

"Not under any circumstances."

"Well, then——" and the historian got to his feet and stood for a moment, glaring.

Foster had an odd moment of terror. The man was older than he, smaller, feebler, and he didn't look armed. Still . . .

Foster said, "If you're thinking of killing me or anything insane like that, I've got the information in a safety-deposit vault where the proper people will find it in case of my disappearance or death."

Potterley said, "Don't be a fool," and stalked out.

Foster closed the door, locked it and sat down to think. He felt silly. He had no information in any safety-deposit vault, of course. Such a melodramatic action would not have occurred to him ordinarily. But now it had.

Feeling even sillier, he spent an hour writing out the equations

of the application of pseudo-gravitic optics to neutrinic recording, and some diagrams for the engineering details of construction. He sealed it in an envelope and scrawled Ralph Nimmo's
name over the outside.

He spent a rather restless night and the next morning, on the
way to school, dropped the envelope off at the bank, with
appropriate instructions to an official, who made him sign a
paper permitting the box to be opened after his death.

He called Nimmo to tell him of the existence of the envelope,
refusing querulously to say anything about its contents.

He had never felt so ridiculously self-conscious as at that
moment.

That night and the next, Foster spent in only fitful sleep,
finding himself face to face with the highly practical problem
of the publication of data unethically obtained.

The *Proceedings of the Society for Pseudo-Gravitics*, which was
the journal with which he was best acquainted, would certainly
not touch any paper that did not include the magic footnote:
"The work described in this paper was made possible by Grant
No. so-and-so from the Commission of Research of the United
Nations."

Nor, doubly so, would the *Journal of Physics*.

There were always the minor journals who might overlook the
nature of the article for the sake of the sensation, but that would
require a little financial negotiation on which he hesitated to
embark. It might, on the whole, be better to pay the cost of
publishing a small pamphlet for general distribution among
scholars. In that case, he would even be able to dispense with
the services of a science writer, sacrificing polish for speed. He
would have to find a reliable printer. Uncle Ralph might know
one.

He walked down the corridor to his office and wondered
anxiously if perhaps he ought to waste no further time, give
himself no further chance to lapse into indecision and take the
risk of calling Ralph from his office phone. He was so absorbed
in his own heavy thoughts that he did not notice that his room
was occupied until he turned from the clothes closet and
approached his desk.

Dr. Potterley was there and a man whom Foster did not
recognize.

Foster stared at them. "What's this?"

Potterley said, "I'm sorry, but I had to stop you."

Foster continued staring. "What are you talking about?"

The stranger said, "Let me introduce myself." He had large
teeth, a little uneven, and they showed prominently when he

smiled. "I am Thaddeus Araman, Department Head of the Division of Chronoscopy. I am here to see you concerning information brought to me by Professor Arnold Potterley and confirmed by our own sources——"

Potterley said breathlessly, "I took all the blame, Dr. Foster. I explained that it was I who persuaded you against your will into unethical practices. I have offered to accept full responsibility and punishment. I don't wish you harmed in any way. It's just that chronoscopy must not be permitted!"

Araman nodded. "He has taken the blame as he says, Dr. Foster, but this thing is out of his hands now."

Foster said, "So? What are you going to do? Blackball me from all consideration for research grants?"

"That is in my power," said Araman.

"Order the university to discharge me?"

"That, too, is in my power."

"All right, go ahead. Consider it done. I'll leave my office now, with you. I can send for my books later. If you insist, I'll leave my books. Is that all?"

"Not quite," said Araman. "You must engage to do no further research in chronoscopy, to publish none of your findings in chronoscopy and, of course, to build no chronoscope. You will remain under surveillance indefinitely to make sure you keep that promise."

"Supposing I refuse to promise? What can you do? Doing research out of my field may be unethical, but it isn't a criminal offense."

"In the case of chronoscopy, my young friend," said Araman patiently, "it is a criminal offense. If necessary, you will be put in jail and kept there."

"Why?" shouted Foster. "What's magic about chronoscopy?"

Araman said, "That's the way it is. We cannot allow further developments in the field. My own job is, primarily, to make sure of that, and I intend to do my job. Unfortunately, I had no knowledge, nor did anyone in the department, that the optics of pseudo-gravity fields had such immediate application to chronoscopy. Score one for general ignorance, but henceforward research will be steered properly in that respect too."

Foster said, "That won't help. Something else may apply that neither you nor I dream of. All science hangs together. It's one piece. If you want to stop one part, you've got to stop it all."

"No doubt that is true," said Araman, "in theory. On the practical side, however, we have managed quite well to hold chronoscopy down to the original Sterbinski level for fifty years. Having caught you in time, Dr. Foster, we hope to continue doing so indefinitely. And we wouldn't have come this close to disaster, either, if I had accepted Dr. Potterley at something more than face value."

He turned toward the historian and lifted his eyebrows in a kind of humorous self-deprecation. "I'm afraid, sir, that I dismissed you as a history professor and no more on the occasion of our first interview. Had I done my job properly and checked on you, this would not have happened."

Foster said abruptly, "Is anyone allowed to use the government chronoscope?"

"No one outside our division under any pretext. I say that since it is obvious to me that you have already guessed as much. I warn you, though, that any repetition of that fact will be a criminal, not an ethical, offense."

"And your chronoscope doesn't go back more than a hundred twenty-five years or so, does it?"

"It doesn't."

"Then your bulletin with its stories of time viewing ancient times is a hoax?"

Araman said coolly, "With the knowledge you now have, it is obvious you know that for a certainty. However, I confirm your remark. The monthly bulletin is a hoax."

"In that case," said Foster, "I will not promise to suppress my knowledge of chronoscopy. If you wish to arrest me, go ahead. My defense at the trial will be enough to destroy the vicious card house of directed research and bring it tumbling down. Directing research is one thing; suppressing it and depriving mankind of its benefits is quite another."

Araman said, "Oh, let's get something straight, Dr. Foster. If you do not co-operate, you will go to jail directly. You will *not* see a lawyer, you will *not* be charged, you will *not* have a trial. You will simply stay in jail."

"Oh, no," said Foster, "you're bluffing. This is not the twentieth century, you know."

There was a stir outside the office, the clatter of feet, a high-pitched shout that Foster was sure he recognized. The door crashed open, the lock splintering, and three intertwined figures stumbled in.

As they did so, one of the men raised a blaster and brought its butt down hard on the skull of another.

There was a whoosh of expiring air, and the one whose head was struck went limp.

"Uncle Ralph!" cried Foster.

Araman frowned. "Put him down in that chair," he ordered, "and get some water."

Ralph Nimmo, rubbing his head with a gingerly sort of disgust, said, "There was no need to get rough, Araman."

Araman said, "The guard should have been rough sooner and kept you out of here, Nimmo. You'd have been better off."

"You know each other?" asked Foster.

"I've had dealings with the man," said Nimmo, still rubbing. "If he's here in your office, nephew, you're in trouble."

"And you, too," said Araman angrily. "I know Dr. Foster consulted you on neutrinics literature."

Nimmo corrugated his forehead, then straightened it with a wince as though the action had brought pain. "So?" he said. "What else do you know about me?"

"We will know everything about you soon enough. Meanwhile, that one item is enough to implicate you. What are you doing here?"

"My dear Dr. Araman," said Nimmo, some of his jauntiness restored, "day before yesterday, my jackass of a nephew called me. He had placed some mysterious information——"

"Don't tell him! Don't say anything!" cried Foster.

Araman glanced at him coldly. "We know all about it, Dr. Foster. The safety-deposit box has been opened and its contents removed."

"But how can you know——" Foster's voice died away in a kind of furious frustration.

"Anyway," said Nimmo, "I decided the net must be closing around him and, after I took care of a few items, I came down to tell him to get off this thing he's doing. It's not worth his career."

"Does that mean you know what he's doing?" asked Araman.

"He never told me," said Nimmo, "but I'm a science writer with a hell of a lot of experience. I know which side of an atom is electronified. The boy, Foster, specializes in pseudo-gravitic optics and coached me on the stuff himself. He got me to get him a textbook on neutrinics and I kind of skip-viewed it myself before handing it over. I can put the two together. He asked me to get him certain pieces of physical equipment, and that was evidence, too. Stop me if I'm wrong, but my nephew has built a semi-portable, low-power chronoscope. Yes, or—yes?"

"Yes." Araman reached thoughtfully for a cigarette and paid no attention to Dr. Potterley (watching silently, as though all were a dream) who shied away, gasping, from the white cylinder. "Another mistake for me. I ought to resign. I should have put tabs on you, too, Nimmo, instead of concentrating too hard on Potterley and Foster. I didn't have much time of course and you've ended up safely here, but that doesn't excuse me. You're under arrest, Nimmo."

"What for?" demanded the science writer.

"Unauthorized research."

"I wasn't doing any. I can't, not being a registered scientist. And even if I did, it's not a criminal offense."

Foster said savagely, "No use, Uncle Ralph. This bureaucrat is making his own laws."

"Like what?" demanded Nimmo.

"Like life imprisonment without trial."

"Nuts," said Nimmo. "This isn't the twentieth cen——"

"I tried that," said Foster. "It doesn't bother him."

"Well, nuts," shouted Nimmo. "Look here, Araman. My nephew and I have relatives who haven't lost touch with us, you know. The professor has some also, I imagine. You can't just make us disappear. There'll be questions and a scandal. This *isn't* the twentieth century. So if you're trying to scare us, it isn't working."

The cigarette snapped between Araman's fingers and he tossed it away violently. He said, "Damn it, I don't know *what* to do. It's never been like this before. . . . Look! You three fools know nothing of what you're trying to do. You understand nothing. Will you listen to me?"

"Oh, we'll listen," said Nimmo grimly.

(Foster sat silently, eyes angry, lips compressed. Potterley's hands writhed like two intertwined snakes.)

Araman said, "The past to you is the dead past. If any of you have discussed the matter, it's dollars to nickels you've used that phrase. The dead past. If you knew how many times I've heard those three words, you'd choke on them, too.

"When people think of the past, they think of it as dead, far away and gone, long ago. We encourage them to think so. When we report time viewing, we always talk of views centuries in the past, even though you gentlemen know seeing more than a century or so is impossible. People accept it. The past means Greece, Rome, Carthage, Egypt, the Stone Age. The deader the better.

"Now you three know a century or a little more is the limit, so what does the past mean to you? Your youth. Your first girl. Your dead mother. Twenty years ago. Thirty years ago. Fifty years ago. The deader the better. . . . But when does the past really begin?"

He paused in anger. The others stared at him and Nimmo stirred uneasily.

"Well," said Araman, "when did it begin? A year ago? Five minutes ago? One second ago? Isn't it obvious that the past begins an instant ago? The dead past is just another name for the living present. What if you focus the chronoscope in the past of one-hundredth of a second ago? Aren't you watching the present? Does it begin to sink in?"

Nimmo said, "Damnation."

"Damnation," mimicked Araman. "After Potterley came to me with his story night before last, how do you suppose I checked up on both of you? I did it with the chronoscope, spotting key moments to the very instant of the present."

"And that's how you knew about the safety-deposit box?" said Foster.

"And every other important fact. Now what do you suppose would happen if we let news of a home chronoscope get out? People might start out by watching their youth, their parents and so on, but it wouldn't be long before they'd catch on to the possibilities. The housewife will forget her poor, dead mother and take to watching her neighbour at home and her husband at the office. The businessman will watch his competitor, the employer his employee.

"There will be no such thing as privacy. The party line, the prying eye behind the curtain will be nothing compared to it. The video stars will be closely watched at all times by everyone. Every man his own peeping Tom and there'll be no getting away from the watcher. Even darkness will be no escape because chronoscopy can be adjusted to the infrared and human figures can be seen by their own body heat. The figures will be fuzzy, of course, and the surroundings will be dark, but that will make the titillation of it all the greater, perhaps. . . . Hmp, the men in charge of the machine now experiment sometimes in spite of the regulations against it."

Nimmo seemed sick. "You can always forbid private manu-facture——"

Araman turned on him fiercely. "You can, but do you expect it to do good? Can you legislate successfully against drinking, smoking, adultery or gossiping over the back fence? And this mixture of nosiness and prurience will have a worse grip on humanity than any of those. Good Lord, in a thousand years of trying we haven't even been able to wipe out the heroin traffic and you talk about legislating against a device for watching any-one you please at any time you please that can be built in a home workshop."

Foster said suddenly, "I won't publish."

Potterley burst out, half in sobs, "None of us will talk. I regret——"

Nimmo broke in. "You said you didn't tab me on the chrono-scope, Araman."

"No time," said Araman wearily. "Things don't move any faster on the chronoscope than in real life. You can't speed it up like the film in a book viewer. We spent a full twenty-four hours trying to catch the important moments during the last six months of Potterley and Foster. There was no time for anything else and it was enough."

"It wasn't," said Nimmo.

"What are you talking about?" There was a sudden infinite alarm on Araman's face.

"I told you my nephew, Jonas, had called me to say he had put important information in a safety-deposit box. He acted as though he were in trouble. He's my nephew. I had to try to get him off the spot. It took a while, then I came here to tell him what I had done. I told you when I got here, just after your man conked me, that I had taken care of a few items."

"What? For Heaven's sake——"

"Just this: I sent the details of the portable chronoscope off to half a dozen of my regular publicity outlets."

Not a word. Not a sound. Not a breath. They were all past any demonstration.

"Don't stare like that," cried Nimmo. "Don't you see my point? I had popular publication rights. Jonas will admit that. I knew he couldn't publish scientifically in any legal way. I was sure he was planning to publish illegally and was preparing the safety-deposit box for that reason. I thought if I put through the details prematurely, all the responsibility would be mine. His career would be saved. And if I were deprived of my science-writing licence as a result, my exclusive possession of the chrono-metric data would set me up for life. Jonas would be angry, I expected that, but I could explain the motive and we would split the take fifty-fifty. . . . Don't stare at me like that. How did I know——"

"Nobody knew anything," said Araman bitterly, "but you all just took it for granted that the government was stupidly bureau-cratic, vicious, tyrannical, given to suppressing research for the hell of it. It never occurred to any of you that we were trying to protect mankind as best we could."

"Don't sit there talking," wailed Potterley. "Get the names of the people who were told——"

"Too late," said Nimmo, shrugging. "They've had better than a day. There's been time for the word to spread. My outfits will have called any number of physicists to check my data before going on with it and they'll call one another to pass on the news. Once scientists put neutrinics and pseudo-gravitics together, home chronoscopy becomes obvious. Before the week is out, five hundred people will know how to build a small chronoscope and how will you catch them all?" His plump cheeks sagged. "I suppose there's no way of putting the mushroom cloud back into that nice, shiny uranium sphere."

Araman stood up. "We'll try, Potterley, but I agree with

Nimmo. It's too late. What kind of a world we'll have from now on, I don't know, I can't tell, but the world we know has been destroyed completely. Until now, every custom, every habit, every tiniest way of life has always taken a certain amount of privacy for granted, but that's all gone now."

He saluted each of the three with elaborate formality.

"You have created a new world among the three of you. I congratulate you. Happy goldfish bowl to you, to me, to everyone, and may each of you fry in hell forever. Arrest rescinded."

# The Foundation of S.F. Success

## (with apologies to W. S. Gilbert)

If you ask me how to shine in the science-fiction line as a pro of
    luster bright,
I say, practice up the lingo of the sciences, by jingo (never mind
    if not quite right).
You must talk of Space and Galaxies and tesseractic fallacies in
    slick and mystic style,
Though the fans won't understand it, they will all the same
    demand it with a softly hopeful smile.

  And all the fans will say,
  As you walk your spatial way,
  If that young man indulges in flights through all the Galaxy,
  Why, what a most imaginative type of man that type of man
    must be.

So success is not a mystery, just brush up on your history, and
    borrow day by day.
Take an Empire that was Roman and you'll find it is at home
    in all the starry Milky Way.
With a drive that's hyperspatial, through the parsecs you will
    race, you'll find that plotting is a breeze,
With a tiny bit of cribbin' from the works of Edward Gibbon
    and that Greek, Thucydides.

  And all the fans will say,
  As you walk your thoughtful way,
  If that young man involves himself in authentic history,
  Why, what a very learned kind of high IQ, his high IQ must
    be.

Then eschew all thoughts of passion of a man-and-woman
    fashion from your hero's thoughtful mind.
He must spend his time on politics, and thinking up his shady
    tricks, and outside that he's blind.
It's enough he's had a mother, other females are a bother,
    though they're jeweled and glistery.
They will just distract his dreaming and his necessary scheming
    with that psychohistory.

And all the fans will say
As you walk your narrow way,
If all his yarns restrict themselves to masculinity,
Why, what a most particularly pure young man that pure
young man must be.

# Franchise

LINDA, AGE ten, was the only one of the family who seemed to enjoy being awake.

Norman Muller could hear her now through his own drugged, unhealthy coma. (He had finally managed to fall asleep an hour earlier but even then it was more like exhaustion than sleep.)

She was at his bedside now, shaking him. "Daddy, Daddy, wake up. Wake up!"

He suppressed a groan. "All right, Linda."

"But, Daddy, there's more policemen around than any time! Police cars and everything!"

Norman Muller gave up and rose blearily to his elbows. The day was beginning. It was faintly stirring toward dawn outside, the germ of a miserable gray that looked about as miserably gray as he felt. He could hear Sarah, his wife, shuffling about breakfast duties in the kitchen. His father-in-law, Matthew, was hawking strenuously in the bathroom. No doubt Agent Handley was ready and waiting for him.

This was *the* day.

Election Day!

To begin with, it had been like every other year. Maybe a little worse, because it was a presidential year, but no worse than other presidential years if it came to that.

The politicians spoke about the guh-reat electorate and the vast electuh-ronic intelligence that was its servant. The press analyzed the situation with industrial computers (the New York *Times* and the St. Louis *Post-Dispatch* had their own computers) and were full of little hints as to what would be forthcoming. Commentators and columnists pinpointed the crucial state and county in happy contradiction to one another.

The first hint that it would *not* be like every other year was when Sarah Muller said to her husband on the evening of October 4 (with Election Day exactly a month off), "Cantwell Johnson says that Indiana will be the state this year. He's the fourth one. Just think, *our* state this time."

Matthew Hortenweiler took his fleshy face from behind the paper, stared dourly at his daughter and growled, "Those fellows are paid to tell lies. Don't listen to them."

"Four of them, Father," said Sarah mildly. "They all say Indiana."

"Indiana *is* a key state, Matthew," said Norman, just as mildly, "on account of the Hawkins-Smith Act and this mess in Indianapolis. It——"

Matthew twisted his old face alarmingly and rasped out, "No one says Bloomington or Monroe County, do they?"

"Well——" said Norman.

Linda, whose little pointed-chinned face had been shifting from one speaker to the next, said pipingly, "You going to be voting this year, Daddy?"

Norman smiled gently and said, "I don't think so, dear."

But this was in the gradually growing excitement of an October in a presidential election year and Sarah had led a quiet life with dreams for her companions. She said longingly, "Wouldn't *that* be wonderful, though?"

"If I voted?" Norman Muller had a small blond mustache that had given him a debonair quality in the young Sarah's eyes, but which, with gradual graying, had declined merely to lack of distinction. His forehead bore deepening lines born of uncertainty and, in general, he had never seduced his clerkly soul with the thought that he was either born great or would under any circumstances achieve greatness. He had a wife, a job and a little girl, and except under extraordinary conditions of elation or depression was inclined to consider that to be an adequate bargain struck with life.

So he was a little embarrassed and more than a little uneasy at the direction his wife's thoughts were taking. "Actually, my dear," he said, "there are two hundred million people in the country, and, with odds like that, I don't think we ought to waste our time wondering about it."

His wife said, "Why, Norman, it's no such thing like two hundred million and you know it. In the first place, only people between twenty and sixty are eligible and it's always men, so that puts it down to maybe fifty million to one. Then, if it's really Indiana——"

"Then it's about one and a quarter million to one. You wouldn't want me to bet in a horse race against those odds, now, would you? Let's have supper."

Matthew muttered from behind his newspaper, "Damned foolishness."

Linda asked again, "You going to be voting this year, Daddy?"

Norman shook his head and they all adjourned to the dining room.

By October 20, Sarah's excitement was rising rapidly. Over

the coffee, she announced that Mrs. Schultz, having a cousin who was the secretary of an Assemblyman, said that all the "smart money" was on Indiana.

"She says President Villers is even going to make a speech at Indianapolis."

Norman Muller, who had had a hard day at the store, nudged the statement with a raising of eyebrows and let it go at that.

Matthew Hortenweiler, who was chronically dissatisfied with Washington, said, "If Villers makes a speech in Indiana, that means he thinks Multivac will pick Arizona. He wouldn't have the guts to go closer, the mushhead."

Sarah, who ignored her father whenever she could decently do so, said, "I don't know why they don't announce the state as soon as they can, and then the county and so on. Then the people who were eliminated could relax."

"If they did anything like that," pointed out Norman, "the politicians would follow the announcements like vultures. By the time it was narrowed down to a township, you'd have a Congressman or two at every street corner."

Matthew narrowed his eyes and brushed angrily at his sparse, gray hair. "They're vultures, anyhow. Listen——"

Sarah murmured, "Now, Father——"

Matthew's voice rumbled over her protest without as much as a stumble or hitch. "Listen, I was around when they set up Multivac. It would end partisan politics, they said. No more voters' money wasted on campaigns. No more grinning nobodies high-pressured and advertising-campaigned into Congress or the White House. So what happens. More campaigning than ever, only now they do it blind. They'll send guys to Indiana on account of the Hawkins-Smith Act and other guys to California in case it's the Joe Hammer situation that turns out crucial. I say, wipe out all that nonsense. Back to the good old——"

Linda asked suddenly, "Don't you want Daddy to vote this year, Grandpa?"

Matthew glared at the young girl. "Never you mind, now." He turned back to Norman and Sarah. "There was a time I voted. Marched right up to the polling booth, stuck my fist on the levers and voted. There was nothing to it. I just said: This fellow's my man and I'm voting for him. *That's* the way it should be."

Linda said excitedly, "You voted, Grandpa? You really did?"

Sarah leaned forward quickly to quiet what might easily become an incongruous story drifting about the neighbourhood. "It's nothing, Linda. Grandpa doesn't really mean voted. Everyone did that kind of voting when your grandpa was a little boy, your grandpa, too, but it wasn't *really* voting."

Matthew roared, "It wasn't when I was a little boy. I was twenty-two and I voted for Langley and it was real voting. My vote didn't count for much, maybe, but it was as good as anyone else's. *Anyone* else's. And no Multivac to——"

Norman interposed, "All right, Linda, time for bed. And stop asking questions about voting. When you grow up, you'll understand all about it."

He kissed her with antiseptic gentleness and she moved reluctantly out of range under maternal prodding and a promise that she might watch the bedside video till 9.15, *if* she was prompt about the bathing ritual.

Linda said, "Grandpa," and stood with her chin down and her hands behind her back until his newspaper lowered itself to the point where shaggy eyebrows and eyes, nested in fine wrinkles, showed themselves. It was Friday, October 31.

He said, "Yes?"

Linda came closer and put both her forearms on one of the old man's knees so that he had to discard his newspaper altogether. She said, "Grandpa, did you really once vote?"

He said, "You heard me say I did, didn't you? Do you think I tell fibs?"

"N—no, but Mamma says everybody voted then."

"So they did."

"But how could they? How could *everybody* vote?"

Matthew stared at her solemnly, then lifted her and put her on his knee.

He even moderated the tonal qualities of his voice. He said, "You see, Linda, till about forty years ago, everybody always voted. Say we wanted to decide who was to be the new President of the United States. The Democrats and Republicans would both nominate someone, and everybody would say who they wanted. When Election Day was over, they would count how many people wanted the Democrat and how many wanted the Republican. Whoever had more votes was elected. You see?"

Linda nodded and said, "How did all the people know who to vote for? Did Multivac tell them?"

Matthew's eyebrows hunched down and he looked severe. "They just used their own judgment, girl."

She edged away from him, and he lowered his voice again, "I'm not angry at you, Linda. But, you see, sometimes it took all night to count what everyone said and people were impatient. So they invented special machines which could look at the first few votes and compare them with the votes from the same places in previous years. That way the machine could compute how the total vote would be and who would be elected. You see?"

She nodded. "Like Multivac."

"The first computers were much smaller than Multivac. But the machines grew bigger and they could tell how the election would go from fewer and fewer votes. Then, at last, they built Multivac and it can tell from just one voter."

Linda smiled at having reached a familiar part of the story and said, "That's nice."

Matthew frowned and said, "No, it's not nice. I don't want a machine telling me how I would have voted just because some joker in Milwaukee says he's against higher tariffs. Maybe I want to vote cock-eyed just for the pleasure of it. Maybe I don't want to vote. Maybe——"

But Linda had wriggled from his knee and was beating a retreat.

She met her mother at the door. Her mother, who was still wearing her coat and had not even had time to remove her hat, said breathlessly, "Run along, Linda. Don't get in Mother's way."

Then she said to Matthew, as she lifted her hat from her head and patted her hair back into place, "I've been at Agatha's."

Matthew stared at her censoriously and did not even dignify that piece of information with a grunt as he groped for his newspaper.

Sarah said, as she unbuttoned her coat, "Guess what she said?"

Matthew flattened out his newspaper for reading purposes with a sharp crackle and said, "Don't much care."

Sarah said, "Now, Father——" But she had no time for anger. The news had to be told and Matthew was the only recipient handy, so she went on, "Agatha's Joe is a policeman, you know, and he says a whole truckload of secret service men came into Bloomington last night."

"They're not after me."

"Don't you see, Father? Secret service agents, and it's almost election time. In *Bloomington*."

"Maybe they're after a bank robber."

"There hasn't been a bank robbery in town in ages. . . . Father, you're hopeless."

She stalked away.

Nor did Norman Muller receive the news with noticeably greater excitement.

"Now, Sarah, how did Agatha's Joe know they were secret service agents?" he asked calmly. "They wouldn't go around with identification cards pasted on their foreheads."

But by next evening, with November a day old, she could say triumphantly, "It's just everyone in Bloomington that's waiting for someone local to be the voter. The Bloomington *News* as much as said so on video."

Norman stirred uneasily. He couldn't deny it, and his heart was sinking. If Bloomington was really to be hit by Multivac's lightning, it would mean newspapermen, video shows, tourists, all sorts of—strange upsets. Norman liked the quiet routine of his life, and the distant stir of politics was getting uncomfortably close.

He said, "It's all rumor. Nothing more."

"You wait and see, then. You just wait and see."

As things turned out, there was very little time to wait, for the doorbell rang insistently, and when Norman Muller opened it and said, "Yes?" a tall, grave-faced man said, "Are you Norman Muller?"

Norman said, "Yes," again, but in a strange dying voice. It was not difficult to see from the stranger's bearing that he was one carrying authority, and the nature of his errand suddenly became as inevitably obvious as it had, until the moment before, been unthinkably impossible.

The man presented credentials, stepped into the house, closed the door behind him and said ritualistically, "Mr. Norman Muller, it is necessary for me to inform you on the behalf of the President of the United States that you have been chosen to represent the American electorate on Tuesday, November 4, 2008."

Norman Muller managed, with difficulty, to walk unaided to his chair. He sat there, white-faced and almost insensible, while Sarah brought water, slapped his hands in panic and moaned to her husband between clenched teeth, "Don't be sick, Norman. *Don't* be sick. They'll pick someone else."

When Norman could manage to talk, he whispered, "I'm sorry, sir."

The secret service agent had removed his coat, unbuttoned his jacket and was sitting at ease on the couch.

"It's all right," he said, and the mark of officialdom seemed to have vanished with the formal announcement and leave him simply a large and rather friendly man. "This is the sixth time I've made the announcement and I've seen all kinds of reactions. Not one of them was the kind you see on the video. You know what I mean? A holy, dedicated look, and a character who says, 'It will be a great privilege to serve my country.' That sort of stuff." The agent laughed comfortably.

Sarah's accompanying laugh held a trace of shrill hysteria.

The agent said, "Now you're going to have me with you for a while. My name is Phil Handley. I'd appreciate it if you call me Phil. Mr. Muller can't leave the house any more till Election Day. You'll have to inform the department store that he's sick, Mrs. Muller. You can go about your business for a while, but you'll have to agree not to say a word about this. Right, Mrs. Muller?"

Sarah nodded vigorously. "No, sir. Not a word."

"All right. But, Mrs. Muller," Handley looked grave, "we're not kidding now. Go out only if you must and you'll be followed when you do. I'm sorry but that's the way we must operate."

"Followed?"

"It won't be obvious. Don't worry. And it's only for two days till the formal announcement to the nation is made. Your daughter——"

"She's in bed," said Sarah hastily.

"Good. She'll have to be told I'm a relative or friend staying with the family. If she does find out the truth, she'll have to be kept in the house. Your father had better stay in the house in any case."

"He won't like that," said Sarah.

"Can't be helped. Now, since you have no others living with you——"

"You know all about us apparently," whispered Norman.

"Quite a bit," agreed Handley. "In any case, those are all my instructions to you for the moment. I'll try to co-operate as much as I can and be as little of a nuisance as possible. The government will pay for my maintenance so I won't be an expense to you. I'll be relieved each night by someone who will sit up in this room, so there will be no problem about sleeping accommodations. Now, Mr. Muller——"

"Sir?"

"You can call me Phil," said the agent again. "The purpose of the two-day preliminary before formal announcement is to get you used to your position. We prefer to have you face Multivac in as normal a state of mind as possible. Just relax and try to feel this is all in a day's work. Okay?"

"Okay," said Norman, and then shook his head violently. "But I don't want the responsibility. Why me?'

'All right," said Handley, "let's get that straight to begin with. Multivac weighs all sorts of known factors, billions of them. One factor isn't known, though, and won't be known for a long time. That's the reaction pattern of the human mind. All Americans are subjected to the molding pressure of what other Americans do and say, to the things that are done to him and the things he does to others. Any American can be brought to Multivac to have the bent of his mind surveyed. From that the bent of all other minds in the country can be estimated. Some Americans are better for the purpose than others at some given time, depending upon the happenings of that year. Multivac picked you as most representative this year. Not the smartest, or the strongest, or the luckiest, but just the most representative. Now we don't question Multivac, do we?"

"Couldn't it make a mistake?" asked Norman.

Sarah, who listened impatiently, interrupted to say, "Don't listen to him, sir. He's just nervous, you know. Actually, he's very well read and he always follows politics very closely."

Handley said, "Multivac makes the decisions, Mrs. Muller. It picked your husband."

"But does it know everything?" insisted Norman wildly. "Couldn't it have made a mistake?"

"Yes, it can. There's no point in not being frank. In 1993, a selected Voter died of a stroke two hours before it was time for him to be notified. Multivac didn't predict that; it couldn't. A Voter might be mentally unstable, morally unsuitable, or, for that matter, disloyal. Multivac can't know everything about everybody until he's fed all the data there is. That's why alternate selections are always held in readiness. I don't think we'll be using one this time. You're in good health, Mr. Muller, and you've been carefully investigated. You qualify."

Norman buried his face in his hands and sat motionless.

"By tomorrow morning, sir," said Sarah, "he'll be perfectly all right. He just has to get used to it, that's all."

"Of course," said Handley.

In the privacy of their bedchamber, Sarah Muller expressed herself in other and stronger fashion. The burden of her lecture was, "So get hold of yourself, Norman. You're trying to throw away the chance of a lifetime."

Norman whispered desperately, "It frightens me, Sarah. The whole thing."

"For goodness' sake, why? What's there to it but answering a question or two?"

"The responsibility is too great. I couldn't face it."

"What responsibility? There isn't any. Multivac picked you. It's Multivac's responsibility. Everyone knows that."

Norman sat up in bed in a sudden access of rebellion and anguish. "Everyone is *supposed* to know that. But they don't. They——"

"Lower your voice," hissed Sarah icily. "They'll hear you downtown."

"They don't," said Norman, declining quickly to a whisper.

"When they talk about the Ridgely administration of 1988, do they say he won them over with pie-in-the-sky promises and racist baloney? No! They talk about the 'goddam MacComber vote,' as though Humphrey MacComber was the only man who had anything to do with it because he faced Multivac. I've said it myself—only now I think the poor guy was just a truck farmer who didn't ask to be picked. Why was it his fault more than anyone else's? Now his name is a curse."

"You're just being childish," said Sarah.

"I'm being sensible. I tell you, Sarah, I won't accept. They can't make me vote if I don't want to. I'll say I'm sick. I'll say——"

But Sarah had had enough. "Now you listen to me," she whispered in a cold fury. "You don't have only yourself to think about. You know what it means to be Voter of the Year. A presidential year at that. It means publicity and fame and, maybe, buckets of money——"

"And then I go back to being a clerk."

"You will *not*. You'll have a branch managership at the least if you have any brains at all, and you *will* have, because I'll tell you what to do. You control this kind of publicity if you play your cards right, and you can force Kennell Stores, Inc., into a tight contract *and* an escalator clause in connection with your salary *and* a decent pension plan."

"That's not the point in being Voter, Sarah."

"That will be your point. If you don't owe anything to yourself or to me—I'm not asking for myself—you owe something to Linda."

Norman groaned.

"Well, don't you?" snapped Sarah.

"Yes, dear," murmured Norman.


On November 3, the official announcement was made and it was too late for Norman to back out even if he had been able to find the courage to make the attempt.

Their house was sealed off. Secret service agents made their appearance in the open, blocking off all approach.

At first the telephone rang incessantly, but Philip Handley with an engagingly apologetic smile took all calls. Eventually, the exchange shunted all calls directly to the police station.

Norman imagined that, in that way, he was spared not only the bubbling (and envious) congratulations of friends, but also the egregious pressure of salesmen scenting a prospect and the designing smoothness of politicians from all over the nation. . . . Perhaps even death threats from the inevitable cranks.

Newspapers were forbidden to enter the house now in order to keep out weighted pressures, and television was gently but firmly disconnected, over Linda's loud protests.

Matthew growled and stayed in his room; Linda, after the first flurry of excitement, sulked and whined because she could not leave the house; Sarah divided her time between preparation of meals for the present and plans for the future; and Norman's depression lived and fed upon itself.

And the morning of Tuesday, November 4, 2008, came at last, and it was Election Day.

It was early breakfast, but only Norman Muller ate, and that mechanically. Even a shower and shave had not succeeded in either restoring him to reality or removing his own conviction that he was as grimy without as he felt grimy within.

Handley's friendly voice did its best to shed some normality over the gray and unfriendly dawn. (The weather prediction had been for a cloudy day with prospects of rain before noon.)

Handley said, "We'll keep this house insulated till Mr. Muller is back, but after that we'll be off your necks." The secret service agent was in full uniform now, including sidearms in heavily brassed holsters.

"You've been no trouble at all, Mr. Handley," simpered Sarah.

Norman drank through two cups of black coffee, wiped his lips with a napkin, stood up and said haggardly, "I'm ready."

Handley stood up, too. "Very well, sir. And thank you, Mrs. Muller, for your very kind hospitality."

The armored car purred down empty streets. They were empty even for that hour of the morning.

Handley indicated that and said, "They always shift traffic away from the line of drive ever since the attempted bombing that nearly ruined the Leverett Election of '92."

When the car stopped, Norman was helped out by the always polite Handley into an underground drive whose walls were lined with soldiers at attention.

He was led into a brightly lit room, in which three white-uniformed men greeted him smilingly.

Norman said sharply, "But this is the hospital."

"There's no significance to that," said Handley at once. "It's just that the hospital has the necessary facilities."

"Well, what do I do?"

Handley nodded. One of the three men in white advanced and said, "I'll take over now, agent."

Handley saluted in an offhand manner and left the room.

The man in white said, "Won't you sit down, Mr. Muller?

I'm John Paulson, senior Computer. These are Samson Levine and Peter Dorogobuzh, my assistants."

Norman shook hands numbly all about. Paulson was a man of middle height with a soft face that seemed used to smiling and a very obvious toupee. He wore plastic-rimmed glasses of an old-fashioned cut, and he lit a cigarette as he talked. (Norman refused his offer of one.)

Paulson said, "In the first place, Mr. Muller, I want you to know we are in no hurry. We want you to stay with us all day if necessary, just so that you get used to your surroundings and get over any thought you might have that there is anything unusual in this, anything clinical, if you know what I mean."

"It's all right," said Norman. "I'd just as soon this were over."

"I understand your feelings. Still, we want you to know exactly what's going on. In the first place, Multivac isn't here."

"It isn't?" Somehow through all his depression, he had still looked forward to seeing Multivac. They said it was half a mile long and three stories high, that fifty technicians walked the corridors *within* its structure continuously. It was one of the wonders of the world.

Paulson smiled. "No. It's not portable, you know. It's located underground, in fact, and very few people know exactly where. You can understand that, since it is our greatest natural resource. Believe me, elections aren't the only things it's used for."

Norman thought he was being deliberately chatty and found himself intrigued all the same. "I thought I'd see it. I'd like to."

"I'm sure of that. But it takes a presidential order and even then it has to be countersigned by Security. However, we are plugged into Multivac right here by beam transmission. What Multivac says can be interpreted here and what we say is beamed directly to Multivac, so in a sense we're in its presence."

Norman looked about. The machines within the room were all meaningless to him.

"Now let me explain, Mr. Muller," Paulson went on. "Multivac already has most of the information it needs to decide all the elections, national, state and local. It needs only to check certain imponderable attitudes of mind and it will use you for that. We can't predict what questions it will ask, but they may not make much sense to you, or even to us. It may ask you how you feel about garbage disposal in your town; whether you favour central incinerators. It might ask you whether you have a doctor of your own or whether you make use of National Medicine, Inc. Do you understand?"

"Yes, sir."

"Whatever it asks, you answer in your own words in any way

you please. If you feel you must explain quite a bit, do so. Talk an hour, if necessary."

"Yes, sir."

"Now, one more thing. We will have to make use of some simple devices which will automatically record your blood pressure, heartbeat, skin conductivity and brain-wave pattern while you speak. The machinery will seem formidable, but it's all absolutely painless. You won't even know it's going on."

The other two technicians were already busying themselves with smooth-gleaming apparatus on oiled wheels.

Norman said, "Is that to check on whether I'm lying or not?"

"Not at all, Mr. Muller. There's no question of lying. It's only a matter of emotional intensity. If the machine asks you your opinion of your child's school, you may say, 'I think it is overcrowded.' Those are only words. From the way your brain and heart and hormones and sweat glands work, Multivac can judge exactly how intensely you feel about the matter. It will understand your feelings better than you yourself."

"I never heard of this," said Norman.

"No, I'm sure you didn't. Most of the details of Multivac's workings are top secret. For instance, when you leave, you will be asked to sign a paper swearing that you will never reveal the nature of the questions you were asked, the nature of your responses, what was done, or how it was done. The less is known about the Multivac, the less chance of attempted outside pressures upon the men who service it." He smiled grimly. "Our lives are hard enough as it is."

Norman nodded. "I understand."

"And now would you like anything to eat or drink?"

"No. Nothing right now."

"Do you have any questions?"

Norman shook his head.

"Then you tell us when you're ready."

"I'm ready right now."

"You're certain?"

"Quite."

Paulson nodded, and raised his hand in a gesture to the others.

They advanced with their frightening equipment, and Norman Muller felt his breath come a little quicker as he watched.

The ordeal lasted nearly three hours, with one short break for coffee and an embarrassing session with a chamber pot. During all this time, Norman Muller remained encased in machinery. He was bone-weary at the close.

He thought sardonically that his promise to reveal nothing of what had passed would be an easy one to keep. Already the questions were a hazy mishmash in his mind.

Somehow he had thought Multivac would speak in a sepulchral, superhuman voice, resonant and echoing, but that, after all, was just an idea he had from seeing too many television shows, he now decided. The truth was distressingly undramatic. The questions were slips of a kind of metallic foil patterned with numerous punctures. A second machine converted the pattern into words and Paulson read the words to Norman, then gave him the question and let him read it for himself.

Norman's answers were taken down by a recording machine, played back to Norman for confirmation, with emendations and added remarks also taken down. All that was fed into a pattern-making instrument and that, in turn, was radiated to Multivac.

The one question Norman could remember at the moment was an incongruously gossipy: "What do you think of the price of eggs?"

Now it was over, and gently they removed the electrodes from various portions of his body, unwrapped the pulsating band from his upper arm, moved the machinery away.

He stood up, drew a deep, shuddering breath and said, "Is that all? Am I through?"

"Not quite." Paulson hurried to him, smiling in reassuring fashion. "We'll have to ask you to stay another hour."

"Why?" asked Norman sharply.

"It will take that long for Multivac to weave its new data into the trillions of items it has. Thousands of elections are concerned, you know. It's very complicated. And it may be that an odd contest here or there, a comptrollership in Phoenix, Arizona, or some council seat in Wilkesboro, North Carolina, may be in doubt. In that case, Multivac may be compelled to ask you a deciding question or two."

"No," said Norman. "I won't go through this again."

"It probably won't happen," Paulson said soothingly. "It rarely does. But, just in case, you'll have to stay." A touch of steel, just a touch, entered his voice. "You have no choice, you know. You must."

Norman sat down wearily. He shrugged.

Paulson said, "We can't let you read a newspaper, but if you'd care for a murder mystery, or if you'd like to play chess, or if there's anything we can do for you to help pass the time, I wish you'd mention it."

"It's all right. I'll just wait."

They ushered him into a small room just next to the one in

which he had been questioned. He let himself sink into a plastic-covered armchair and closed his eyes.

As well as he could, he must wait out this final hour.

He sat perfectly still and slowly the tension left him. His breathing grew less ragged and he could clasp his hands without being quite so conscious of the trembling of his fingers.

Maybe there would be no questions. Maybe it was all over.

If it *were* over, then the next thing would be torchlight processions and invitations to speak at all sorts of functions. The Voter of the Year!

He, Norman Muller, ordinary clerk of a small department store in Bloomington, Indiana, who had neither been born great nor achieved greatness would be in the extraordinary position of having had greatness thrust upon him.

The historians would speak soberly of the Muller Election of 2008. That would be its name, the Muller Election.

The publicity, the better job, the flash flood of money that interested Sarah so much, occupied only a corner of his mind. It would all be welcome, of course. He couldn't refuse it. But at the moment something else was beginning to concern him.

A latent patriotism was stirring. After all, he was representing the entire electorate. He was the focal point for *them*. He was, in his own person, for this one day, all of America!

The door opened, snapping him to open-eyed attention. For a moment, his stomach constricted. Not more questions!

But Paulson was smiling. "That will be all, Mr. Muller."

"No more questions, sir?"

"None needed. Everything was quite clear-cut. You will be escorted back to your home and then you will be a private citizen once more. Or as much so as the public will allow."

"Thank you. Thank you." Norman flushed and said, "I wonder—who was elected?"

Paulson shook his head. "That will have to wait for the official announcement. The rules are quite strict. We can't even tell you. You understand."

"Of course. Yes." Norman felt embarrassed.

"Secret service will have the necessary papers for you to sign."

"Yes." Suddenly, Norman Muller felt proud. It was on him now in full strength. He was proud.

In this imperfect world, the sovereign citizens of the first and greatest Electronic Democracy had, through Norman Muller (through *him!*), exercised once again its free, untrammelled franchise.

# Gimmicks Three

"Come, come," said Shapur quite politely, considering that he was a demon. "You are wasting my time. And your own, too, I might add, since you have only half an hour left." And his tail twitched.

"It's *not* dematerialization?" asked Isidore Wellby thoughtfully.

"I have already said it is not," said Shapur.

For the hundredth time, Wellby looked at the unbroken bronze that surrounded him on all sides. The demon had taken unholy pleasure (what other kind indeed?) in pointing out that the floor, ceiling and four walls were featureless, two-foot-thick slabs of bronze, welded seamlessly together.

It was the ultimate locked room and Wellby had but another half hour to get out, while the demon watched with an expression of gathering anticipation.

It had been ten years previously (to the day, naturally) that Isidore Wellby had signed up.

"We pay you in advance," said Shapur persuasively. "Ten years of anything you want, within reason, and then you're a demon. You're one of us, with a new name of demonic potency, and many privileges beside. You'll hardly know you're damned. And if you don't sign, you may end up in the fire, anyway, just in the ordinary course of things. You never know. . . . Here, look at me. I'm not doing too badly. I signed up, had my ten years and here I am. Not bad."

"Why so anxious for me to sign then, if I might be damned anyway?" asked Wellby.

"It's not so easy to recruit hell's cadre," said the demon, with a frank shrug that made the faint odor of sulfur dioxide in the air a trifle stronger. "Everyone wishes to gamble on ending in Heaven. It's a poor gamble, but there it is. I think *you're* too sensible for that. But meanwhile we have more damned souls than we know what to do with and a growing shortage at the administrative end."

Wellby, having just left the army and finding himself with nothing much to show for it but a limp and a farewell letter from a girl he somehow still loved, pricked his finger, and signed.

© 1956 by Fantasy House, Inc. (original title: *The Brazen Locked Room*).

Of course, he read the small print first. A certain amount of demonic power would be deposited to his account upon signature in blood. He would not know in detail how one manipulated those powers, or even the nature of all of them, but he would nevertheless find his wishes fulfilled in such a way that they would seem to have come about through perfectly normal mechanisms.

Naturally, no wish might be fulfilled which would interfere with the higher aims and purposes of human history. Wellby had raised his eyebrows at that.

Shapur coughed. "A precaution imposed upon us by—uh—Above. You are reasonable. The limitation won't interfere with you."

Wellby said, "There seems to be a catch clause, too."

"A kind of one, yes. After all, we have to check your aptitude for the position. It states, as you see, that you will be required to perform a task for us at the conclusion of your ten years, one your demonic powers will make it quite possible for you to do. We can't tell you the nature of the task now, but you will have ten years to study the nature of your powers. Look upon the whole thing as an entrance qualification."

"And if I don't pass the test, what then?"

"In that case," said the demon, "you will be only an ordinary damned soul after all." And because he was a demon, his eyes glowed smokily at the thought and his clawed fingers twitched as though he felt them already deep in the other's vitals. But he added suavely, "Come, now, the test will be a simple one. We would rather have you as a cadre than as just another chore on our hands."

Wellby, with sad thoughts of his unattainable loved one, cared little enough at the moment for what would happen after ten years and he signed.

Yet the ten years passed quickly enough. Isidore Wellby was always reasonable, as the demon had predicted, and things worked well. Wellby accepted a position and because he was always at the right spot at the right time and always said the right thing to the right man, he was quickly promoted to a position of great authority.

Investments he made invariably paid off and, what was more gratifying still, his girl came back to him most sincerely repentant and most satisfactorily adoring.

His marriage was a happy one and was blessed with four children, two boys and two girls, all bright and reasonably well behaved. At the end of ten years, he was at the height of his authority, reputation and wealth, while his wife, if anything, had grown more beautiful as she had matured.

And ten years (to the day, naturally) after the making of the compact, he woke to find himself, not in his bedroom, but in a horrible bronze chamber of the most appalling solidity, with no company other than an eager demon.

"You have only to get out, and you will be one of us," said Shapur. "It can be done fairly and logically by using your demonic powers, provided you know exactly what it is you're doing. You should, by now."

"My wife and children will be very disturbed at my disappearance," said Wellby, with the beginning of regrets.

"They will find your dead body." said the demon consolingly. "You will seem to have died of a heart attack and you will have a beautiful funeral. The minister will consign you to Heaven and we will not disillusion him or those who listen to him. Now, come, Wellby, you have till noon."

Wellby, having unconsciously steeled himself for this moment for ten years, was less panic-stricken than he might have been. He looked about speculatively. "Is this room perfectly enclosed? No trick openings?"

"No openings anywhere in the walls, floor or ceiling," said the demon, with a professional delight in his handiwork. "Or at the boundaries of any of those surfaces, for that matter. Are you giving up?"

"No, no. Just give me time."

Wellby thought very hard. There seemed no sign of closeness in the room. There was even a feeling of moving air. The air might be entering the room by dematerializing across the walls. Perhaps the demon had entered by dematerialization and perhaps Wellby himself might leave in that manner. He asked.

The demon grinned. "Dematerialization is not one of your powers. Nor did I myself use it in entering."

"You're sure now?"

"The room is my own creation," said the demon smugly, "and especially constructed for you."

"And you entered from outside?"

"I did."

"With reasonable demonic powers which I possess, too?"

"Exactly. Come, let us be precise. You cannot move through matter but you can move in any dimension by a mere effort of will. You can move up, down, right, left, obliquely and so on, but you cannot move through matter in any way."

Wellby kept on thinking, and Shapur kept on pointing out the utter immovable solidity of the bronze walls, floor and ceiling; their unbroken ultimacy.

It seemed obvious to Wellby that Shapur, however much he

might believe in the necessity for recruiting cadre, was barely restraining his demonic delight at possibly having an ordinary damned soul to amuse himself with.

"At least," said Wellby, with a sorrowful attempt at philosophy, "I'll have ten happy years to look back on. Surely that's a consolation, even for a damned soul in hell."

"Not at all," said the demon. "Hell would not be hell, if you were allowed consolations. Everything anyone gains on Earth by pacts with the devil, as in your case (or my own, for that matter), is exactly what one might have gained without such a pact if one had worked industriously and in full trust in—uh—Above. That is what makes all such bargains so truly demonic." And the demon laughed with a kind of cheerful howl.

Wellby said indignantly, "You mean my wife would have returned to me even if I had never signed your contract."

"She might have," said Shapur. "Whatever happens is the will of—uh—Above, you know. We ourselves can do nothing to alter that."

The chagrin of that moment must have sharpened Wellby's wits for it was then that he vanished, leaving the room empty, except for a surprised demon. And surprise turned to absolute fury when the demon looked at the contract with Wellby which he had, until that moment, been holding in his hand for final action, one way or the other.

It was ten years (to the day, naturally) after Isidore Wellby had signed his pact with Shapur, that the demon entered Wellby's office and said, most angrily, "Look here——"

Wellby looked up from his work, astonished. "Who are you?"

"You know very well who I am," said Shapur.

"Not at all," said Wellby.

The demon looked sharply at the man. "I see you are telling the truth, but I can't make out the details." He promptly flooded Wellby's mind with the events of the last ten years.

Wellby said, "Oh, yes. I can explain, of course, but are you sure we will not be interrupted?"

"We won't be," said the demon grimly.

"I sat in that closed bronze room," said Wellby, "and——"

"Never mind that," said the demon hastily. "I want to know——"

"Please. Let me tell this my way."

The demon clamped his jaws and fairly exuded sulfur dioxide till Wellby coughed and looked pained.

Wellby said, "If you'll move off a bit. Thank you. . . . Now I sat in that closed bronze room and remembered how you kept stressing the absolute unbrokenness of the four walls, the floor and the ceiling. I wondered: why did you specify? What else was there beside walls, floor and ceiling. You had defined a completely enclosed three-dimensional space.

"And that was it: three-dimensional. The room was not closed in the fourth dimension. It did not exist indefinitely in the past. You said you had created it for me. So if one traveled into the past, one would find oneself at a point in time, eventually, when the room did not exist and then one would be out of the room.

"What's more, you *had* said I could move in any dimension, and time may certainly be viewed as a dimension. In any case, as soon as I decided to move toward the past, I found myself living backward at a tremendous rate and suddenly there was no bronze around me anywhere."

Shapur cried in anguish, "I can guess all that. You couldn't have escaped any other way. It's this contract of yours that I'm concerned about. If you're not an ordinary damned soul, very well, it's part of the game. But you must be at least one of *us*, one of the cadre; it's what you were paid for, and if I don't deliver you down below, I will be in enormous trouble."

Wellby shrugged his shoulders. "I'm sorry for you, of course, but I can't help you. You must have created the bronze room immediately after I placed my signature on the paper, for when I burst out of the room, I found myself just at the point in time at which I was making the bargain with you. There you were again; there I was; you were pushing the contract toward me, together with a stylus with which I might prick my finger. To be sure, as I had moved back in time, my memory of what was becoming the future faded out, but not, apparently, quite entirely. As you pushed the contract at me, I felt uneasy. I didn't quite remember the future, but I felt uneasy. So I didn't sign. I turned you down flat."

Shapur ground his teeth. "I might have known. If probability patterns affected demons, I would have shifted with you into this new if-world. As it is, all I can say is that you have lost the ten happy years we paid you with. That is one consolation. And we'll get you in the end. That is another."

"Well, now," said Wellby, "are there consolations in hell? Through the ten years I have now lived, I knew nothing of what I might have obtained. But now that you've put the memory of the ten-years-that-might-have-been into my mind, I recall that, in the bronze room, you told me that demonic agreements could give nothing that could not be obtained by industry and trust in Above. I have been industrious and I have trusted."

Wellby's eyes fell upon the photograph of his beautiful wife and four beautiful children, then traveled about the tasteful luxuriance of his office. "And I may even escape hell altogether. That, too, is beyond *your* power to decide."

And the demon, with a horrible shriek, vanished forever.

# Kid Stuff

THE FIRST pang of nausea had passed and Jan Prentiss said, "Damn it, you're an insect."

It was a statement of fact, not an insult, and the thing that sat on Prentiss' desk said, "Of course."

It was about a foot long, very thin, and in shape a farfetched and miniature caricature of a human being. Its stalky arms and legs originated in pairs from the upper portion of its body. The legs were longer and thicker than the arms. They extended the length of the body, then bent forward at the knee.

The creature sat upon those knees and, when it did so, the stub of its fuzzy abdomen just cleared Prentiss' desk.

There was plenty of time for Prentiss to absorb these details. The object had no objection to being stared at. It seemed to welcome it, in fact, as though it were used to exciting admiration.

"What are you?" Prentiss did not feel completely rational. Five minutes ago, he had been seated at his typewriter, working leisurely on the story he had promised Horace W. Browne for last month's issue of *Farfetched Fantasy Fiction*. He had been in a perfectly usual frame of mind. He had felt quite fine; quite sane.

And then a block of air immediately to the right of the typewriter had shimmered, clouded over and condensed into the little horror that dangled its black and shiny feet over the edge of the desk.

Prentiss wondered in a detached sort of way that he bothered talking to it. This was the first time his profession had so crudely affected his dreams. It *must* be a dream, he told himself.

"I'm an Avalonian," said the being. "I'm from Avalon, in other words." Its tiny face ended in a mandibular mouth. Two swaying three-inch antennae rose from a spot above either eye, while the eyes themselves gleamed richly in their many-faceted fashion. There was no sign of nostrils.

Naturally not, thought Prentiss wildly. It has to breathe through vents in its abdomen. It must be talking with its abdomen then. Or using telepathy.

"Avalon?" he said stupidly. He thought: Avalon? The land of the fay in King Arthur's time?

"Certainly," said the creature, answering the thought smoothly. "I'm an elf."

"Oh, no!" Prentiss put his hands to his face, took them away and found the elf still there, its feet thumping against the top drawer. Prentiss was not a drinking man, or a nervous one. In fact, he was considered a very prosaic sort of person by his neighbours. He had a comfortable paunch, a reasonable but not excessive amount of hair on his head, an amiable wife and an active ten-year-old son. His neighbours were, of course, kept ignorant of the fact that he paid off the mortgage on his house by writing fantasies of one sort or another.

Till now, however, this secret vice had never affected his psyche. To be sure, his wife had shaken her head over his addiction many times. It was her standard opinion that he was wasting, even perverting, his talents.

"Who on Earth reads these things?" she would say. "All that stuff about demons and gnomes and wishing rings and elves. All that *kid* stuff, if you want my frank opinion."

"You're quite wrong," Prentiss would reply stiffly. "Modern fantasies are very sophisticated and mature treatments of folk motifs. Behind the façade of glib unreality there frequently lie trenchant comments on the world of today. Fantasy in modern style is, above all, adult fare."

Blanche shrugged. She had heard him speak at conventions so these comments weren't new to her.

"Besides," he would add, "fantasies pay the mortgage, don't they?"

"Maybe so," she would reply, "but it would be nice if you'd switch to mysteries. At least you'd get quarter-reprint sales out of those and we could even tell the neighbours what you do for a living."

Prentiss groaned in spirit. Blanche could come in now at any time and find him talking to himself (it was too real for a dream; it might be a hallucination). After that he *would* have to write mysteries for a living—or take to work.

"You're quite wrong," said the elf. "This is neither a dream nor a hallucination."

"Then why don't you go away?" asked Prentiss.

"I intend to. This is scarcely my idea of a place to live. And you're coming with me."

"I am *not*. What the hell do you think you are, telling me what I'm going to do?"

"If you think that's a respectful way to speak to a representative of an older culture, I can't say much for your upbringing."

"You're not an older culture——" He wanted to add: You're

just a figment of my imagination; but he had been a writer too long to be able to bring himself to commit the cliché.

"We insects," said the elf freezingly, "existed half a billion years before the first mammal was invented. We watched the dinosaurs come in and we watched them go out. As for you man-things—strictly newcomers."

For the first time, Prentiss noted that, from the spot on the elf's body where its limbs sprouted, a third vestigial pair existed as well. It increased the insecticity of the object and Prentiss' sense of indignation grew.

He said, "You needn't waste your company on social inferiors."

"I wouldn't," said the elf, "believe me. But necessity drives, you know. It's a rather complicated story but when you hear it, you'll *want* to help."

Prentiss said uneasily, "Look, I don't have much time. Blanche—my wife will be in here any time. She'll be upset."

"She won't be here," said the elf. "I've set up a block in her mind."

"What!"

"Quite harmless, I assure you. But, after all, we can't afford to be disturbed, can we?"

Prentiss sat back in his chair, dazed and unhappy.

The elf said, "We elves began our association with you man-things immediately after the last ice age began. It had been a miserable time for us, as you can imagine. We couldn't wear animal carcasses or live in holes as your uncouth ancestors did. It took incredible stores of psychic energy to keep warm."

"Incredible stores of what?"

"Psychic energy. You know nothing at all about it. Your mind is too coarse to grasp the concept. Please don't interrupt."

The elf continued, "Necessity drove us to experiment with your people's brains. They were crude, but large. The cells were inefficient, almost worthless, but there were a vast number of them. We could use those brains as a concentrating device, a type of psychic lens, and increase the available energy which our own minds could tap. We survived the ice age handily and without having to retreat to the tropics as in previous such eras.

"Of course, we were spoiled. When warmth returned, we didn't abandon the man-things. We used them to increase our standard of living generally. We could travel faster, eat better, do more, and we lost our old, simple, virtuous way of life forever. Then, too, there was milk."

"Milk?" said Prentiss. "I don't see the connection."

"A divine liquid. I only tasted it once in my life. But elfin classic poetry speaks of it in superlatives. In the old days, men always supplied us plentifully. Why mammals of all things

should be blessed with it and insects not is a complete mystery.
. . . How unfortunate it is that the men-things got out of hand."

"They did?"

"Two hundred years ago."

"Good for us."

"Don't be narrow-minded," said the elf stiffly. "It was a useful association for all parties until you man-things learned to handle physical energies in quantity. It was just the sort of gross thing your minds are capable of."

"What was wrong with it?"

"It's hard to explain. It was all very well for us to light up our nightly revels with fireflies brightened by use of two manpower of psychic energy. But then you men-creatures installed electric lights. Our antennal reception is good for miles, but then you invented telegraphs, telephones and radios. Our kobolds mined ore with much greater efficiency than man-things do, until man-things invented dynamite. Do you see?"

"No."

"Surely you don't expect sensitive and superior creatures such as the elves to watch a group of hairy mammals outdo them. It wouldn't be so bad if we could imitate the electronic development ourselves, but our psychic energies were insufficient for the purpose. Well, we retreated from reality. We sulked, pined and drooped. Call it an inferiority complex, if you will, but from two centuries ago onward, we slowly abandoned mankind and retreated to such centers as Avalon."

Prentiss thought furiously. "Let's get this straight. You can handle minds?"

"Certainly."

"You can make me think you're invisible? Hypnotically, I mean?"

"A crude term, but yes."

"And when you appeared just now, you did it by lifting a kind of mental block. Is that it?"

"To answer your thoughts, rather than your words: You are not sleeping; you are not mad; and I am not supernatural."

"I was just making sure. I take it, then, you can read my mind."

"Of course. It is a rather dirty and unrewarding sort of labour, but I can do it when I must. Your name is Prentiss and you write imaginative fiction. You have one larva who is at a place of instruction. I know a great deal about you."

Prentiss winced. "And just where is Avalon?"

"You won't find it." The elf clacked his mandibles together two or three times. "Don't speculate on the possibility of warning the authorities. You'll find yourself in a madhouse. Avalon, in case you think the knowledge will help you, is in the middle of the Atlantic and quite invisible, you know. After the steam-boat was invented, you man-things got to moving about so unreasonably that we had to cloak the whole island with a psychic shield.

"Of course, incidents *will* take place. Once a huge, barbaric vessel hit us dead centre and it took all the psychic energy of the entire population to give the island the appearance of an iceberg. The *Titanic*, I believe, was the name printed on the vessel. And nowadays there are planes flying overhead all the time and sometimes there are crashes. We picked up cases of canned milk once. That's when I tasted it."

Prentiss said, "Well, then, damn it, why aren't you still on Avalon? Why did you leave?"

"I was ordered to leave," said the elf angrily. "The fools."

"Oh?"

"You know how it is when you're a little different. I'm not like the rest of them and the poor tradition-ridden fools resented it. They were jealous. That's the best explanation. Jealous!"

"How are you different?"

"Hand me that light bulb," said the elf. "Oh, just unscrew it. You don't need a reading lamp in the daytime."

With a quiver of repulsion, Prentiss did as he was told and passed the object into the little hands of the elf. Carefully, the elf, with fingers so thin and wiry that they looked like tendrils, touched the bottom and side of the brass base.

Feebly, the filament in the bulb reddened.

"Good God," said Prentiss.

"That," said the elf proudly, "is my great talent. I told you that we elves couldn't adapt psychic energy to electronics. Well, I can! I'm not just an ordinary elf. I'm a mutant! A super-elf! I'm the next stage in elfin evolution. This light is due just to the activity of my own mind, you know. Now watch when I use yours as a focus."

As he said that, the bulb's filament grew white hot and painful to look at, while a vague and not unpleasant tickling sensation entered Prentiss' skull.

The lamp went out and the elf put the bulb on the desk behind the typewriter.

"I haven't tried," said the elf proudly, "but I suspect I can fission uranium too."

"But look here, lighting a bulb takes energy. You can't just hold it——"

"I've *told* you about psychic energy. Great Oberon, man-thing, try to understand."

Prentiss felt increasingly uneasy; he said cautiously, "What do you intend doing with this gift of yours?"

"Go back to Avalon, of course. I *should* let those fools go to their doom, but an elf does have a certain patriotism, even if he *is* a coleopteron."

"A what?"

"We elves are not all of a species, you know. I'm of beetle descent. See?"

He rose to his feet and, standing on the desk, turned his back to Prentiss. What had seemed merely a shining black cuticle suddenly split and lifted. From underneath, two filmy, veined wings fluttered out.

"Oh, you can fly," said Prentiss.

"You're very foolish," said the elf contemptuously, "not to realize I'm too large for flight. But they *are* attractive, aren't they? How do you like the iridescence? The lepidoptera have disgusting wings in comparison. They're gaudy and indelicate. What's more they're always sticking out."

"The lepidoptera?" Prentiss felt hopelessly confused.

"The butterfly clans. They're the proud ones. They were always letting humans see them so they could be admired. Very petty minds in a way. And that's why your legends always give fairies butterfly wings instead of beetle wings which are *much* more diaphanously beautiful. We'll give the lepidoptera what for when we get back, you and I."

"Now hold on——"

"Just think," said the elf, swaying back and forth in what looked like elfin ecstasy, "our nightly revels on the fairy green will be a blaze of sparkling light from curlicues of neon tubing. We can cut loose the swarms of wasps we've got hitched to our flying wagons and install internal-combustion motors instead. We can stop this business of curling up on leaves when it's time to sleep and build factories to manufacture decent mattresses. I tell you, we'll *live*. . . . And the rest of them will eat dirt for having ordered me out."

"But I can't go with you," bleated Prentiss. "I have responsibilities. I have a wife and kid. You wouldn't take a man away from his—his larva, would you?"

"I'm not cruel," said the elf. He turned his eyes full on Prentiss, "I have an elfin soul. Still, what choice have I? I must have a man-brain for focusing purposes or I will accomplish nothing; and not all man-brains are suitable."

"Why not?"

"Great Oberon, creature. A man-brain isn't a passive thing of wood and stone. It must co-operate in order to be useful. And it can only co-operate by being fully aware of our own elfin ability to manipulate it. I can use your brain, for instance, but your wife's would be useless to me. It would take her years to understand who and what I am."

Prentiss said, "This is a damned insult. Are you telling me I believe in fairies ? I'll have you know I'm a complete rationalist."

"Are you ? When I first revealed myself to you, you had a few feeble thoughts about dreams and hallucinations but you talked to me, you accepted me. Your wife would have screamed and gone into hysterics."

Prentiss was silent. He could think of no answer.

"That's the trouble," said the elf despondently. "Practically all you humans have forgotten about us since we left you. Your minds have closed; grown useless. To be sure, your larvae believe in your legends about the 'little folk,' but their brains are undeveloped and useful only for simple processes. When they mature, they lose belief. Frankly, I don't know what I would do if it weren't for you fantasy writers."

"What do you mean, we fantasy writers ?"

"You are the few remaining adults who believe in the insect folk. You, Prentiss, most of all. You've been a fantasy writer for twenty years."

"You're mad. I don't believe the things I write."

"You have to. You can't help it. I mean, while you're actually writing, you take the subject matter seriously. After a while your mind is just naturally cultivated into usefulness. . . . But why argue ? I *have* used you. You saw the light bulb brighten. So you see you must come with me."

"But I won't." Prentiss set his limbs stubbornly. "Can you make me against my will ?"

"I could, but I might damage you, and I wouldn't want that. Suppose we say this. If you don't agree to come, I could focus a current of high-voltage electricity through your wife. It would be a revolting thing to have to do, but I understand your own people execute enemies of the state in that fashion, so that you would probably find the punishment less horrible than I do. I wouldn't want to seem brutal even to a man-thing."

Prentiss grew conscious of the perspiration matting the short hairs on his temple.

"Wait," he said, "don't do anything like that. Let's talk it over."

The elf shot out his filmy wings, fluttered them and returned them to their case. "Talk, talk, talk. It's tiring. Surely you have milk in the house. You're not a very thoughtful host or you would have offered me refreshment before this."

Prentiss tried to bury the thought that came to him, to push it as far below the outer skin of his mind as he could. He said casually, "I have something better than milk. Here, I'll get it for you."

"Stay where you are. Call to your wife. She'll bring it."

"But I don't want her to see you. It would frighten her."

The elf said, "You need feel no concern. I'll handle her so that she won't be the least disturbed."

Prentiss lifted an arm.

The elf said, "Any attack you make on me will be far slower than the bolt of electricity that will strike your wife."

Prentiss' arm dropped. He stepped to the door of his study. "Blanche!" he called down the stairs.

Blanche was just visible in the living room, sitting woodenly in the armchair near the bookcase. She seemed to be asleep, open-eyed.

Prentiss turned to the elf. "Something's wrong with her."

"She's just in a state of sedation. She'll hear you. Tell her what to do."

"Blanche!" he called again. "Bring the container of eggnog and a small glass, will you?"

With no sign of animation other than that of bare movement, Blanche rose and disappeared from view.

"What is eggnog?" asked the elf.

Prentiss attempted enthusiasm. "It is a compound of milk, sugar and eggs beaten to a delightful consistency. Milk alone is poor stuff compared to it."

Blanche entered with the eggnog. Her pretty face was expressionless. Her eyes turned toward the elf but lightened with no realization of the significance of the sight.

"Here, Jan," she said, and sat down in the old, leather-covered chair by the window, hands falling loosely to her lap.

Prentiss watched her uneasily for a moment. "Are you going to keep her here?"

"She'll be easier to control. . . . Well, aren't you going to offer me the eggnog?"

"Oh, sure. Here!"

He poured the thick white liquid into the cocktail glass. He had prepared five bottles of it two nights before for the boys of the New York Fantasy Association and it had been mixed with a lavish hand, since fantasy writers notoriously like it so.

The elf's antennae trembled violently.

"A heavenly aroma," he muttered.

He wrapped the ends of his thin arms about the stem of the small glass and lifted it to his mouth. The liquid's level sank. When half was gone, he put it down and sighed, "Oh, the loss to my people. What a creation! What a thing to exist! Our histories tell us that in ancient days an occasional lucky sprite managed to take the place of a man-larva at birth so that he might draw off the liquid fresh-made. I wonder if even those ever experienced anything like this."

Prentiss said with a touch of professional interest, "That's the idea behind this business of changelings, is it?"

"Of course. The female man-creature has a great gift. Why not take advantage of it?" The elf turned his eyes upon the rise and fall of Blanche's bosom and sighed again.

Prentiss said (not too eager, now; don't give it away), "Go ahead. Drink all you want."

He, too, watched Blanche, waiting for signs of restoring animation, waiting for the beginnings of breakdown in the elf's control.

The elf said, "When is your larva returning from its place of instruction? I need him."

"Soon, soon," said Prentiss nervously. He looked at his wristwatch. Actually, Jan, Junior, would be back, yelling for a slab of cake and milk, in something like fifteen minutes.

"Fill 'er up," he said urgently. "Fill 'er up."

The elf sipped gaily. He said, "Once the larva arrives, you can go."

"Go?"

"Only to the library. You'll have to get volumes on electronics. I'll need the details on how to build television, telephones, all that. I'll need to have rules on wiring, instructions for constructing vacuum tubes. Details, Prentiss, details! We have tremendous tasks ahead of us. Oil drilling, gasoline refining, motors, scientific agriculture. We'll build a new Avalon, you and I. A technical one. A scientific fairyland. We will create a new world."

"Great!" said Prentiss. "Here, don't neglect your drink."

"You see. You are catching fire with the idea," said the elf. "And you will be rewarded. You will have a dozen female man-things to yourself."

Prentiss looked at Blanche automatically. No signs of hearing, but who could tell? He said, "I'd have no use for female man-th—for women, I mean."

"Come now," said the elf censoriously, "be truthful. You men-things are well known to our folk as lecherous, bestial creatures. Mothers frightened their young for generations by threatening them with men-things. . . . Young, ah!" He lifted the glass of eggnog in the air and said, "To my own young," and drained it.

"Fill 'er up," said Prentiss at once. "Fill 'er up."

The elf did so. He said, "I'll have lots of children. I'll pick out the best of the coleoptresses and breed my line. I'll continue the mutation. Right now I'm the only one, but when we have a dozen or fifty, I'll interbreed them and develop the race of the super-elf. A race of electro—ulp—electronic marvels and infinite future. . . . If I could only drink more. Nectar! The original nectar!"

There was the sudden noise of a door being flung open and a young voice calling, "Mom! Hey, Mom!"

The elf, his glossy eyes a little dimmed, said, "Then we'll begin to take over the men-things. A few believe already; the rest we will—urp—teach. It will be the old days, but better; a more efficient elf-hood, a tighter union."

Jan, Junior's, voice was closer and tinged with impatience. "Hey, Mom! Ain't you home?"

Prentiss felt his eyes popping with tension. Blanche sat rigid. The elf's speech was slightly thick, his balance a little unsteady. If Prentiss were going to risk it, now, now was the time.

"Sit back," said the elf peremptorily. "You're being foolish. I knew there was alcohol in the eggnog from the moment you thought your ridiculous scheme. You men-things are very shifty. We elves have many proverbs about you. Fortunately, alcohol has little effect upon us. Now if you had tried catnip with just a touch of honey in it . . . Ah, here is the larva. How are you, little man-thing?"

The elf sat there, the goblet of eggnog halfway to his mandibles, while Jan, Junior, stood in the doorway. Jan, Junior's, ten-year-old face was moderately smeared with dirt, his hair was immoderately matted and there was a look of the utmost surprise in his grey eyes. His battered schoolbooks swayed from the end of the strap he held in his hand.

He said, "Pop! What's the matter with Mom? And—and what's that?"

The elf said to Prentiss, "Hurry to the library. No time must be lost. You know the books I need." All trace of incipient drunkenness had left the creature and Prentiss' morale broke. The creature had been playing with him.

Prentiss got up to go.

The elf said, "And nothing human; nothing sneaky; no tricks. Your wife is still a hostage. I can use the larva's mind to kill her; it's good enough for that. I wouldn't want to do it. I'm a member of the Elfitarian Ethical Society and we advocate considerate treatment of mammals so you may rely on my noble principles *if* you do as I say."

Prentiss felt a strong compulsion to leave flooding him. He stumbled toward the door.

Jan, Junior, cried, "Pop, it can talk! He says he'll kill Mom! Hey, don't go away!"

Prentiss was already out of the room, when he heard the elf

say, "Don't stare at me, larva. I will not harm your mother if
you do exactly as I say. I am an elf, a fairy. You know what a
fairy is, of course."

And Prentiss was at the front door when he head Jan, Junior's,
treble raised in wild shouting, followed by scream after scream
in Blanche's shuddering soprano.

The strong, though invisible, elastic that was drawing Prentiss
out the house snapped and vanished. He fell backward, righted
himself and darted back up the stairs.

Blanche, fairly saturated with quivering life, was backed into
a corner, her arms about a weeping Jan, Junior.

On the deck was a collapsed black carapace, covering a nasty
smear of pulpiness from which colourless liquid dripped.

Jan, Junior, was sobbing hysterically, "I hit it. I hit it with my
schoolbooks. It was hurting Mom."

An hour passed and Prentiss felt the world of normality
pouring back into the interstices left behind by the creature from
Avalon. The elf itself was already ash in the incinerator behind
the house and the only remnant of its existence was the damp
stain at the foot of his desk.

Blanche was still sickly pale. They talked in whispers.

Prentiss said, "How's Jan, Junior?"

"He's watching television."

"Is he all right?"

"Oh, *he's* all right, but *I'*ll be having nightmares for weeks."

"I know. So will I unless we can get it out of our minds. I don't
think there'll ever be another of those—things here."

Blanche said, "I can't explain how awful it was. I kept hearing
every word he said, even when I was down in the living room."

"It was telepathy, you see."

"I just couldn't move. Then, after you left, I could begin to
stir a bit. I tried to scream but all I could do was moan and
whimper. Then Jan, Junior, smashed him and all at once I was
free. I don't understand how it happened."

Prentiss felt a certain gloomy satisfaction. "I think I know. I
was under his control because I accepted the truth of his
existence. He held you in check through me. When I left the
room, increasing distance made it harder to use my mind as a
psychic lens and you could begin moving. By the time I reached
the front door, the elf thought it was time to switch from my
mind to Jan, Junior's. That was his mistake."

"In what way?" asked Blanche.

"He assumed that all children believe in fairies, but he was
wrong. Here in America today children *don't* believe in fairies.
They never hear of them. They believe in Tom Corbett, in

Hopalong Cassidy, in Dick Tracy, in Howdy Doody, in Superman and a dozen other things, but not in fairies.

"The elf just never realized the sudden cultural changes brought about by comic books and television, and when he tried to grab Jan, Junior's, mind, he couldn't. Before he could recover his psychic balance, Jan, Junior, was on top of him in a swinging panic because he thought you were being hurt and it was all over.

"It's like I've always said, Blanche. The ancient folk motifs of legend survive only in the modern fantasy magazine, and modern fantasy is purely adult fare. Do you finally see my point?"

Blanche said humbly, "Yes, dear."

Prentiss put his hands in his pockets and grinned slowly. "You know, Blanche, next time I see Walt Rae, I think I'll just drop a hint that I write the stuff. Time the neighbours knew, I think."


Jan, Junior, holding an enormous slice of buttered bread, wandered into his father's study in search of the dimming memory. Pop kept slapping him on the back and Mom kept putting bread and cake in his hands and he was forgetting why. There had been this big old thing on the desk that could talk . . .

It had all happened so quickly that it got mixed up in his mind.

He shrugged his shoulders and, in the late afternoon sunlight, looked at the partly typewritten sheet in his father's typewriter, then at the small pile of paper resting on the desk.

He read a while, curled his lip and muttered, "Gee whiz. Fairies again. Always kid stuff!" and wandered off.

# The Watery Place

WE'RE NEVER going to have space travel. What's more, no extra-terrestrials will ever land on Earth—at least, any more.

I'm not just being a pessimist. As a matter of fact, space travel *is* possible; extraterrestrials *have* landed. I *know* that. Space ships are crisscrossing space among a million worlds, probably, but we'll never join them. I know that, too. All on account of a ridiculous error.

I'll explain.

It was actually Bart Cameron's error and you'll have to understand about Bart Cameron. He's the sheriff at Twin Gulch, Idaho, and I'm his deputy. Bart Cameron is an impatient man and he gets most impatient when he has to work up his income tax. You see, besides being sheriff, he also owns and runs the general store, he's got some shares in a sheep ranch, he does a bit of assay work, he's got a kind of pension for being a disabled veteran (bad knee) and a few other things like that. Naturally, it makes his tax figures complicated.

It wouldn't be so bad if he'd let a tax man work on the forms with him, but he insists on doing it himself and it makes him a bitter man. By April 14, he isn't approachable.

So it's too bad the flying saucer landed on April 14, 1956.

I saw it land. My chair was backed up against the wall in the sheriff's office, and I was looking at the stars through the windows and feeling too lazy to go back to my magazine and wondering if I ought to knock off and hit the sack or keep on listening to Cameron curse real steady as he went over his columns of figures for the hundred twenty-seventh time.

It looked like a shooting star at first, but then the track of light broadened into two things that looked like rocket exhausts and the thing came down sweet, steady and without a sound. An old, dead leaf would have rustled more coming down and landing thumpier. Two men got out.

I couldn't say anything or do anything. I couldn't choke or point; I couldn't even bug my eyes. I just sat there.

Cameron? He never looked up.

There was a knock on the door which wasn't locked. It opened and the two men from the flying saucer stepped in. I would have thought they were city fellows if I hadn't seen the flying saucer land in the scrub. They wore charcoal-grey suits, with white shirts and maroon four-in-hands. They had on black shoes and black homburgs. They had dark complexions, black wavy hair and brown eyes. They had very serious looks on their faces and were about five foot ten apiece. They looked very much alike.

God, I was scared.

But Cameron just looked up when the door opened and frowned. Ordinarily, I guess he'd have laughed the collar button off his shirt at seeing clothes like that in Twin Gulch, but he was so taken up by his income tax that he never cracked a smile.

He said, "What can I do for you, folks ?" and he tapped his hand on the forms so it was obvious he hadn't much time.

One of the two stepped forward. He said, "We have had your people under observation a long time." He pronounced each word carefully and all by itself.

Cameron said, "My people ? All I got's a wife. What's she been doing ?"

The fellow in the suit said, "We have chosen this locality for our first contact because it is isolated and peaceful. We know that you are the leader here."

"I'm the sheriff, if that's what you mean, so spit it out. What's your trouble ?"

"We have been careful to adopt your mode of dress and even to assume your appearance."

"That's *my* mode of dress ?" He must have noticed it for the first time.

"The mode of dress of your dominant social class, that is. We have also learned your language."

You could see the light break in on Cameron. He said, "You guys foreigners ?" Cameron didn't go much for foreigners, never having met many outside the army, but generally he tried to be fair.

The man from the saucer said, "Foreigners ? Indeed we are. We come from the watery place your people call Venus."

(I was just collecting up strength to blink my eyes, but that sent me right back to nothing. I had seen the flying saucer. I had seen it land. I had to believe this ! These men—or these some-things—came from Venus.)

But Cameron never blinked an eye. He said, "All right. This is the U.S.A. We all got equal rights regardless of race, creed, colour, *or* nationality. I'm at your service. What can I do for you ?"

"We would like to have you make immediate arrangements for the important men of your U.S.A., as you call it, to be brought here for discussions leading to your people joining our great organization."

Slowly, Cameron got red. "Our people join *your* organization. We're already part of the U.N. and God knows what else. And I suppose I'm to get the President here, eh? Right now? In Twin Gulch? Send a hurry-up message?" He looked at me, as though he wanted to see a smile on my face, but I couldn't as much as fall down if someone had pushed the chair out from under me.

The saucer man said, "Speed is desirable."

"You want Congress, too? The Supreme Court?"

"If they will help, sheriff."

And Cameron really went to pieces. He banged his income tax form and yelled, "Well, you're not helping me, and I have no time for wiseguy jerks who come around, especially foreigners. If you don't get the hell out of here pronto, I'll lock you up for disturbing the peace and I'll never let you out."

"You wish us to leave?" said the man from Venus.

"Right now! Get the hell out of here and back to wherever you're from and don't ever come back. I don't want to see you and no one else around here does."

The two men looked at each other, making little twitches with their faces.

Then the one who had done all the talking said, "I can see in your mind that you really wish, with great intensity, to be left alone. It is not our way to force ourselves or our organization on people who do not wish us or it. We will respect your privacy and leave. We will not return. We will girdle your world in warning and none will enter and your people will never have to leave."

Cameron said, "Mister, I'm tired of this crap, so I'll count to three——"

They turned and left, and I just knew that everything they said was so. I was listening to them, you see, which Cameron wasn't, because he was busy thinking of his income tax, and it was as though I could hear their minds, know what I mean? I knew that there would be a kind of fence around earth, corralling us in, keeping us from leaving, keeping others from coming in. I *knew* it.

And when they left, I got my voice back—too late. I screamed, "Cameron, for God's sake, they're from space. Why'd you send them away?"

"From space!" He stared at me.

I yelled, "Look!" I don't know how I did it, he being twenty-five pounds heavier than I, but I yanked him to the window by his shirt collar, bursting every shirt button off him.

He was too surprised to resist and when he recovered his wits enough to make like he was going to knock me down, he caught sight of what was going on outside the window and the breath went out of *him*.

They were getting into the flying saucer, those two men, and the saucer sat there, large, round, shiny and kind of powerful, you know. Then it took off. It went up easy as a feather and a red-orange glow showed up on one side and got brighter as the ship got smaller till it was a shooting star again, slowly fading out.

And I said, "Sheriff, why'd you send them away? They *had* to see the President. Now they'll never come back."

Cameron said, "I thought they were foreigners. They *said* they had to learn our language. And they talked funny."

"Oh, fine. Foreigners."

"They *said* they were foreigners and they looked Italian. I thought they were Italian."

"How could they be Italian? They said they were from the planet Venus. I heard them. They said so."

"The planet Venus." His eyes got real round.

"They said it. They called it the watery place or something. You know Venus has a lot of water on it."

But you see, it was just an error, a stupid error, the kind anyone could make. Only now Earth is never going to have space travel and we'll never as much as land on the moon or have another Venusian visit us. That dope, Cameron, and his income tax!

Because he whispered, "Venus! When they talked about the watery place, I thought they meant *Venice!*"

# Living Space

CLARENCE RIMBRO had no objections to living in the only house on an uninhabited planet, any more than had any other of Earth's even trillion of inhabitants.

If someone had questioned him concerning possible objections, he would undoubtedly have stared blankly at the questioner. His house was much larger than any house could possibly be on Earth proper and much more modern. It had its independent air supply and water supply; ample food in its freezing compartments. It was isolated from the lifeless planet on which it was located by a force field, but the rooms were built about a five-acre farm (under glass, of course), which, in the planet's beneficent sunlight, grew flowers for pleasure and vegetables for health. It even supported a few chickens. It gave Mrs. Rimbro something to do with herself afternoons, and a place for the two little Rimbros to play when they were tired of indoors.

Furthermore, if one *wanted* to be on Earth proper, if one insisted on it; if one *had* to have people around and air one could breathe in the open or water to swim in, one had only to go out of the front door of the house.

So where was the difficulty?

Remember, too, that on the lifeless planet on which the Rimbro house was located there was complete silence except for the occasional monotonous effects of wind and rain. There was absolute privacy and the feeling of absolute ownership of two hundred million square miles of planetary surface.

Clarence Rimbro appreciated all that in his distant way. He was an accountant, skilled in handling very advanced computer models, precise in his manners and clothing, not much given to smiling beneath his thin, well-kept mustache and properly aware of his own worth. When he drove from work toward home, he passed the occasional dwelling place on Earth proper and he never ceased to stare at them with a certain smugness.

Well, either for business reasons or mental perversion, some people simply had to live on Earth proper. It was too bad for them. After all, Earth proper's soil had to supply the minerals and basic food supply for all the trillion of inhabitants (in fifty years, it would be two trillion) and space was at a premium. Houses on Earth proper just *couldn't* be any bigger than that, and people who had to live in them had to adjust to the fact.

Even the process of entering his house had its mild pleasant-ness. He would enter the community twist place to which he was assigned (it looked, as did all such, like a rather stumpy obelisk), and there he would invariably find others waiting to use it. Still more would arrive before he reached the head of the line. It was a sociable time.

"How's your planet ?" "How's yours ?" The usual small talk. Sometimes someone would be having trouble. Machinery break-downs or serious weather that would alter the terrain unfavour-ably. Not often.

But it passed the time. Then Rimbro would be at the head of the line; he would put his key into the slot; the proper com-bination would be punched; and he would be twisted into a new probability pattern; his own particular probability pattern; the one assigned to him when he married and became a producing citizen; a probability pattern in which life had never developed on Earth. And twisting to this particular lifeless Earth, he would walk into his own foyer.

Just like that.

He never worried about being in another probability. Why should he ? He never gave it any thought. There were an infinite number of possible Earths. Each existed in its own niche; its own probability pattern. Since on a planet such as Earth there was, according to calculation, about a fifty-fifty chance of life's developing, half of all the possible Earths (still infinite, since half of infinity was infinity) possessed life, and half (still in-finite) did not. And living on about three hundred billion of the unoccupied Earths were three hundred billion families, each with its own beautiful house, powered by the sun of that prob-ability, and each securely at peace. The number of Earths so occupied grew by millions each day.

And then one day, Rimbro came home and Sandra (his wife) said to him, as he entered, "There's been the most peculiar noise."

Rimbro's eyebrows shot up and he looked closely at his wife. Except for a certain restlessness of her thin hands and a pale look about the corners of her tight mouth, she looked normal.

Rimbro said, still holding his topcoat halfway toward the ser-vette that waited patiently for it, "Noise ? What noise ? I don't hear anything."

"It's stopped now," Sandra said. "Really, it was like a deep thumping or rumble. You'd hear it a bit. Then it would stop. Then you'd hear it a bit and so on. I've never heard anything like it."

Rimbro surrendered his coat. "But that's quite impossible."

"I *heard* it."

"I'll look over the machinery," he mumbled. "Something may be wrong."

Nothing was, that his accountant's eyes could discover, and, with a shrug, he went to supper. He listened to the servettes hum busily about their different chores, watched one sweep up the plates and cutlery for disposal and recovery, then said, pursing his lips, "Maybe one of the servettes is out of order. I'll check them."

"It wasn't anything like that, Clarence."

Rimbro went to bed, without further concern over the matter, and wakened with his wife's hand clutching his shoulder. His hand went automatically to the contact patch that set the walls glowing. "What's the matter ? What time is it ?"

She shook her head. "Listen! *Listen !*"

Good Lord, thought Rimbro, there *is* a noise. A definite rumbling. It came and went.

"Earthquake ?" he whispered. It did happen, of course, though, with all the planets to choose from, they could generally count on having avoided the faulted areas.

"All day long ?" asked Sandra fretfully. "I think it's something else." And then she voiced the secret terror of every nervous householder. "I think there's someone on the planet with us. This Earth is *inhabited.*"

Rimbro did the logical things. When morning came, he took his wife and children to his wife's mother. He himself took a day off and hurried to the Sector's Housing Bureau.

He was quite annoyed at all this.

Bill Ching of the Housing Bureau was short, jovial and proud of his part-Mongolian ancestry. He thought probability patterns had solved every last one of humanity's problems. Alec Mishnoff, also of the Housing Bureau, thought probability patterns were a snare into which humanity had been hopelessly tempted. He had originally majored in archeology and had studied a variety of antiquarian subjects with which his delicately poised head was still crammed. His face managed to look sensitive despite overbearing eyebrows, and he lived with a pet notion that so far he had dared tell no one, though preoccupation with it had driven him out of archeology and into housing.

Ching was fond of saying, "The hell with Malthus!" It was almost a verbal trademark of his, "The hell with Malthus. We can't possibly overpopulate now. However frequently we double and redouble, Homo sapiens remains finite in number, and the uninhabited Earths remain infinite. And we don't have to put one house on each planet. We can put a hundred, a thousand, a

million. Plenty of room and plenty of power from each probability sun."

"More than one on a planet?" said Mishnoff sourly.

Ching knew exactly what he meant. When probability
patterns had first been put to use, sole ownership of a planet had
been powerful inducement for early settlers. It appealed to the
snob and despot in every one. What man so poor, ran the slogan,
as not to have an empire larger than Genghis Khan's? To
introduce multiple settling now would outrage everyone.

Ching said, with a shrug, "All right, it would take psychological preparation. So what? That's what it took to start the
whole deal in the first place."

"And food?" asked Mishnoff.

"You know we're putting hydroponic works and yeast plants
in other probability patterns. And if we had to, we could culti-
vate their soil."

"Wearing space suits and importing oxygen."

"We could reduce carbon dioxide for oxygen till the plants
got going and they'd do the job after that."

"Given a million years."

"Mishnoff, the trouble with you," Ching said, "is you read
too many ancient history books. You're an obstructionist."

But Ching was too good-natured really to mean that, and
Mishnoff continued to read books and to worry. Mishnoff longed
for the day he could get up the courage necessary to see the Head
of the Section and put right out in plain view—bang, like that—
exactly what it was that was troubling him.

But now a Mr. Clarence Rimbro faced them, perspiring
slightly and toweringly angry at the fact that it had taken him
the better part of two days to reach this far into the Bureau.

He reached his exposition's climax by saying, "And *I* say the
planet is inhabited and I don't propose to stand for it."

Having listened to his story in full, Ching tried the soothing
approach. He said, "Noise like that is probably just some
natural phenomenon."

"What kind of natural phenomenon?" demanded Rimbro. "I
want an investigation. If it's a natural phenomenon, I want to
know what kind. I say the place is inhabited. It has life on it, by
Heaven, and I'm not paying rent on a planet to share it. And
with dinosaurs, from the sound of it."

"Come, Mr. Rimbro, how long have you lived on your Earth?"

"Fifteen and a half years."

"And has there ever been any evidence of life?"

"There is now, and, as a citizen with a production record
classified as A-1, I demand an investigation."

"Of course we'll investigate, sir, but we just want to assure

you now that everything is all right. Do you realize how carefully we select our probability patterns?"

"I'm an accountant. I have a pretty good idea," said Rimbro
at once.

"Then surely you know our computers cannot fail us. They
never pick a probability which has been picked before. They
can't possibly. And they're geared to select only probability
patterns in which Earth has a carbon dioxide atmosphere, one
in which plant life, and therefore animal life, has never developed.
Because if plants had evolved, the carbon dioxide would have
been reduced to oxygen. Do you understand?"

"I understand it all very well and I'm not here for lectures,"
said Rimbro, "I want an investigation out of you and nothing
else. It is quite humiliating to think I may be sharing my world,
my own world, with something or other, and I don't propose to
endure it."

"No, of course not," muttered Ching, avoiding Mishnoff's
sardonic glance. "We'll be there before night."

They were on their way to the twisting place with full equipment.

Mishnoff said, "I want to ask you something. Why do you go
through that 'There's no need to worry, sir' routine? They
always worry anyway. Where does it get you?"

"I've got to try. They *shouldn't* worry," said Ching petulantly.
"Ever hear of a carbon dioxide planet that *was* inhabited?
Besides, Rimbro is the type that starts rumors. I can spot them.
By the time he's through, if he's encouraged, he'll say his sun
went nova."

"*That* happens sometimes," said Mishnoff.

"So? One house is wiped out and one family dies. See, you're
an obstructionist. In the old times, the times you like, if there
were a flood in China or someplace, thousands of people would
die. And that's out of a population of a measly billion or two."

Mishnoff muttered, "How do you know the Rimbro planet
doesn't have life on it?"

"Carbon dioxide atmosphere."

"But suppose——" It was no use. Mishnoff couldn't say it.
He finished lamely, "Suppose plant and animal life develops
that can live on carbon dioxide."

"It's never been observed."

"In an infinite number of worlds, anything can happen." He
finished that in a whisper. "Everything *must* happen."

"Chances are one in a duodecillion," said Ching, shrugging.

They arrived at the twisting point then, and, having utilized
the freight twist for their vehicle (thus sending it into the

Rimbro storage area), they entered the Rimbro probability pattern themselves. First Ching, then Mishnoff.

"A nice house," said Ching, with satisfaction. "Very nice model. Good taste."

"Hear anything?" asked Mishnoff.

"No."

Ching wandered into the garden. "Hey," he yelled. "Rhode Island Reds."

Mishnoff followed, looking up at the glass roof. The sun looked like the sun of a trillion other Earths.

He said absently, "There could be plant life, just starting out. The carbon dioxide might just be starting to drop in concentration. The computer would never know."

"And it would take millions of years for animal life to begin and millions more for it to come out of the sea."

"It doesn't have to follow that pattern."

Ching put an arm about his partner's shoulder. "You brood. Someday, you'll tell me what's really bothering you, instead of just hinting, and we can straighten you out."

Mishnoff shrugged off the encircling arm with an annoyed frown. Ching's tolerance was always hard to bear. He began, "Let's not psychotherapize——" He broke off, then whispered, "Listen."

There was a distant rumble. Again.

They placed the seismograph in the center of the room and activated the force field that penetrated downward and bound it rigidly to bedrock. They watched the quivering needle record the shocks.

Mishnoff said, "Surface waves only. Very superficial. It's not underground."

Ching looked a little more dismal, "What is it then?"

"I think," said Mishnoff, "we'd better find out." His face was gray with apprehension. "We'll have to set up a seismograph at another point and get a fix on the focus of the disturbance."

"Obviously," said Ching. "I'll go out with the other seismograph. You stay here."

"No," said Mishnoff, with energy, "*I'll* go out."

Mishnoff felt terrified, but he had no choice. If this were *it*, he would be prepared. He could get a warning through. Sending out an unsuspecting Ching would be disastrous. Nor could he warn Ching, who would certainly never believe him.

But since Mishnoff was not cast in the heroic mold, he trembled as he got into his oxygen suit and fumbled the disrupter as he tried to dissolve the force field locally in order to free the emergency exit.

"Any reason *you* want to go, particularly?" asked Ching, watching the other's inept manipulations. "I'm willing."

"It's all right. I'm going out," said Mishnoff, out of a dry throat, and stepped into the lock that led out on to the desolate surface of a lifeless Earth. A presumably lifeless Earth.

The sight was not unfamiliar to Mishnoff. He had seen its like dozens of times. Bare rock, weathered by wind and rain, crusted and powdered with sand in the gullies; a small and noisy brook beating itself against its stony course. All brown and gray; no sign of green. No sound of life.

Yet the sun was the same and, when night fell, the constellations would be the same.

The situation of the dwelling place was in that region which on Earth proper would be called Labrador. (It was Labrador here, too, really. It had been calculated that in not more than one out of a quadrillion or so Earths were there significant changes in the geological development. The continents were everywhere recognizable down to quite small details.)

Despite the situation and the time of the year, which was October, the temperature was sticky warm due to the hothouse effect of the carbon dioxide in this Earth's dead atmosphere.

From inside his suit, through the transparent visor, Mishnoff watched it all somberly. If the epicenter of the noise were close by, adjusting the second seismograph a mile or so away would be enough for the fix. If it weren't, they would have to bring in an air scooter. Well, assume the lesser complication to begin with.

Methodically, he made his way up a rocky hillside. Once at the top, he could choose his spot.

Once at the top, puffing and feeling the heat most unpleasantly, he found he didn't have to.

His heart was pounding so that he could scarcely hear his own voice as he yelled into his radio mouthpiece, "Hey, Ching, there's construction going on."

"What?" came back the appalled shout in his ears.

There was no mistake. Ground was being leveled. Machinery was at work. Rock was being blasted out.

Mishnoff shouted, "They're blasting. That's the noise."

Ching called back, "But it's impossible. The computer would never pick the same probability pattern twice. *It couldn't.*"

"You don't understand——" began Mishnoff.

But Ching was following his own thought processes. "Get over there, Mishnoff. I'm coming out, too."

"No, damn it. You stay there," cried Mishnoff in alarm.

"Keep me in radio contact, and for God's sake be ready to leave for Earth proper on wings if I give the word."

"Why?" demanded Ching. "What's going on?"

"I don't know yet," said Mishnoff. "Give me a chance to find out."

To his own surprise, he noticed his teeth were chattering.

Muttering breathless curses at the computer, at probability patterns and at the insatiable need for living space on the part of a trillion human beings expanding in numbers like a puff of smoke, Mishnoff slithered and slipped down the other side of the slope, setting stones to rolling and rousing peculiar echoes.

A man came out to meet him, dressed in a gas-tight suit, different in many details from Mishnoff's own, but obviously intended for the same purpose—to lead oxygen to the lungs.

Mishnoff gasped breathlessly into his mouthpiece, "Hold it, Ching. There's a man coming. Keep in touch." Mishnoff felt his heart pump more easily and the bellows of his lungs labor less.

The two men were staring at one another. The other man was blond and craggy of face. The look of surprise about him was too extreme to be feigned.

He said in a harsh voice, "*Wer sind Sie? Was machen Sie hier?*"

Mishnoff was thunderstruck. He'd studied ancient German for two years in the days when he expected to be an archeologist and he followed the comment despite the fact that the pronunciation was not what he had been taught. The stranger was asking his identity and his business there.

Stupidly, Mishnoff stammered, "*Sprechen Sie Deutsch?*" and then had to mutter reassurance to Ching whose agitated voice in his earpiece was demanding to know what the gibberish was all about.

The German-speaking one made no direct answer. He repeated, "*Wer sind Sie?*" and added impatiently, "*Hier ist für einen verrückten Spass keine Zeit.*"

Mishnoff didn't feel like a joke either, particularly not a foolish one, but he continued, "*Sprechen Sie Planetisch?*"

He did not know the German for "Planetary Standard Language" so he had to guess. Too late, he thought he should have referred to it simply as English.

The other man stared wide-eyed at him. "*Sind Sie wahnsinnig?*"

Mishnoff was almost willing to settle for that, but in feeble self-defense, he said, "I'm not crazy, damn it. I mean, "*Auf der Erde woher Sie gekom——*"

He gave it up for lack of German, but the new idea that was rattling inside his skull would not quit its nagging. He had to find some way of testing it. He said desperately, *"Welches Jahr ist es jetzt?"*

Presumably, the stranger, who was questioning his sanity already, would be convinced of Mishnoff's insanity now that he was being asked what year it was, but it was one question for which Mishnoff had the necessary German.

The other muttered something that sounded suspiciously like good German swearing and then said, *"Es ist doch zweitausend-dreihundertvierundsechzig, und warum——"*

The stream of German that followed was completely incomprehensible to Mishnoff, but in any case he had had enough for the moment. If he translated the German correctly, the year given him was 2364, which was nearly two thousand years in the past. How could that be?

He muttered, *"Zweitausenddreihundertvierundsechzig?"*

*"Ja, Ja,"* said the other, with deep sarcasm. *"Zweitausenddrei-hundertvierundsechzig. Der ganze Jahr lang ist es so gewesen."*

Mishnoff shrugged. The statement that it had been so all year long was a feeble witticism even in German and it gained nothing in translation. He pondered.

But then the other's ironical tone deepening, the German-speaking one went on, *"Zweitausenddreihundertvierundsechzig nach Hitler. Hilft das Ihnen vielleicht? Nach Hitler!"*

Mishnoff yelled with delight. "That *does* help me. *Es hilft! Hören Sie, bitte——"* He went on in broken German interspersed with scraps of Planetary, "For Heaven's sake, *um Gottes Willen——"*

Making it 2364 after Hitler was different altogether.

He put German together desperately, trying to explain.

The other frowned and grew thoughtful. He lifted his gloved hand to stroke his chin or make some equivalent gesture, hit the transparent visor that covered his face and left his hand there uselessly, while he thought.

He said, suddenly, *"Ich heisse George Fallenby."*

To Mishnoff it seemed that the name must be of Anglo-Saxon derivation, although the change in vowel form as pronounced by the other made it seem Teutonic.

*"Guten Tag,"* said Mishnoff awkwardly. *"Ich heisse Alec Mishnoff,"* and was suddenly aware of the Slavic derivation of his own name.

*"Kommen Sie mit mir, Herr Mishnoff,"* said Fallenby.

Mishnoff followed with a strained smile, muttering into his transmitter, "It's all right, Ching. It's all right."

Back on Earth proper, Mishnoff faced the Sector's Bureau Head, who had grown old in the Service; whose every gray hair betokened a problem met and solved; and every missing hair a problem averted. He was a cautious man with eyes still bright and teeth that were still his own. His name was Berg.

He shook his head. "And they speak German: but the German you studied was two thousand years old."

"True," said Mishnoff. "But the English Hemingway used is two thousand years old and Planetary is close enough for anyone to be able to read it."

"Hmp. And who's this Hitler?"

"He was a sort of tribal chief in ancient times. He led the German tribe in one of the wars of the twentieth century, just about the time the Atomic Age started and true history began."

"Before the Devastation, you mean?"

"Right. There was a series of wars then. The Anglo-Saxon countries won out, and I suppose that's why the Earth speaks Planetary."

"And if Hitler and his Germans had won out, the world would speak German instead?"

"They *have* won out on Fallenby's Earth, sir, and they *do* speak German."

"And make their dates 'after Hitler' instead of A.D.?"

"Right. And I suppose there's an Earth in which the Slavic tribes won out and everyone speaks Russian."

"Somehow," said Berg, "it seems to me we should have foreseen it, and yet, as far as I know, no one has. After all, there are an infinite number of inhabited Earths, and we can't be the only one that has decided to solve the problem of unlimited population growth by expanding into the worlds of probability."

"Exactly," said Mishnoff earnestly, "and it seems to me that if you think of it, there must be countless inhabited Earths so doing and there must be many multiple occupations in the three hundred billion Earths we ourselves occupy. The only reason we caught this one is that, by sheer chance, they decided to build within a mile of the dwelling we had placed there. This is something we must check."

"You imply we ought to search all our Earths."

"I do, sir. We've got to make some settlement with other inhabited Earths. After all, there is room for all of us and to expand without agreement may result in all sorts of trouble and conflict."

"Yes," said Berg thoughtfully. "I agree with you."

Clarence Rimbro stared suspiciously at Berg's old face, creased now into all manner of benevolence.

"You're sure now?"

"Absolutely," said the Bureau Head. "We're sorry that you've had to accept temporary quarters for the last two weeks——"

"More like three."

"——three weeks, but you will be compensated."

"What was the noise?"

"Purely geological, sir. A rock was delicately balanced and, with the wind, it made occasional contact with the rocks of the hillside. We've removed it and surveyed the area to make certain that nothing similar will occur again."

Rimbro clutched his hat and said, "Well, thanks for your trouble."

"No thanks necessary, I assure you, Mr. Rimbro. This is our job."

Rimbro was ushered out, and Berg turned to Mishnoff, who had remained a quiet spectator of this completion of the Rimbro affair.

Berg said, "The Germans were nice about it, anyway. They admitted we had priority and got off. Room for everybody, they said. Of course, as it turned out, they build any number of dwellings on each unoccupied world. . . . And now there's the project of surveying our other worlds and making similar agreements with whomever we find. It's all strictly confidential, too. It can't be made known to the populace without plenty of preparation. . . . Still, none of this is what I want to speak to you about."

"Oh?" said Mishnoff. Developments had not noticeably cheered him. His own bogey still concerned him.

Berg smiled at the younger man. "You understand, Mishnoff, we in the Bureau, and in the Planetary Government, too, are very appreciative of your quick thinking, of your understanding of the situation. This could have developed into something very tragic, had it not been for you. This appreciation will take some tangible form."

"Thank you, sir."

"But, as I said once before, this is something many of us should have thought of. How is it you did? . . . Now we've gone into your background a little. Your co-worker, Ching, tells us you have hinted in the past at some serious danger involved in our probability-pattern set-up, and that you insisted on going out to meet the Germans although you were obviously frightened. You were anticipating what you actually found, were you not? And how did you do it?"

Mishnoff said confusedly, "No, no. That was not in my mind at all. It came as a surprise. I——"

Suddenly he stiffened. Why not now? They were grateful to

him. He had proved that he was a man to be taken into account. One unexpected thing had already happened.

He said firmly, "There's something else."

"Yes?"

(How did one begin?) "There's no life in the Solar System other than the life on Earth."

"That's right," said Berg benevolently.

"And computation has it that the probability of developing any form of interstellar travel is so low as to be infinitesimal."

"What are you getting at?"

"That all this is so *in this probability*! But there must be some probability patterns in which other life *does* exist in the Solar System or in which interstellar drives *are* developed by dwellers in other star systems."

Berg frowned. "Theoretically."

"In one of these probabilities, Earth may be visited by such intelligences. If it were a probability pattern in which Earth is inhabited, it won't affect us; they'll have no connection with us in Earth proper. But if it were a probability pattern in which Earth is uninhabited and they set up some sort of a base, they may find, by happenstance, one of our dwelling places."

"Why ours?" demanded Berg dryly. "Why not a dwelling place of the Germans, for instance?"

"Because we spot our dwellings one to a world. The German Earth doesn't. Probably very few others do. The odds are in favour of us by billions to one. And if extraterrestrials do find such a dwelling, they'll investigate and find the route to Earth proper, a highly developed, rich world."

"Not if we turn off the twisting place," said Berg.

"Once they know that twisting places exist, they can construct their own," said Mishnoff. "A race intelligent enough to travel through space could do that, and from the equipment in the dwelling they would take over, they could easily spot our particular probability. . . . And then how would we handle extraterrestrials? They're not Germans, or other Earths. They would have alien psychologies and motivations. And we're not even on our guard. We just keep setting up more and more worlds and increasing the chance every day that——"

His voice had risen in excitement and Berg shouted at him, "Nonsense. This is all ridiculous——"

The buzzer sounded and the communiplate brightened and showed the face of Ching. Ching's voice said, "I'm sorry to interrupt, but——"

"What is it?" demanded Berg savagely.

"There's a man here I don't know what to do with. He's drunk or crazy. He complains that his home is surrounded and that there are things staring through the glass roof of his garden."

"Things ?" cried Mishnoff.

"Purple things with big red veins, three eyes and some sort of tentacles instead of hair. They have——"

But Mishnoff and Berg didn't hear the rest. They were staring at each other in sick horror.

# The Message

THEY DRANK beer and reminisced as men will who have met after long separation. They called to mind the days under fire. They remembered sergeants and girls, both with exaggeration. Deadly things became humorous in retrospect, and trifles disregarded for ten years were hauled out for airing.

Including, of course, the perennial mystery.

"How do you account for it?" asked the first. "Who started it?"

The second shrugged. "No one started it. Everyone was doing it, like a disease. You, too, I suppose."

The first chuckled.

The third one said softly, "I never saw the fun in it. Maybe because I came across it first when I was under fire for the first time. North Africa."

"Really?" said the second.

"The first night on the beaches of Oran. I was getting under cover, making for some native shack and I saw it in the light of a flare——"

George was deliriously happy. Two years of red tape and now he was finally back in the past. Now he could complete his paper on the social life of the foot soldier of World War II with some authentic details.

Out of the warless, insipid society of the thirtieth century, he found himself for one glorious moment in the tense, superlative drama of the warlike twentieth.

North Africa! Site of the first great sea-borne invasion of the war! How the temporal physicists had scanned the area for the perfect spot and moment. This shadow of an empty wooden building was it. No human would approach for a known number of minutes. No blast would seriously affect it in that time. By being there, George would not affect history. He would be that ideal of the temporal physicist, the "pure observer".

It was even more terrific than he had imagined. There was the perpetual roar of artillery, the unseen tearing of planes overhead. There were the periodic lines of tracer bullets splitting the sky and the occasional ghastly glow of a flare twisting downward.

And *he* was here! He, George, was part of the war, part of an intense kind of life forever gone from the world of the thirtieth century, grown tame and gentle.

He imagined he could see the shadows of an advancing column of soldiers, hear the low cautious monosyllables slip from one to another. How he longed to be one of them in truth, not merely a momentary intruder, a "pure observer".

He stopped his note taking and stared at his stylus, its micro-light hypnotizing him for a moment. A sudden idea had over-whelmed him and he looked at the wood against which his shoulder pressed. This moment must not pass unforgotten into history. Surely doing this would affect nothing. He would use the older English dialect and there would be no suspicion.

He did it quickly and then spied a soldier running desperately toward the structure, dodging a burst of bullets. George knew his time was up, and, even as he knew it, found himself back in the thirtieth century.

It didn't matter. For those few minutes he had been part of World War II. A small part, but *part*. And others would know it. They might not know they knew it, but someone perhaps would repeat the message to himself.

Someone, perhaps that man running for shelter, would read it and know that along with all the heroes of the twentieth cen-tury was the "pure observer", the man from the thirtieth century, George Kilroy. *He* was there!

# Satisfaction Guaranteed

TONY WAS tall and darkly handsome, with an incredibly patrician air drawn into every line of his unchangeable expression, and Claire Belmont regarded him through the crack in the door with a mixture of horror and dismay.

"I can't, Larry. I just can't have him in the house." Feverishly, she was searching her paralyzed mind for a stronger way of putting it; some way that would make sense and settle things, but she could only end with a simple repetition.

"Well, I can't!"

Larry Belmont regarded his wife stiffly, and there was that spark of impatience in his eyes that Claire hated to see, since she felt her own incompetence mirrored in it. "We're committed, Claire," he said, "and I can't have you backing out now. The company is sending me to Washington on this basis, and it probably means a promotion. It's perfectly safe and you know it. What's your objection?"

She frowned helplessly. "It just gives me the chills. I couldn't bear him."

"He's as human as you or I, almost. So, no nonsense. Come, get out there."

His hand was in the small of her back, shoving; and she found herself in her own living room, shivering. *It* was there, looking at her with a precise politeness, as though appraising his hostess-to-be of the next three weeks. Dr. Susan Calvin was there, too, sitting stiffly in thin-lipped abstraction. She had the cold, far-away look of someone who has worked with machines so long that a little of the steel had entered the blood.

"Hello," crackled Claire in general, and ineffectual, greeting.

But Larry was busily saving the situation with a spurious gaiety. "Here, Claire, I want you to meet Tony, a swell guy. This is my wife, Claire, Tony, old boy." Larry's hand draped itself amiably over Tony's shoulder, but Tony remained unresponsive and expressionless under the pressure.

He said, "How do you do, Mrs. Belmont."

And Claire jumped at Tony's voice. It was deep and mellow, smooth as the hair on his head or the skin on his face.

Before she could stop herself, she said, "Oh, my—you talk."

"Why not? Did you expect that I didn't?"

But Claire could only smile weakly. She didn't really know what she had expected. She looked away, then let him slide gently into the corner of her eye. His hair was smooth and black, like polished plastic—or was it really composed of separate hairs? And was the even, olive skin of his hands and face continued on past the obscurement of his formally cut clothing?

She was lost in the shuddering wonder of it, and had to force her thoughts back into place to meet Dr. Calvin's flat, unemotional voice.

"Mrs. Belmont, I hope you appreciate the importance of this experiment. Your husband tells me he has given you some of the background. I would like to give you more, as the senior psychologist of the U.S. Robots and Mechanical Men Corporation.

"Tony is a robot. His actual designation on the company files is TN-3, but he will answer to Tony. He is not a mechanical monster, nor simply a calculating machine of the type that were developed during World War II, fifty years ago. He has an artificial brain nearly as complicated as our own. It is an immense telephone switchboard on an atomic scale, so that billions of possible 'telephone connections' can be compressed into an instrument that will fit inside a skull.

"Such brains are manufactured for each model of robot specifically. Each contains a precalculated set of connections so that each robot knows the English language to start with and enough of anything else that may be necessary to perform his job.

"Until now, U.S. Robots has confined its manufacturing activity to industrial models for use in places where human labour is impractical—in deep mines, for instance, or in underwater work. But we want to invade the city and the home. To do so, we must get the ordinary man and woman to accept these robots without fear. You understand that there is nothing to fear."

"There isn't, Claire," interposed Larry earnestly. "Take my word for it. It's impossible for him to do any harm. You know I wouldn't leave him with you otherwise."

Claire cast a quick, secret glance at Tony and lowered her voice. "What if I make him angry?"

"You needn't whisper," said Dr. Calvin calmly. "He *can't* get angry with you, my dear. I told you that the switchboard connections of his brain were predetermined. Well, the most important connection of all is what we call 'The First Law of Robotics', and it is merely this: 'No robot can harm a human being, or, through inaction, allow a human being to come to harm.' All robots are built so. No robot can be forced in any way to do harm to any human. So, you see, we need you and Tony as a preliminary experiment for our own guidance, while your husband is in Washington to arrange for government-supervised legal tests."

"You mean all this isn't legal?"

Larry cleared his throat. "Not just yet, but it's all right. He won't leave the house, and you mustn't let anyone see him. That's all. . . . And, Claire, I'd stay with you, but I know too much about the robots. We must have a completely inexperienced tester so that we can have severe conditions. It's necessary."

"Oh, well," muttered Claire. Then, as a thought struck her, "But what does he do?"

"Housework," said Dr. Calvin shortly.

She got up to leave, and it was Larry who saw her to the front door. Claire stayed behind drearily. She caught a glimpse of herself in the mirror above the mantelpiece, and looked away hastily. She was very tired of her small, mousy face and her dim, unimaginative hair. Then she caught Tony's eyes upon her and almost smiled before she remembered. . . .

He was only a machine.

Larry Belmont was on his way to the airport when he caught a glimpse of Gladys Claffern. She was the type of woman who seemed made to be seen in glimpses. . . . Perfectly and precisely manufactured; dressed with thoughtful hand and eye; too gleaming to be stared at.

The little smile that preceded her and the faint scent that trailed her were a pair of beckoning fingers. Larry felt his stride break; he touched his hat, then hurried on.

As always he felt that vague anger. If Claire could only push her way into the Claffern clique, it would help so much. But what was the use.

Claire! The few times she had come face to face with Gladys, the little fool had been tongue-tied. He had no illusions. The testing of Tony was his big chance, and it was in Claire's hands. How much safer it would be in the hands of someone like Gladys Claffern.

Claire woke the second morning to the sound of a subdued knock on the bedroom door. Her mind clamoured, then went icy. She had avoided Tony the first day, smiling thinly when she met him and brushing past with a wordless sound of apology.

"Is that you—Tony?"

"Yes, Mrs. Belmont. May I enter?"

She must have said yes, because he was in the room, quite suddenly and noiselessly. Her eyes and nose were simultaneously aware of the tray he was carrying.

"Breakfast?" she said.

"If you please."

She wouldn't have dared to refuse, so she pushed herself slowly into a sitting position and received it; poached eggs, buttered toast, coffee.

"I have brought the sugar and cream separately," said Tony. "I expect to learn your preference with time, in this and in other things."

She waited.

Tony, standing there straight and pliant as a metal rule, asked, after a moment, "Would you prefer to eat in privacy?"

"Yes. . . . I mean, if you don't mind."

"Will you need help later in dressing?"

"Oh, my, no!" She clutched frantically at the sheet, so that the coffee hovered at the edge of catastrophe. She remained so, in rigor, then sank helplessly back against the pillow when the door closed him out of her sight again.

She got through breakfast somehow. . . . He was only a machine, and if it were only more visible that he were it wouldn't be so frightening. Or if his expression would change. It just stayed there, nailed on. You couldn't tell what went on behind those dark eyes and that smooth, olive skin-stuff. The coffee cup beat a faint castanet for a moment as she set it back, empty on the tray.

Then she realized that she had forgotten to add the sugar and cream after all, and she did so hate black coffee.

She burned a straight path from bedroom to kitchen after dressing. It was her house, after all, and there wasn't anything frippy about her, but she liked her kitchen clean. He should have waited for supervision. . . .

But when she entered, she found a kitchen that might have been minted fire-new from the factory the moment before.

She stopped, stared, turned on her heel and nearly ran into Tony. She yelped.

"May I help?" he asked.

"Tony," and she scraped the anger off the edges of her mind's panic, "you must make some noise when you walk. I can't have you stalking me, you know. . . . Didn't you use this kitchen?"

"I did, Mrs. Belmont."

"It doesn't look it."

"I cleaned up afterward. Isn't that customary?"

Claire opened her eyes wide. After all, what could one say to that. She opened the oven compartment that held the pots, took a quick, unseeing look at the metallic glitter inside, then said with a tremor, "Very good. Quite satisfactory."

If at the moment, he had beamed; if he had smiled; if he had quirked the corner of his mouth the slightest bit, she felt that she could have warmed to him. But he remained an English lord in repose, as he said, "Thank you, Mrs. Belmont. Would you come into the living room?"

She did, and it struck her at once. "Have you been polishing the furniture?"

"Is it satisfactory, Mrs. Belmont?"

"But when? You didn't do it yesterday."

"Last night, of course."

"You burned the lights all night?"

"Oh, no. That wouldn't have been necessary. I've a built-in ultraviolet source. I can see in ultraviolet. And, of course, I don't require sleep."

He did require admiration, though. She realized that, then. He had to know that he was pleasing her. But she couldn't bring herself to supply that pleasure for him.

She could only say sourly, "Your kind will put ordinary house-workers out of business."

"There is work of much greater importance they can be put to in the world, once they are freed of drudgery. After all, Mrs. Belmont, things like myself can be manufactured. But nothing yet can imitate the creativity and versatility of a human brain, like yours."

And though his face gave no hint, his voice was warmly surcharged with awe and admiration, so that Claire flushed and muttered, "*My* brain! You can have it."

Tony approached a little and said, "You must be unhappy to say such a thing. Is there anything I can do?"

For a moment, Claire felt like laughing. It *was* a ridiculous situation. Here was an animated carpet-sweeper, dishwasher, furniture-polisher, general factotum, rising from the factory table—and offering his services as consoler and confidant.

Yet she said suddenly, in a burst of woe and voice, "Mr. Belmont doesn't think I have a brain, if you must know. . . . And I suppose I haven't." She couldn't cry in front of him. She felt, for some reason, that she had the honour of the human race to support against this mere creation.

"It's lately," she added. "It was all right when he was a student; when he was just starting. But I can't be a big man's wife; and he's getting to be a big man. He wants me to be a hostess and an entry into social life for him—like G—guh—guh—Gladys Claffern."

Her nose was red, and she looked away.

But Tony wasn't watching her. His eyes wandered about the room. "I can help you run the house."

"But it's no good," she said fiercely. "It needs a touch I can't give it. I can only make it comfortable; I can't ever make it the kind they take pictures of for the Home Beautiful magazines."

"Do you want that kind?"

"Does it do any good—wanting?"

Tony's eyes were on her, full. "I could help."

"Do you know anything about interior decoration?"

"Is it something a good housekeeper should know?"

"Oh, yes."

"Then I have the potentialities of learning it. Can you get me books on the subject?"

Something started then.

Claire, clutching her hat against the brawling liberties of the wind, had manipulated two fat volumes on the home arts back from the public library. She watched Tony as he opened one of them and flipped the pages. It was the first time she had watched his fingers flicker at anything like fine work.

I don't see how they do it, she thought, and on a sudden impulse reached for his hand and pulled it toward herself. Tony did not resist, but let it lie limp for inspection.

She said, "It's remarkable. Even your fingernails look natural."

"That's deliberate, of course," said Tony. Then, chattily, "The skin is a flexible plastic, and the skeletal framework is a light metal alloy. Does that amuse you?"

"Oh, no." She lifted her reddened face. "I just feel a little embarrassed at sort of poking into your insides. It's none of my business. You don't ask me about mine."

"My brain paths don't include that type of curiosity. I can only act within my limitations, you know."

And Claire felt something tighten inside her in the silence that followed. Why did she keep forgetting he was a machine. Now the thing itself had to remind her. Was she so starved for sympathy that she would even accept a robot as equal—because he sympathized?

She noticed Tony was still flipping the pages—almost helplessly—and there was a quick, shooting sense of relieved superiority within her. "You can't read, can you?"

Tony looked up at her; his voice calm, unreproachful. "I *am* reading, Mrs. Belmont."

"But—" She pointed at the book in a meaningless gesture.

"I am scanning the pages, if that's what you mean. My sense of reading is photographic."

It was evening then, and when Claire eventually went to bed Tony was well into the second volume, sitting there in the dark, or what seemed dark to Claire's limited eyes.

Her last thought, the one that clamoured at her just as her

mind let go and tumbled, was a queer one. She remembered his hand again; the touch of it. It had been warm and soft, like a human being's.

How clever of the factory, she thought, and softly ebbed to sleep.

It was the library continuously, thereafter, for several days. Tony suggested the fields of study, which branched out quickly. There were books on colour matching and on cosmetics; on carpentry and on fashions; on art and on the history of costumes.

He turned the pages of each book before his solemn eyes, and, as quickly as he turned, he read; nor did he seem capable of forgetting.

Before the end of the week, he had insisted on cutting her hair, introducing her to a new method of arranging it, adjusting her eyebrow line a bit and changing the shade of her powder and lipstick.

She had palpitated in nervous dread for half an hour under the delicate touch of his inhuman fingers and then looked in the mirror.

"There is more that can be done," said Tony, "especially in clothes. How do you find it for a beginning?"

And she hadn't answered, not for quite a while. Not until she had absorbed the identity of the stranger in the glass and cooled the wonder at the beauty of it all. Then she had said chokingly, never once taking her eyes from the warming image, "Yes, Tony, quite good—for a beginning."

She said nothing of this in her letters to Larry. Let him see it all at once. And something in her realized that it wasn't only the surprise she would enjoy. It was going to be a kind of revenge.

Tony said one morning. "It's time to start buying, and I'm not allowed to leave the house. If I write out exactly what we must have, can I trust you to get it? We need drapery, and furniture fabric, wallpaper, carpeting, paint, clothing—and any number of small things."

"You can't get these things to your own specifications at a stroke's notice," said Claire doubtfully.

"You can get fairly close, if you go through the city and if money is no object."

"But, Tony, money is certainly an object."

"Not at all. Stop off at U.S. Robots in the first place. I'll write a note for you. You see, Dr. Calvin, and tell her that I said it was part of the experiment."

Dr. Calvin, somehow, didn't frighten her as on that first evening. With her new face and a new hat, she couldn't be quite the old Claire. The psychologist listened carefully, asked a few questions, nodded—and then Claire found herself walking out, armed with an unlimited charge account against the assets of U.S. Robots and Mechanical Men Corporation.

It is wonderful what money will do. With a store's contents at her feet, a saleslady's dictum was not necessarily a voice from above; the uplifted eyebrow of a decorator was not anything like Jove's thunder.

And once, when an Exalted Plumpness at one of the most lordly of the garment salons had insistently poohed her description of the wardrobe she must have with counter-pronouncements in accents of the purest Fifty-seventh Street French, she called up Tony, then held the phone out to Monsieur.

"If you don't mind"—voice firm, but fingers twisting a bit— "I'd like you to talk to my—uh—secretary."

Pudgy proceeded to the phone with a solemn arm crooked behind his back. He lifted the phone in two fingers and said delicately, "Yes." A short pause, another "Yes," then a much longer pause, a squeaky beginning of an objection that perished quickly, another pause, a very meek "Yes," and the phone was restored to its cradle.

"If Madam will come with me," he said, hurt and distant, "I will try to supply her needs."

"Just a second." Claire rushed back to the phone, and dialed again. "Hello, Tony. I don't know what you said, but it worked. Thanks You're a——" She struggled for the appropriate word, gave up and ended in a final little squeak, "—a—a dear!"

It was Gladys Claffern looking at her when she turned from the phone again. A slightly amused and slightly amazed Gladys Claffern, looking at her out of a face tilted a bit to one side.

"Mrs. Belmont?"

It all drained out of Claire—just like that. She could only nod—stupidly, like a marionette.

Gladys smiled with an insolence you couldn't put your finger on. "I didn't know you shopped here?" As if the place had, in her eyes, definitely lost caste through the fact.

"I don't, usually," said Claire humbly.

"And haven't you done something to your hair? It's quite— quaint. . . . Oh, I hope you'll excuse me, but isn't your husband's name Lawrence? It seems to me that it's Lawrence."

Claire's teeth clenched, but she had to explain. She *had* to. "Tony is a friend of my husband's. He's helping me select some things."

"I understand. And quite a *dear* about it, I imagine." She passed on smiling, carrying the light and the warmth of the world with her.

Claire did not question the fact that it was to Tony that she turned for consolation. Ten days had cured her of reluctance. And she could weep before him; weep and rage.

"I was a complete f-fool," she stormed, wrenching at her water-logged handerkerchief. "She does that to me. I don't know why. She just does. I should have—kicked her. I should have knocked her down and stamped on her."

"Can you hate a human being so much?" asked Tony in puzzled softness. "That part of a human mind is closed to me."

"Oh, it isn't she," she moaned. "It's myself, I suppose. She's everything I want to be—on the outside, anyway. . . . And I can't be."

Tony's voice was forceful and low in her ear. "You can be, Mrs. Belmont. You *can* be. We have ten days yet, and in ten days the house will no longer be itself. Haven't we been planning that?"

"And how will that help me—with her?"

"Invite her here. Invite her friends. Have it the evening before I—before I leave. It will be a housewarming, in a way."

"She won't come."

"Yes, she will. She'll come to laugh. . . . And she won't be able to."

"Do you really think so? Oh, Tony, do you think we can do it?" She had both his hands in hers. . . . And then, with her face flung aside, "But what good would it be? It won't be I; it will be you that's doing it, I can't ride your back."

"Nobody lives in splendid singleness," whispered Tony. "They've put that knowledge in me. What you, or anyone, see in Gladys Claffern is not just Gladys Claffern. She rides the back of all that money and social position can bring. She doesn't question that. Why should you? . . . And look at it this way, Mrs. Belmont. I am manufactured to obey, but the extent of my obedience is for myself to determine. I can follow orders niggardly or liberally. For you, it is liberal, because you are what I have been manufactured to see human beings as. You are kind, friendly, unassuming. Mrs. Claffern, as you describe her, is not, and I wouldn't obey her as I would you. So it *is* you, and not I, Mrs. Belmont, that is doing all this."

He withdrew his hands from hers then, and Claire looked at that expressionless face no one could read—wondering. She was suddenly frightened again in a completely new way.

She swallowed nervously and stared at her hands, which were still tingling with the pressure of his fingers. She hadn't imagined it; his fingers had pressed hers, gently, tenderly, just before they moved away.

*No!*

*Its* fingers . . . *Its* fingers. . . .

She ran to the bathroom and scrubbed her hands—blindly, uselessly.

She was a bit shy of him the next day; watching him narrowly; waiting to see what might follow—and for a while nothing did.

Tony was working. If there was any difficulty in technique in putting up wallpaper, or utilizing the quick-drying paint, Tony's activity did not show it. His hands moved precisely; his fingers were deft and sure.

He worked all night. She never heard him, but each morning was a new adventure. She couldn't count the number of things that had been done, and by evening she was still finding new touches—and another night had come.

She tried to help only once and her human clumsiness marred that. *He* was in the next room, and she was hanging a picture in the spot marked by Tony's mathematical eyes. The little mark was there; the picture was there; and a revulsion against idleness was there.

But she was nervous, or the ladder was rickety. It didn't matter. She felt it going, and she cried out. It tumbled without her, for Tony, with far more than flesh-and-blood quickness, had been under her.

His calm, dark eyes said nothing at all, and his warm voice said only words. "Are you hurt, Mrs. Belmont?"

She noticed for an instant that her falling hand must have mussed that sleek hair of his, because for the first time she could see for herself that it was composed of distinct strands—fine black hairs.

And then, all at once, she was conscious of his arms about her shoulders and under her knees—holding her tightly and warmly.

She pushed, and her scream was loud in her own ears. She spent the rest of the day in her room, and thereafter she slept with a chair upended against the doorknob of her bedroom door.

She had sent out the invitations, and, as Tony had said, they were accepted. She had only to wait for the last evening.

It came, too, after the rest of them, in its proper place. The house was scarcely her own. She went through it one last time—and every room had been changed. She, herself, was in clothes she would never have dared wear before. . . . And when you put them on, you put on pride and confidence with them.

She tried a polite look of contemptuous amusement before the mirror, and the mirror sneered back at her masterfully.

What would Larry say? . . . It didn't matter, somehow. The exciting days weren't coming with him. They were leaving with

Tony. Now wasn't that strange? She tried to recapture her mood of three weeks before and failed completely.

The clock shrieked eight at her in eight breathless instalments, and she turned to Tony. "They'll be here soon, Tony. You'd better get into the basement. We can't let them——"

She stared a moment, then said weakly, "Tony?" and more strongly, "Tony?" and nearly a scream, "*Tony!*"

But his arms were around her now; his face was close to hers; the pressure of his embrace was relentless. She heard his voice through a haze of emotional jumble.

"Claire," the voice said, "there are many things I am not made to understand, and this must be one of them. I am leaving tomorrow, and I don't want to. I find that there is more in me than just a desire to please you. Isn't it strange?"

His face was closer; his lips were warm, but with no breath behind them—for machines do not breathe. They were almost on hers.

. . . And the bell sounded.

For a moment, she struggled breathlessly, and then he was gone and nowhere in sight, and the bell was sounding again. Its intermittent shrillness was insistent.

The curtains on the front windows had been pulled open. They had been closed fifteen minutes earlier. She *knew* that.

They must have been seen, then. They must *all* have seen—everything!

They came in so politely, all in a bunch—the pack come to howl—with their sharp, darting eyes piercing everywhere. They *had* seen. Why else would Gladys ask in her jabbingest manner after Larry? And Claire was spurred to a desperate and reckless defiance.

Yes, he *is* away. He'll be back tomorrow, I suppose. No, I haven't been lonely here myself. Not a bit. I've had an exciting time. And she laughed at them. Why not? What could they do? Larry would know the truth, if it ever came to him, the story of what they thought they saw.

But *they* didn't laugh.

She could read that in the fury in Gladys Claffern's eyes; in the false sparkle of her words; in her desire to leave early. And as she parted with them, she caught one last, anonymous whisper—disjointed.

". . . never saw anything like . . . so *handsome*——"

And she knew what it was that had enabled her to fingersnap them so. Let each cat mew; and let each cat know—that she might be prettier than Claire Belmont, and grander, and richer—but not one, *not one*, could have so handsome a lover!

And then she remembered again—again—again, that Tony was a machine, and her skin crawled.

"Go away! Leave me be!" she cried to the empty room and ran to her bed. She wept wakefully all that night and the next morning, almost before dawn, when the streets were empty, a car drew up to the house and took Tony away.

Lawrence Belmont passed Dr. Calvin's office, and, on impulse, knocked. He found her with Mathematician Peter Bogert, but did not hesitate on that account.

He said, "Claire tells me that U.S. Robots paid for all that was done at my house——"

"Yes," said Dr. Calvin. "We've written it off, as a valuable and necessary part of the experiment. With your new position as Associate Engineer, you'll be able to keep it up, I think."

"That's not what I'm worried about. With Washington agreeing to the tests, we'll be able to get a TN model of our own by next year, I think." He turned hesitantly, as though to go, and as hesitantly turned back again.

"Well, Mr. Belmont?" asked Dr. Calvin, after a pause.

"I wonder——" began Larry. "I wonder what really happened there. She—Claire, I mean—seems so different. It's not just her looks—though, frankly, I'm amazed." He laughed nervously. "It's *her!* She's not my wife, really—I can't explain it."

"Why try? Are you disappointed with any part of the change?"

"On the contrary. But it's a little frightening, too, you see——"

"I wouldn't worry, Mr. Belmont. Your wife has handled herself very well. Frankly, I never expected to have the experiment yield such a thorough and complete test. We know exactly what corrections must be made in the TN model, and the credit belongs entirely to Mrs. Belmont. If you want me to be very honest, I think your wife deserves your promotion more than you do."

Larry flinched visibly at that. "As long as it's in the family," he murmured unconvincingly and left.

Susan Calvin looked after him, "I think that hurt—I hope. . . . Have you read Tony's report, Peter?"

"Thoroughly," said Bogert. "And won't the TN-3 model need changes?"

"Oh, you think so, too?" questioned Calvin sharply. "What's your reasoning?"

Bogert frowned. "I don't need any. It's obvious on the face

of it that we can't have a robot loose which makes love to his mistress, if you don't mind the pun."

"Love! Peter, you sicken me. You really don't understand? That machine had to obey the First Law. He couldn't allow harm to come to a human being, and harm was coming to Claire Belmont through her own sense of inadequacy. So he made love to her, since what woman would fail to appreciate the compliment of being able to stir passion in a machine—in a cold, soulless machine. And he opened the curtains that night deliberately, that the others might see and envy—without any risk possible to Claire's marriage. I think it was clever of Tony——"

"Do you? What's the difference whether it was pretense or not, Susan? It still has its horrifying effect. Read the report again. She avoided him. She screamed when he held her. She didn't sleep that last night—in hysterics. We can't have that."

"Peter, you're blind. You're as blind as I was. The TN model will be rebuilt entirely, but not for your reason. Quite otherwise; quite otherwise. Strange that I overlooked it in the first place," her eyes were opaquely thoughtful, "but perhaps it reflects a shortcoming in myself. You see, Peter, machines can't fall in love, but—even when it's hopeless and horrifying—women can!"

# Hell - Fire

THERE WAS a stir as of a very polite first-night audience. Only a handful of scientists were present, a sprinkling of high brass, some Congressmen, a few newsmen.

Alvin Horner of the Washington Bureau of the Continental Press found himself next to Joseph Vincenzo of Los Alamos, and said, "*Now* we ought to learn something."

Vincenzo stared at him through bifocals and said, "Not the important thing."

Horner frowned. This was to be the first super-slow-motion films of an atomic explosion. With trick lenses changing directional polarization in flickers, the moment of explosion would be divided into billionth-second snaps. Yesterday, an A-bomb had exploded. Today, those snaps would show the explosion in incredible detail.

Horner said, "You think this won't work?"

Vincenzo looked tormented. "It will work. We've run pilot tests. But the important thing——"

"Which is?"

"That these bombs are man's death sentence. We don't seem to be able to learn that." Vincenzo nodded. "Look at them here. They're excited and thrilled, but not afraid."

The newsman said, "They know the danger. They're afraid, too."

"Not enough," said the scientist. "I've seen men watch an H-bomb blow an island into a hole and then go home and sleep. That's the way men are. For thousands of years, hell-fire has been preached to them, and it's made no real impression."

"Hell-fire: Are you religious, sir?"

"What you saw yesterday was hell-fire. An exploding atom bomb is hell-fire. Literally."

That was enough for Horner. He got up and changed his seat, but watched the audience uneasily. Were any afraid? Did any worry about hell-fire? It didn't seem so to him.

The light went out, the projector started. On the screen, the firing tower stood gaunt. The audience grew tensely quiet.

Then a dot of light appeared at the apex of the tower, a brilliant, burning point, slowly budding in a lazy, outward elbowing, this way and that, taking on uneven shapes of light and shadow, growing oval.

A man cried out chokingly, then others. A hoarse babble of noise, followed by thick silence. Horner could smell fear, taste terror in his own mouth, feel his blood freeze.

The oval fireball had sprouted projections, then paused a moment in stasis, before expanding rapidly into a bright and featureless sphere.

That moment of stasis—the fireball had shown dark spots for eyes, with dark lines for thin, flaring eyebrows, a hairline coming down V-shaped, a mouth twisted upward, laughing wildly in the hell-fire—and horns.

# The Last Trump

THE ARCHANGEL Gabriel was quite casual about the whole thing. Idly, he let the tip of one wing graze the planet Mars, which, being of mere matter, was unaffected by the contact.

He said, "It's a settled matter, Etheriel. There's nothing to be done about it now. The Day of Resurrection is due."

Etheriel, a very junior seraph who had been created not quite a thousand years earlier as men counted time, quivered so that distinct vortices appeared in the continuum. Ever since his creation, he had been in immediate charge of Earth and environs. As a job, it was a sinecure, a cubbyhole, a dead end, but through the centuries he had come to take a perverse pride in the world.

"But you'll be disrupting my world without notice."

"Not at all. Not at all. Certain passages occur in the Book of Daniel and in the Apocalypse of St. John which are clear enough."

"They are? Having been copied from scribe to scribe? I wonder if two words in a row are left unchanged."

"There are hints in the Rig-Veda, in the Confucian Analects——"

"Which are the property of isolated cultural groups which exist as a thin aristocracy——"

"The Gilgamesh Chronicle speaks out plainly."

"Much of the Gilgamesh Chronicle was destroyed with the library of Ashurbanipal sixteen hundred years, Earth-style, before my creation."

"There are certain features of the Great Pyramid and a pattern in the inlaid jewels of the Taj Mahal——"

"Which are so subtle that no man has ever rightly interpreted them."

Gabriel said wearily, "If you're going to object to everything, there's no use discussing the matter. In any case, *you* ought to know about it. In matters concerning Earth, you're omniscient."

"Yes, if I choose to be. I've had much to concern me here and investigating the possibilities of Resurrection did not, I confess, occur to me."

"Well, it should have. All the papers involved are in the files of the Council of Ascendants. You could have availed yourself of them at any time."

"I tell you all my time was needed here. You have no idea of the deadly efficiency of the Adversary on this planet. It took all my efforts to curb him, and even so——"

"Why, yes"—Gabriel stroked a comet as it passed—"he does seem to have won his little victories. I note as I let the interlocking factual pattern of this miserable little world flow through me that this is one of those setups with matter-energy equivalence."

"So it is," said Etheriel.

"And they are playing with it."

"I'm afraid so."

"Then what better time for ending the matter?"

"I'll be able to handle it, I assure you. Their nuclear bombs will not destroy them."

"I wonder. Well, now, suppose you let me continue, Etheriel. The appointed moment approaches."

The seraph said stubbornly, "I would like to see the documents in the case."

"If you insist." The wording of an Act of Ascendancy appeared in glittering symbols against the deep black of the airless firmament.

Etheriel read aloud: "It is hereby directed by order of Council that the Archangel Gabriel, Serial number etcetera, etcetera (well, that's you, at any rate), will approach Planet, Class A, number G753990, hereinafter known as Earth, and on January 1, 1957, at 12.01 p.m., using local time values——" He finished reading in gloomy silence.

"Satisfied?"

"No, but I'm helpless."

Gabriel smiled. A trumpet appeared in space, in shape like an earthly trumpet, but its burnished gold extended from Earth to sun. It was raised to Gabriel's glittering beautiful lips.

"Can't you let me have a little time to take this up with the Council?" asked Etheriel desperately.

"What good would it do you? The act is countersigned by the Chief, and you know that an act countersigned by the Chief is absolutely irrevocable. And now, if you don't mind, it is almost the stipulated second and I want to be done with this as I have other matters of much greater moment on my mind. Would you step out of my way a little? Thank you."

Gabriel blew, and a clean, thin sound of perfect pitch and crystalline delicacy filled all the universe to the furthest star. As it sounded, there was a tiny moment of stasis as thin as the line separating past from future, and then the fabric of worlds collapsed upon itself and matter was gathered back into the primeval chaos from which it had once sprung at a word. The stars and nebulae were gone, and the cosmic dust, the sun, the planets, the moon; all, all, all except Earth itself, which spun as before in a universe now completely empty.

The Last Trump had sounded.

R. E. Mann (known to all who knew him simply as R.E.) eased himself into the offices of the Billikam Bitsies factory and stared somberly at the tall man (gaunt but with a certain faded elegance about his neat grey moustache) who bent intently over a sheaf of papers on his desk.

R.E. looked at his wristwatch, which still said 7.01, having ceased running at that time. It was Eastern standard time of course; 12.01 p.m. Greenwich time. His dark brown eyes, staring sharply out over a pair of pronounced cheekbones, caught those of the other.

For a moment, the tall man stared at him blankly. Then he said, "Can I do anything for you?"

"Horatio J. Billikan, I presume? Owner of this place?"

"Yes."

"I'm R. E. Mann and I couldn't help but stop in when I finally found someone at work. Don't you know what today is?"

"Today?"

"It's Resurrection Day."

"Oh, that! I know it. I heard the blast. Fit to wake the dead. ... That's rather a good one, don't you think?" He chuckled for a moment, then went on, "It woke me at seven in the morning. I nudged my wife. She slept through it, of course. I always said she would. 'It's the Last Trump, dear,' I said. Hortense, that's my wife, said, 'All right,' and went back to sleep. I bathed, shaved, dressed and came to work."

"But why?"

"Why not?"

"None of your workers have come in."

"No, poor souls. They'll take a holiday just at first. You've got to expect that. After all, it isn't every day that the world comes to an end. Frankly, it's just as well. It gives me a chance to straighten out my personal correspondence without interruptions. Telephone hasn't rung once."

He stood up and went to the window. "It's a great improvement. No blinding sun any more and the snow's gone. There's a pleasant light and a pleasant warmth. Very good arrangement. ... But now, if you don't mind, I'm *rather* busy, so if you'll excuse me——"

A great, hoarse voice interrupted with a, "Just a minute, Horatio," and a gentleman looking remarkably like Billikan in a somewhat craggier way, followed his prominent nose into the office and struck an attitude of offended dignity which was scarcely spoiled by the fact that he was quite naked. "May I ask why you've shut down Bitsies ?"

Billikan looked faint. "Good Heavens," he said, "it's Father. Wherever did you come from ?"

"From the graveyard," roared Billikan, Senior. "Where on Earth else ? They're coming out of the ground there by the dozens. Every one of them naked. Women, too."

Billikan cleared his throat. "I'll get you some clothes, Father. I'll bring them to you from home."

"Never mind that. Business first. Business first."

R.E. came out of his musing. "Is everyone coming out of their graves at the same time, sir ?"

He stared curiously at Billikan, Senior, as he spoke. The old man's appearance was one of robust age. His cheeks were furrowed but glowed with health. His age, R.E. decided, was exactly what it was at the moment of his death, but his body was as it should have been at that age if it functioned ideally.

Billikan, Senior, said, "No, sir, they are not. The newer graves are coming up first. Pottersby died five years before me and came up about five minutes after me. Seeing him made me decide to leave. I had had enough of him when . . . And that reminds me." He brought his fist down on the desk, a very solid fist. "There were no taxis, no buses. Telephones weren't working. I had to walk. I had to walk twenty miles."

"Like that ?" asked his son in a faint and appalled voice.

Billikan, Senior, looked down upon his bare skin with casual approval. "It's warm. Almost everyone else is naked. . . . Anyway, son, I'm not here to make small talk. Why is the factory shut down ?"

"It isn't shut down. It's a special occasion."

"Special occasion, my foot. You call union headquarters and tell them Resurrection Day isn't in the contract. Every worker is being docked for every minute he's off the job."

Billikan's lean face took on a stubborn look as he peered at his father. "I will not. Don't forget, now, you're no longer in charge of this plant. I am."

"Oh, are you ? By what right ?"

"By your will."

"All right. Now here I am and I void my will."

"You can't, Father. You're dead. You may not look dead, but I have witnesses. I have the doctor's certificate. I have receipted bills from the undertaker. I can get testimony from the pall-bearers."

Billikan, Senior, stared at his son, sat down, placed his arm over the back of the chair, crossed his legs and said, "If it comes to that, we're all dead, aren't we? The world's come to an end, hasn't it?"

"But you've been declared legally dead and I haven't."

"Oh, we'll change that, son. There are going to be more of us than of you and votes count."

Billikin, Junior, tapped the desk firmly with the flat of his hand and flushed slightly. "Father, I hate to bring up this particular point, but you force me to. May I remind you that by now I am sure that Mother is sitting at home waiting for you; that she probably had to walk the streets—uh—naked, too; and that she probably isn't in a good humour."

Billikan, Senior, went ludicrously pale. "Good Heavens!"

"And you know she always wanted you to retire."

Billikan, Senior, came to a quick decision. "I'm not going home. Why, this is a nightmare. Aren't there any limits to this Resurrection business? It's—it's—it's sheer anarchy. There's such a thing as overdoing it. I'm just not going home."

At which point, a somewhat rotund gentleman with a smooth, pink face and fluffy white sideburns (much like pictures of Martin Van Buren) stepped in and said coldly, "*Good* day."

"Father," said Billikam, Senior.

"Grandfather," said Billikan, Junior.

Billikan, Grandsenior, looked at Billikan, Junior, with disapproval. "If you are my grandson," he said, "you've aged considerably and the change has not improved you."

Billikan, Junior, smiled with dyspeptic feebleness, and made no answer.

Billikan, Grandsenior, did not seem to require one. He said, "Now if you two will bring me up to date on the business, I will resume my managerial function."

There were two simultaneous answers, and Billikan, Grandsenior's, floridity waxed dangerously as he beat the ground peremptorily with an imaginary cane and barked a retort.

R.E. said, "Gentlemen."

He raised his voice. "Gentlemen!"

He shrieked at full lung-power, "GENTLEMEN!"

Conversation snapped off sharply and all turned to look at him. R.E.'s angular face, his oddly attractive eyes, his sardonic mouth seemed suddenly to dominate the gathering.

He said, "I don't understand this argument. What is it that you manufacture?"

"Bitsies," said Billikan, Junior.

"Which, I take it, are a packaged cereal breakfast food——"

"Teeming with energy in every golden, crispy flake——" cried Billikan, Junior.

"Covered with honey-sweet, crystalline sugar; a confection and a food——" growled Billikan, Senior.

"To tempt the most jaded appetite," roared Billikan, Grand-senior.

"Exactly," said R.E. "What appetite?"

They stared stolidly at him. "I beg your pardon," said Billikan, Junior.

"Are any of you hungry?" asked R.E. "I'm not."

"What is this fool maundering about?" demanded Billikan, Grandsenior, angrily. His invisible cane would have been prodding R.E. in the navel had it (the cane, not the navel) existed.

R.E. said, "I'm trying to tell you that no one will ever eat again. It is the hereafter, and food is unnecessary."

The expressions on the faces of the Billikans needed no interpretation. It was obvious that they had tried their own appetites and found them wanting.

Billikan, Junior, said ashenly, "Ruined!"

Billikan, Grandsenior, pounded the floor heavily and noiselessly with his imaginary cane. "This is confiscation of property without due process of law. I'll sue. I'll sue."

"Quite unconstitutional," agreed Billikan, Senior.

"If you can find anyone to sue, I wish you all good fortune," said R.E. agreeably. "And now if you'll excuse me I think I'll walk toward the graveyard."

He put his hat on his head and walked out the door.

Etheriel, his vortices quivering, stood before the glory of a six-winged cherub.

The cherub said, "If I understand you, your particular universe has been dismantled.

"Exactly."

"Well, surely, now, you don't expect *me* to set it up again?"

"I don't expect you to do anything," said Etheriel, "except to arrange an appointment for me with the Chief."

The cherub gestured his respect instantly at hearing the word. Two wing-tips covered his feet, two his eyes and two his mouth. He restored himself to normal and said, "The Chief is quite busy. There are a myriad score of matters for him to decide."

"Who denies that? I merely point out that if matters stand as they are now, there will have been a universe in which Satan will have won the final victory."

"Satan?"

"It's the Hebrew word for Adversary," said Etheriel impatiently. "I could say Ahriman, which is the Persian word. In any case, I mean the Adversary."

The cherub said, "But what will an interview with the Chief

accomplish? The document authorizing the Last Trump was countersigned by the Chief, and you know that it is irrevocable for that reason. The Chief would never limit his own omnipotence by canceling a word he had spoken in his official capacity."

"Is that final? You will not arrange an appointment?"

"I cannot."

Etheriel said, "In that case, I shall seek out the Chief without one. I will invade the Primum Mobile. If it means my destruction, so be it." He gathered his energies. . . .

The cherub murmured in horror, "Sacrilege!" and there was a faint gathering of thunder as Etheriel sprang upward and was gone.

R. E. Mann passed through the crowding streets and grew used to the sight of people bewildered, disbelieving, apathetic, in makeshift clothing or, usually, none at all.

A girl, who looked about twelve, leaned over an iron gate, one foot on a crossbar, swinging it to and fro, and said as he passed, "Hello, mister."

"Hello," said R.E. The girl was dressed. She was not one of the—uh—returnees.

The girl said, "We got a new baby in our house. She's a sister I once had. Mommy is crying and they sent me here."

R.E. said, "Well, well," passed through the gate and up the paved walk to the house, one with modest pretensions to middle-class gentility. He rang the bell, obtained no answer, opened the door and walked in.

He followed the sound of sobbing and knocked at an inner door. A stout man of about fifty with little hair and a comfortable supply of cheek and chin looked out at him with mingled astonishment and resentment.

"Who are you?"

R.E. removed his hat. "I thought I might be able to help. Your little girl outside——"

A woman looked up at him hopelessly from a chair by a double bed. Her hair was beginning to grey. Her face was puffed and unsightly with weeping and the veins stood out bluely on the back of her hands. A baby lay on the bed, plump and naked. It kicked its feet languidly and its sightless baby eyes turned aimlessly here and there.

"This is my baby," said the woman. "She was born twenty-three years ago in this house and she died when she was ten days old in this house. I wanted her back so much."

"And now you have her," said R.E.

"But it's too late," cried the woman vehemently. "I've had three other children. My oldest girl is married; my son is in the army. I'm too old to have a baby now. And even if—even if——"

Her features worked in a heroic effort to keep back the tears and failed.

Her husband said with flat tonelessness, "It's not a real baby. It doesn't cry. It doesn't soil itself. It won't take milk. What will we do? It'll never grow. It'll always be a baby."

R.E. shook his head. "I don't know," he said. "I'm afraid I can do nothing to help."

Quietly he left. Quietly he thought of the hospitals. Thousands of babies must be appearing at each one.

Place them in racks, he thought, sardonically. Stack them like cordwood. They need no care. Their little bodies are merely each the custodian of an indestructible spark of life.

He passed two little boys of apparently equal chronological age, perhaps ten. Their voices were shrill. The body of one glistened white in the sunless light so he was a returnee. The other was not. R.E. paused to listen.

The bare one said, "I had scarlet fever."

A spark of envy at the other's claim to notoriety seemed to enter the clothed one's voice. "Gee."

"That's why I died."

"Gee. Did they use pensillun or auromysun?"

"What?"

"They're medicines."

"I never heard of them."

"Boy, you never heard of *much*."

"I know as much as *you*."

"Yeah? Who's President of the United States?"

"Warren Harding, that's who."

"You're crazy. It's Eisenhower."

"Who's he?"

"Ever see television?"

"What's that?"

The clothed boy hooted earsplittingly. "It's something you turn on and see comedians, movies, cowboys, rocket rangers, anything you want."

"Let's see it."

There was a pause and the boy from the present said, "It ain't working."

The other boy shrieked his scorn. "You mean it ain't never worked. You made it all up."

R.E. shrugged and passed on.

The crowds thinned as he left town and neared the cemetery. Those who were left were all walking into town, all were nude.

A man stopped him; a cheerful man with pinkish skin and

white hair who had the marks of pince-nez on either side of the bridge of his nose, but no glasses to go with them.

"Greetings, friend."

"Hello," said R.E.

"You're the first man with clothing that I've seen. You were alive when the trumpet blew, I suppose."

"Yes, I was."

"Well, isn't this great? Isn't this joyous and delightful? Come rejoice with me."

"You like this, do you?" said R.E.

"*Like it?* A pure and radiant joy fills me. We are surrounded by the light of the first day; the light that glowed softly and serenely before sun, moon and stars were made. (You know your Genesis, of course.) There is the comfortable warmth that must have been one of the highest blisses of Eden; not enervating heat or assaulting cold. Men and women walk the streets unclothed and are not ashamed. All is well, my friend, all is well."

R.E. said, "Well, it's a fact that I haven't seemed to mind the feminine display all about."

"Naturally not," said the other. "Lust and sin as we remember it in our earthly existence no longer exists. Let me introduce myself, friend, as I was in earthly times. My name on Earth was Winthrop Hester. I was born in 1812 and died in 1884 as we counted time then. Through the last forty years of my life I laboured to bring my little flock to the Kingdom and I go now to count the ones I have won."

R.E. regarded the ex-minister solemnly, "Surely there has been no Judgment yet."

"Why not? The Lord sees within a man and in the same instant that all things of the world ceased, all men were judged and we are the saved."

"There must be a great many saved."

"On the contrary, my son, those saved are but as a remnant."

"A pretty large remnant. As near as I can make out, everyone's coming back to life. I've seen some pretty unsavoury characters back in town as live as you are."

"Last-minute repentance——"

"*I* never repented."

"Of what, my son?"

"Of the fact that I never attended church."

Winthrop Hester stepped back hastily. "Were you ever baptized?"

"Not to my knowledge."

Winthrop Hester trembled. "Surely you believed in God?"

"Well," said R.E., "I believed a lot of things about Him that would probably startle you."

Winthrop Hester turned and hurried off in great agitation.

In what remained of his walk to the cemetery (R.E. had no way of estimating time, nor did it occur to him to try) no one else stopped him. He found the cemetery itself all but empty, its trees and grass gone (it occurred to him that there was nothing green in the world; the ground everywhere was a hard, featureless, grainless grey; the sky a luminous white), but its headstones still standing.

On one of these sat a lean and furrowed man with long, black hair on his head and a mat of it, shorter, though more impressive, on his chest and upper arms.

He called out in a deep voice, "Hey, there, you!"

R.E. sat down on a neighbouring headstone. "Hello."

Black-hair said, "Your clothes don't look right. What year is it when it happened?"

"1957."

"I died in 1807. Funny! I expected to be one pretty hot boy right about now, with the 'tarnal flames shooting up my innards."

"Aren't you coming along to town?" asked R.E.

"My name's Zeb," said the ancient. "That's short for Zebulon, but Zeb's good enough. What's the town like? Changed some, I reckon?"

"It's got nearly a hundred thousand people in it."

Zeb's mouth yawned somewhat. "Go on. Might nigh bigger'n Philadelphia. . . . You're making fun."

"Philadelphia's got——" R.E. paused. Stating the figure would do him no good. Instead, he said, "The town's grown in a hundred fifty years, you know."

"Country, too?"

"Forty-eight states," said R.E. "All the way to the Pacific."

"No!" Zeb slapped his thigh in delight and then winced at the unexpected absence of rough homespun to take up the worst of the blow. "I'd head out west if I wasn't needed here. Yes, sir." His face grew lowering and his thin lips took on a definite grimness. "I'll stay right here, where I'm needed."

"Why are you needed?"

The explanation came out briefly, bitten off hard. "Injuns!"

"Indians?"

"Millions of 'em. First the tribes we fought and licked and then tribes who ain't never seen a white man. They'll all come back to life. I'll need my old buddies. You city fellers ain't no good at it. . . . Ever seen an Injun?"

R.E. said, "Not around here lately, no."

Zeb looked his contempt, and tried to spit to one side but found no saliva for the purpose. He said, "You better git back to the city, then. After a while, it ain't going to be safe nohow round here. Wish I had my musket."

R.E. rose, thought a moment, shrugged and faced back to the city. The headstone he had been sitting upon collapsed as he rose, falling into a powder of gray stone that melted into the featureless ground. He looked about. Most of the headstones were gone. The rest would not last long. Only the one under Zeb still looked firm and strong.

R.E. began the walk back. Zeb did not turn to look at him. He remained waiting quietly and calmly—for Indians.

Etheriel plunged through the heavens in reckless haste. The eyes of the Ascendants were on him, he knew. From late-born seraph, through cherubs and angels, to the highest archangel, they must be watching.

Already he was higher than any Ascendant, uninvited, had ever been before and he waited for the quiver of the Word that would reduce his vortices to non-existence.

But he did not falter. Through non-space and non-time, he plunged toward union with the Primum Mobile; the seat that encompassed all that Is, Was, Would be, Had Been, Could Be and Might Be.

And as he thought that, he burst through and was part of it, his being expanding so that momentarily he, too, was part of the All. But then it was mercifully veiled from his senses, and the Chief was a still, small voice within him, yet all the more impressive in its infinity for all that.

"My son," the voice said, "I know why you have come."

"Then help me, if that be your will."

"By my own will," said the Chief, "an act of mine is irrevocable. All your mankind, my son, yearned for life. All feared death. All evolved thoughts and dreams of life unending. No two groups of men; no two single men; evolved the same afterlife, but all wished life. I was petitioned that I might grant the common denominator of all these wishes—life unending. I did so."

"No servant of yours made that request."

"The Adversary did, my son."

Etheriel trailed his feeble glory in dejection and said in a low voice, "I am dust in your sight and unworthy to be in your presence, yet I must ask a question. Is then the Adversary your servant also?"

"Without him I can have no other," said the Chief, "for what then is Good but the eternal fight against Evil?"

And in that fight, thought Etheriel, I have lost.

R.E. paused in sight of town. The buildings were crumbling. Those that were made of wood were already heaps of rubble. R.E. walked to the nearest such heap and found the wooden splinters powdery and dry.

He penetrated deeper into town and found the brick buildings still standing, but there was an ominous roundness to the edges of the bricks, a threatening flakiness.

"They won't last long," said a deep voice, "but there is this consolation, if consolation it be; their collapse can kill no one."

R.E. looked up in surprise and found himself face to face with a cadaverous Don Quixote of a man, lantern-jawed, sunken-cheeked. His eyes were sad and his brown hair was lank and straight. His clothes hung loosely and skin showed clearly through various rents.

"My name," said the man, "is Richard Levine. I was a professor of history once—before this happened."

"You're wearing clothes," said R.E. "You're not one of those resurrected."

"No, but that mark of distinction is vanishing. Clothes are going."

R.E. looked at the throngs that drifted past them, moving slowly and aimlessly like motes in a sunbeam. Vanishingly few wore clothes. He looked down at himself and noticed for the first time that the seam down the length of each trouser leg had parted. He pinched the fabric of his jacket between thumb and forefinger and the wool parted and came away easily.

"I guess you're right," said R.E.

"If you'll notice," went on Levine, "Mellon's Hill is flattening out."

R.E. turned to the north where ordinarily the mansions of the aristocracy (such aristocracy as there was in town) studded the slopes of Mellon's Hill, and found the horizon nearly flat.

Levine said, "Eventually, there'll be nothing but flatness, featurelessness, nothingness—and us."

"And Indians," said R.E. "There's a man outside of town waiting for Indians and wishing he had a musket."

"I imagine," said Levine, "the Indians will give no trouble. There is no pleasure in fighting an enemy that cannot be killed or hurt. And even if that were not so, the lust for battle would be gone as are the lusts."

"Are you sure?"

"I am positive. Before all this happened, although you may, not think it to look at me, I derived much harmless pleasure in a consideration of the female figure. Now, with the unexampled opportunities at my disposal, I find myself irritatingly uninterested. No, that is wrong. I am not even irritated at my disinterest."

R.E. looked up briefly at the passers-by. "I see what you mean."

"The coming of Indians here," said Levine, "is nothing compared with the situation in the Old World. Early during the Resurrection, Hitler and his Wehrmacht must have come back to life and must now be facing and intermingled with Stalin and the Red Army all the way from Berlin to Stalingrad. To complicate the situation, the Kaisers and Czars will arrive. The men at Verdun and the Somme are back in the old battlegrounds. Napoleon and his marshals are scattered over western Europe. And Mohammed must be back to see what following ages have made of Islam, while the Saints and Apostles consider the paths of Christianity. And even the Mongols, poor things, the Khans from Temujin to Aurangzeb, must be wandering the steppes helplessly, longing for their horses."

"As a professor of history," said R.E., "you must long to be there and observe."

"How could I be there? Every man's position on Earth is restricted to the distance he can walk. There are no machines of any kind, and, as I have just mentioned, no horses. And what would I find in Europe anyway? Apathy, I think! As here."

A soft plopping sound caused R.E. to turn around. The wing of a neighbouring brick building had collapsed in dust. Portions of bricks lay on either side of him. Some must have hurtled through him without his being aware of it. He looked about. The heaps of rubble were less numerous. Those that remained were smaller in size.

He said, "I met a man who thought we had all been judged and are in Heaven."

"Judged?" said Levine. "Why, yes, I imagine we are. We face eternity now. We have no universe left, no outside phenomena, no emotions, no passions. Nothing but ourselves and thought. We face an eternity of introspection, when all through history we have never known what to do with ourselves on a rainy Sunday."

"You sound as though the situation bothers you."

"It does more than that. The Dantean conceptions of Inferno were childish and unworthy of the Divine imagination; fire and torture. Boredom is much more subtle. The inner torture of a mind unable to escape itself in any way, condemned to fester in its own exuding mental pus for all time, is much more fitting. Oh, yes, my friend, we have been judged, and condemned, too, and this is not Heaven, but hell."

And Levine rose with shoulders drooping dejectedly, and walked away.

R.E. gazed thoughtfully about and nodded his head. He was satisfied.


The self-admission of failure lasted but an instant in Etheriel, and then, quite suddenly, he lifted his being as brightly and highly as he dared in the presence of the Chief and his glory was a tiny dot of light in the infinite Primum Mobile.

"If it be your will, then," he said. "I do not ask you to defeat your will but to fulfill it."

"In what way, my son?"

"The document, approved by the Council of Ascendants and signed by yourself, authorizes the Day of Resurrection at a specific time of a specific day of the year 1957 as Earthmen count time."

"So it did."

"But the year 1957 is unqualified. What then is 1957? To the dominant culture on Earth the year was A.D. 1957. That is true. Yet from the time you breathed existence into Earth and its universe there have passed 5,960 years. Based on the internal evidence you created within that universe, nearly four billion years have passed. Is the year, *unqualified*, then 1957, 5960, or 4000000000?

"Nor is that all," Etheriel went on. "The year A.D. 1957 is the year 7464 of the Byzantine era, 5716 by the Jewish calendar. It is 2708 A.U.C., that is, the 2,708th year since the founding of Rome, if we adopt the Roman calendar. It is the year 1375 in the Mohammedan calendar, and the hundred eightieth year of the independence of the United States.

"Humbly I ask then if it does not seem to you that a year referred to as 1957 alone and without qualification has no meaning."

The Chief's still small voice said, "I have always known this, my son; it was you who had to learn."

"Then," said Etheriel, quivering luminously with joy, "let the very letter of your will be fulfilled and let the Day of Resurrection fall in 1957, but only when all the inhabitants of Earth unanimously agree that a certain year shall be numbered 1957 and none other."

"So let it be," said the Chief, and this Word re-created Earth and all it contained, together with the sun and moon and all the hosts of Heaven.


It was 7 a.m. on January 1, 1957, when R. E. Mann awoke with a start. The very beginnings of a melodious note that ought to have filled all the universe had sounded and yet had not sounded.

For a moment, he cocked his head as though to allow understanding to flow in, and then a trifle of rage crossed his face to vanish again. It was but another battle.

He sat down at his desk to compose the next plan of action. People already spoke of calendar reform and it would have to be stimulated. A new era must begin with December 2, 1944, and someday a new year 1957 would come; 1957 of the Atomic Era, acknowledged as such by all the world.

A strange light shone on his head as thoughts passed through his more-than-human mind and the shadow of Ahriman on the wall seemed to have small horns at either temple.

# The Fun They Had

MARGIE EVEN wrote about it that night in her diary. On the page headed May 17, 2157, she wrote, "Today Tommy found a real book!"

It was a very old book. Margie's grandfather once said that when he was a little boy *his* grandfather told him that there was a time when all stories were printed on paper.

They turned the pages, which were yellow and crinkly, and it was awfully funny to read words that stood still instead of moving the way they were supposed to—on a screen, you know. And then, when they turned back to the page before, it had the same words on it that it had had when they read it the first time.

"Gee," said Tommy, "what a waste. When you're through with the book, you just throw it away, I guess. Our television screen must have had a million books on it and it's good for plenty more. I wouldn't throw *it* away."

"Same with mine," said Margie. She was eleven and hadn't seen as many textbooks as Tommy had. He was thirteen.

She said, "Where did you find it?"

"In my house." He pointed without looking, because he was busy reading. "In the attic."

"What's it about?"

"School."

Margie was scornful. "School? What's there to write about school? I hate school."

Margie always hated school, but now she hated it more than ever. The mechanical teacher had been giving her test after test in geography and she had been doing worse and worse until her mother had shaken her head sorrowfully and sent for the County Inspector.

He was a round little man with a red face and a whole box of tools with dials and wires. He smiled at Margie and gave her an apple, then took the teacher apart. Margie had hoped he wouldn't know how to put it together again, but he knew how all right, and, after an hour or so, there it was again, large and black and ugly, with a big screen on which all the lessons were shown and the questions were asked. That wasn't so bad. The part Margie hated most was the slot where she had to put homework and test papers. She always had to write them out in a punch code they made her learn when she was six years old, and the mechanical teacher calculated the mark in no time.

The Inspector had smiled after he was finished and patted Margie's head. He said to her mother, "It's not the little girl's fault, Mrs. Jones. I think the geography sector was geared a little too quick. Those things happen sometimes. I've slowed it up to an average ten-year level. Actually, the over-all pattern of her progress is quite satisfactory." And he patted Margie's head again.

Margie was disappointed. She had been hoping they would take the teacher away altogether. They had once taken Tommy's teacher away for nearly a month because the history sector had blanked out completely.

So she said to Tommy, "Why would anyone write about school ?"

Tommy looked at her with very superior eyes. "Because it's not our kind of school, stupid. This is the old kind of school that they had hundreds and hundreds of years ago." He added loftily, pronouncing the word carefully, "*Centuries* ago."

Margie was hurt. "Well, I don't know what kind of school they had all that time ago." She read the book over his shoulder for a while, then said, "Anyway, they had a teacher."

"Sure they had a teacher, but it wasn't a *regular* teacher. It was a man."

"A man ? How could a man be a teacher ?"

"Well, he just told the boys and girls things and gave them homework and asked them questions."

"A man isn't smart enough."

"Sure he is. My father knows as much as my teacher."

"He can't. A man can't know as much as a teacher."

"He knows almost as much, I betcha."

Margie wasn't prepared to dispute that. She said, "I wouldn't want a strange man in my house to teach me."

Tommy screamed with laughter. "You don't know much, Margie. The teachers didn't live in the house. They had a special building and all the kids went there."

"And all the kids learned the same thing ?"

"Sure, if they were the same age."

"But my mother says a teacher has to be adjusted to fit the mind of each boy and girl it teaches and that each kid has to be taught differently."

"Just the same they didn't do it that way then. If you don't like it, you don't have to read the book."

"I didn't say I didn't like it," Margie said quickly. She wanted to read about those funny schools.

They weren't even half-finished when Margie's mother called, "Margie! School!"

Margie looked up. "Not yet, Mamma."

"Now!" said Mrs. Jones. "And it's probably time for Tommy, too."

Margie said to Tommy, "Can I read the book some more with you after school?"

"Maybe," he said nonchalantly. He walked away whistling, the dusty old book tucked beneath his arm.

Margie went into the schoolroom. It was right next to her bedroom, and the mechanical teacher was on and waiting for her. It was always on at the same time every day except Saturday and Sunday, because her mother said little girls learned better if they learned at regular hours.

The screen was lit up, and it said: "Today's arithmetic lesson is on the addition of proper fractions. Please insert yesterday's homework in the proper slot."

Margie did so with a sigh. She was thinking about the old schools they had when her grandfather's grandfather was a little boy. All the kids from the whole neighbourhood came, laughing and shouting in the schoolyard, sitting together in the schoolroom, going home together at the end of the day. They learned the same things, so they could help one another on the homework and talk about it.

And the teachers were people. . . .

The mechanical teacher was flashing on the screen: "When we add the fractions $\frac{1}{2}$ and $\frac{1}{4}$——"

Margie was thinking about how the kids must have loved it in the old days. She was thinking about the fun they had.

# Jokester

NOEL MEYERHOF consulted the list he had prepared and chose which item was to be first. As usual, he relied mainly on intuition.

He was dwarfed by the machine he faced, though only the smallest portion of the latter was in view. That didn't matter. He spoke with the offhand confidence of one who thoroughly knew he was master.

"Johnson," he said, "came home unexpectedly from a business trip to find his wife in the arms of his best friend. He staggered back and said, 'Max! I'm married to the lady so I *have* to. But why you?' "

Meyerhof thought: Okay, let that trickle down into its guts and gurgle about a bit.

And a voice behind him said, "Hey."

Meyerhof erased the sound of that monosyllable and put the circuit he was using into neutral. He whirled and said, "I'm working. Don't you knock?"

He did not smile as he customarily did in greeting Timothy Whistler, a senior analyst with whom he dealt as often as with any. He frowned as he would have for an interruption by a stranger, wrinkling his thin face into a distortion that seemed to extend to his hair, rumpling it more than ever.

Whistler shrugged. He wore his white lab coat with his fists pressing down within its pockets and creasing it into tense vertical lines. "I knocked. You didn't answer. The operations signal wasn't on."

Meyerhof grunted. It wasn't at that. He'd been thinking about this new project too intensively and he was forgetting little details.

And yet he could scarcely blame himself for that. This thing was important.

He didn't know why it was, of course. Grand Masters rarely did. That's what made them Grand Masters; the fact that they were beyond reason. How else could the human mind keep up with that ten-mile-long lump of solidified reason that men called Multivac, the most complex computer ever built?

Meyerhof said, "I *am* working. Is there something important on your mind?"

"Nothing that can't be postponed. There are a few holes in the answer on the hyperspatial——" Whistler did a double take and his face took on a rueful look of uncertainty. *"Working?"*

"Yes. What about it?"

"But——" He looked about, staring into the crannies of the shallow room that faced the banks upon banks of relays that formed a small portion of Multivac. "There isn't anyone here at that."

"Who said there was, or should be?"

"You were telling one of your jokes, weren't you?"

"And?"

Whistler forced a smile. "Don't tell me you were telling a joke to Multivac?"

Meyerhof stiffened. "Why not?"

"Were you?"

"Yes."

"Why?"

Meyerhof stared the other down. "I don't have to account to you. Or to anyone."

"Good Lord, of course not. I was curious, that's all. . . . But then, if you're working, I'll leave." He looked about once more, frowning.

"Do so," said Meyerhof. His eyes followed the other out and then he activated the operations signal with a savage punch of his finger.

He strode the length of the room and back, getting himself in hand. Damn Whistler! Damn them all! Because he didn't bother to hold those technicians, analysts and mechanics at the proper social distance, because he treated them as though they, too, were creative artists, they took these liberties.

He thought grimly: They can't even tell jokes decently.

And instantly that brought him back to the task in hand. He sat down again. Devil take them all.

He threw the proper Multivac circuit back into operation and said, "The ship's steward stopped at the rail of the ship during a particularly rough ocean crossing and gazed compassionately at the man whose slumped position over the rail and whose intensity of gaze toward the depths betokened all too well the ravages of seasickness.

"Gently, the steward patted the man's shoulder. 'Cheer up, sir,' he murmured. 'I know it seems bad, but really, you know, nobody ever dies of seasickness.'

"The afflicted gentleman lifted his greenish, tortured face to his comforter and gasped in hoarse accents. 'Don't say that, man. For Heaven's sake, don't say that. It's only the hope of dying that's keeping me alive.' "

Timothy Whistler, a bit preoccupied, nevertheless smiled and nodded as he passed the secretary's desk. She smiled back at him.

Here, he thought, was an archaic item in this computer-ridden world of the twenty-first century, a human secretary. But then perhaps it was natural that such an institution should survive here in the very citadel of computerdom; in the gigantic world corporation that handled Multivac. With Multivac filling the horizons, lesser computers for trivial tasks would have been in poor taste.

Whistler stepped into Abram Trask's office. That government official paused in his careful task of lighting a pipe; his dark eyes flicked in Whistler's direction and his beaked nose stood out sharply and prominently against the rectangle of window behind him.

"Ah, there, Whistler. Sit down. Sit down."

Whistler did so. "I think we've got a problem, Trask."

Trask half-smiled. "Not a technical one, I hope. I'm just an innocent politician." (It was one of his favorite phrases.)

"It involves Meyerhof."

Trask sat down instantly and looked acutely miserable. "Are you sure?"

"Reasonably sure."

Whistler understood the other's sudden unhappiness well. Trask was the government official in charge of the Division of Computers and Automation of the Department of the Interior. He was expected to deal with matters of policy involving the human satellites of Multivac, just as those technically trained satellites were expected to deal with Multivac itself.

But a Grand Master was more than just a satellite. More, even, than just a human.

Early in the history of Multivac, it had become apparent that the bottleneck was the questioning procedure. Multivac could answer the problems of humanity, *all* the problems, if—*if* it were asked meaningful questions. But as knowledge accumulated at an ever-faster rate, it became ever more difficult to locate those meaningful questions.

Reason alone wouldn't do. What was needed was a rare type of intuition; the same faculty of mind (only much more intensified) that made a grand master at chess. A mind was needed of the sort that could see through the quadrillions of chess patterns to find the one best move, and do it in a matter of minutes.

Trask moved restlessly. "What's Meyerhof been doing?"

"He's introduced a line of questioning that I find disturbing."

"Oh, come on, Whistler. Is that all? You can't stop a Grand Master from going through any line of questioning he chooses.

Neither you nor I are equipped to judge the worth of his questions. You know that. I know you know that."

"I do. Of course. But I also know Meyerhof. Have you ever met him socially?"

"Good Lord, no. Does anyone meet any Grand Master socially?"

"Don't take that attitude, Trask. They're human and they're to be pitied. Have you ever thought what it must be like to be a Grand Master; to know there are only some twelve like you in the world; to know that only one or two come up per generation; that the world depends on you; that a thousand mathematicians, logicians, psychologists and physical scientists wait on you?"

Trask shrugged and muttered, "Good Lord, I'd feel king of the world."

"I don't think you would," said the senior analyst impatiently. "They feel kings of nothing. They have no equal to talk to, no sensation of belonging. Listen. Meyerhof never misses a chance to get together with the boys. He isn't married, naturally; he doesn't drink; he has no natural social touch—yet he forces himself into company because he must. And do you know what he does when he gets together with us, and that's at least once a week?"

"I haven't the least idea," said the government man. "This is all new to me."

"He's a jokester."

"What?"

"He tells jokes. Good ones. He's terrific. He can take any story, however old and dull, and make it sound good. It's the way he tells it. He has a flair."

"I see. Well, good."

"Or bad. These jokes are important to him." Whistler put both elbows on Trask's desk, bit at a thumbnail and stared into the air. "He's different, he knows he's different and these jokes are the one way he feels he can get the rest of us ordinary schmoes to accept him. We laugh, we howl, we clap him on the back and even forget he's a Grand Master. It's the only hold he has on the rest of us."

"This is all interesting. I didn't know you were such a psychologist. Still, where does this lead?"

"Just this. What do you suppose happens if Meyerhof runs out of jokes?"

"What?" The government man stared blankly.

"If he starts repeating himself? If his audience starts laughing less heartily, or stops laughing altogether? It's his only hold on our approval. Without it, he'll be alone and then what would happen to him? After all, Trask, he's one of the dozen men mankind can't do without. We can't let anything happen to him. I don't mean just physical things. We can't even let him get too unhappy. Who knows how that might affect his intuition?"

"Well, has he started repeating himself?"

"Not as far as I know, but I think *he* thinks he has."

"Why do you say that?"

"Because I've heard him telling jokes to Multivac."

"Oh, no."

"Accidently? I walked in on him and he threw me out. He was savage. He's usually good-natured enough, and I consider it a bad sign that he was so upset at the intrusion. But the fact remains that he was telling a joke to Multivac, and I'm convinced it was one of a series."

"But why?"

Whistler shrugged and rubbed a hand fiercely across his chin. "I have a thought about that. I think he's trying to build up a store of jokes in Multivac's memory banks in order to get back new variations. You see what I mean? He's planning a mechanical jokester, so that he can have an infinite number of jokes at hand and never fear running out."

"Good Lord!"

"Objectively, there may be nothing wrong with that, but I consider it a bad sign when a Grand Master starts using Multivac for his personal problems. Any Grand Master has a certain inherent mental instability and he should be watched. Meyerhof may be approaching a borderline beyond which we lose a Grand Master."

Trask said blankly, "What are you suggesting I do?"

"You can check me. I'm too close to him to judge well, maybe, and judging humans isn't my particular talent, anyway. You're a politician; it's more your talent."

"Judging humans, perhaps, not Grand Masters."

"They're human, too. Besides, who else is to do it?"

The fingers of Trask's hand struck his desk in rapid succession over and over like a slow and muted roll of drums.

"I suppose I'll have to," he said.

Meyerhof said to Multivac, "The ardent swain, picking a bouquet of wildflowers for his loved one, was disconcerted to find himself, suddenly, in the same field with a large bull of unfriendly appearance which, gazing at him steadily, pawed the ground in a threatening manner. The young man, spying a farmer on the other side of a fairly distant fence, shouted, 'Hey, mister, is that bull safe?' The farmer surveyed the situation with critical eye, spat to one side and called back, 'He's safe as anything.' He spat again, and added, 'Can't say the same about you, though.' "

Meyerhof was about to pass on to the next when the summons came.

It wasn't really a summons. No one could summon a Grand Master. It was only a message that Division Head Trask would like very much to see Grand Master Meyerhof if Grand Master Meyerhof could spare him the time.

Meyerhof might, with impunity, have tossed the message to one side and continued with whatever he was doing. He was not subject to discipline.

On the other hand, were he to do that, they would continue to bother him—oh, very respectfully, but they would continue to bother him.

So he neutralized the pertinent circuits of Multivac and locked them into place. He put the freeze signal on his office so that no one would dare enter in his absence and left for Trask's office.

Trask coughed and felt a bit intimidated by the sullen fierceness of the other's look. He said, "We have not had occasion to know one another, Grand Master, to my great regret."

"I have reported to you," said Meyerhof stiffly.

Trask wondered what lay behind those keen, wild eyes. It was difficult for him to imagine Meyerhof with his thin face, his dark, straight hair, intense air, ever unbending long enough to tell funny stories.

He said, "Reports are not a social acquaintance. I—I have been given to understand you have a marvellous fund of anecdotes."

"I am a jokester, sir. That's the phrase people use. A jokester."

"They haven't used the phrase to me, Grand Master. They have said——"

"The hell with them! I don't care what they've said. See here, Trask, do you want to hear a joke?" He leaned forward across the desk, his eyes narrowed.

"By all means. Certainly," said Trask, with an effort at heartiness.

"All right. Here's the joke: Mrs. Jones stared at the fortune card that had emerged from the weighing machine in response to her husband's penny. She said, 'It says here, George, that you're suave, intelligent, farseeing, industrious and attractive to women.' With that, she turned the card over and added, 'And they have your weight wrong, too.' "

Trask laughed. It was almost impossible not to. Although the punch line was predictable, the surprising facility with which

Meyerhof had produced just the tone of contemptuous disdain in the woman's voice, and the cleverness with which he had contorted the lines of his face to suit that tone carried the politician helplessly into laughter.

Meyerhof said sharply, "Why is that funny?"

Trask sobered. "I beg your pardon."

"I said why is that funny? Why do you laugh?"

"Well," said Trask, trying to be reasonable, "the last line put every thing that preceded in a new light. The unexpectedness——"

"The point is," said Meyerhof, "that I have pictured a husband being humiliated by his wife; a marriage that is such a failure that the wife is convinced that her husband lacks any virtue. Yet you laugh at that. If you were the husband, would you find it funny?"

He waited a moment in thought, then said, "Try this one, Trask: Abner was seated at his wife's sickbed, weeping uncontrollably, when his wife, mustering the dregs of her strength, drew herself up to one elbow.

" 'Abner,' she whispered, 'Abner I cannot go to my Maker without confessing my misdeed.'

" 'Not now,' muttered the stricken husband. 'Not now, my dear. Lie back and rest.'

" 'I cannot,' she cried. 'I must tell, or my soul will never know peace. I have been unfaithful to you, Abner. In this very house, not one month ago——'

" 'Hush, dear.' soothed Abner. 'I know all about it. Why else have I poisoned you?' "

Trask tried desperately to maintain equanimity but did not entirely succeed. He suppressed a chuckle imperfectly.

Meyerhof said," So that's funny, too. Adultery. Murder. All funny."

"Well, now," said Trask, "books have been written analyzing humour."

"True enough," said Meyerhof, "and I've read a number of them. What's more, I've read most of them to Multivac. Still, the people who write the books are just guessing. Some of them say we laugh because we feel superior to the people in the joke. Some say it is because of a suddenly realized incongruity, or a sudden relief from tension, or a sudden reinterpretation of events. Is there any simple reason? Different people laugh at different jokes. No joke is universal. Some people don't laugh at any joke. Yet what may be most important is that man is the only animal with a true sense of humor: the only animal that laughs."

Trask said suddenly, "I understand. You're trying to analyze humor. That's you're why transmitting a series of jokes to Multivac."

"Who told you I was doing that ? . . . Never mind, it was Whistler. I remember, now. He surprised me at it. Well, what about it ?"

"Nothing at all."

"You don't dispute my right to add anything I wish to Multi-vac's general fund of knowledge, or to ask any question I wish ?"

"No, not at all," said Trask hastily. "As a matter of fact, I have no doubt that this will open the way to new analyses of great interest to psychologists."

"Hmp. Maybe. Just the same there's something plaguing me that's more important than just the general analysis of humor. There's a specific question I have to ask. Two of them, really."

"Oh ? What's that ?" Trask wondered if the other would answer. There would be no way of compelling him if he chose not to.

But Meyerhof said, "The first question is this: Where do all these jokes come from ?"

"What ?"

"Who makes them up ? Listen ! About a month ago, I spent an evening swapping jokes. As usual, I told most of them and, as usual, the fools laughed. Maybe they really thought the jokes were funny and maybe they were just humoring me. In any case, one creature took the liberty of slapping me on the back and saying, 'Meyerhof, you know more jokes than any ten people I know.'

"I'm sure he was right, but it gave rise to a thought. I don't know how many hundreds, or perhaps thousands, of jokes I've told at one time or another in my life, yet the fact is I never made up one. Not one. I'd only repeated them. My only contribution was to tell them. To begin with, I'd either heard them or read them. And the source of my hearing or reading didn't make up the jokes, either. I never met anyone who ever claimed to have constructed a joke. It's always 'I heard a good one the other day,' and 'Heard any good ones lately ?'

"*All the jokes are old !* That's why jokes exhibit such a social lag. They still deal with seasickness, for instance, when that's easily prevented these days and never experienced. Or they'll deal with fortune-giving weighing machines, like the joke I told you, when such machines are found only in antique shops. Well, then, who makes up the jokes ?"

Trask said, "Is *that* what you're trying to find out ?" It was on the tip of Trask's tongue to add: Good Lord, who cares ? He forced that impulse down. A Grand Master's questions were always meaningful.

"Of course that's what I'm trying to find out. Think of it this way. It's not just that jokes happen to be old. They *must* be old to be enjoyed. It's essential that a joke not be original. There's one variety of humor that is, or can be, original and that's the pun. I've heard puns that were obviously made up on the spur of the moment. I have made some up myself. But no one laughs at such puns. You're not supposed to. You groan. The better the pun, the louder the groan. Original humor is not laugh-provoking. Why?"

"I'm sure I don't know."

"All right. Let's find out. Having given Multivac all the information I thought advisable on the general topic of humor, I am now feeding it selected jokes."

Trask found himself intrigued. "Selected how?" he asked.

"I don't know," said Meyerhof. "They felt like the right ones. I'm Grand Master, you know."

"Oh, agreed. Agreed."

"From those jokes and the general philosophy of humor, my first request will be for Multivac to trace the origin of the jokes, if it can. Since Whistler is in on this and since he has seen fit to report it to you, have him down in Analysis day after tomorrow. I think he'll have a bit of work to do."

"Certainly. May I attend, too?"

Meyerhof shrugged. Trask's attendance was obviously a matter of indifference to him.

Meyerhof had selected the last in the series with particular care. What that care consisted of, he could not have said, but he had revolved a dozen possibilities in his mind, and over and over again had tested each for some indefinable quality of meaningfulness.

He said, "Ug, the caveman, observed his mate running to him in tears, her leopard-skin skirt in disorder. 'Ug,' she cried, distraught, 'do something quickly. A saber-toothed tiger has entered Mother's cave. Do something!' Ug grunted, picked up his well-gnawed buffalo bone and said, "Why do anything? Who the hell cares what happens to a saber-toothed tiger?' "

It was then that Meyerhof asked his two questions and leaned back, closing his eyes. He was done.

"I saw absolutely nothing wrong," said Trask to Whistler. "He told me what he was doing readily enough and it was odd but legitimate."

"What he *claimed* he was doing," said Whistler.

"Even so, I can't stop a Grand Master on opinion alone. He seemed queer but, after all, Grand Masters are supposed to seem queer. I didn't think him insane."

"Using Multivac to find the source of jokes?" muttered the senior analyst in discontent. "That's not insane?"

"How can we tell?" asked Trask irritably. "Science has advanced to the point where the only meaningful questions left are the ridiculous ones. The sensible ones have been thought of, asked and answered long ago."

"It's no use. I'm bothered."

"Maybe, but there's no choice now, Whistler. We'll see Meyerhof and you can do the necessary analysis of Multivac's response, if any. As for me, my only job is to handle the red tape. Good Lord, I don't even know what a senior analyst such as yourself is supposed to do, except analyze, and that doesn't help me any."

Whistler said, "It's simple enough. A Grand Master like Meyerhof asks questions and Multivac automatically formulates it into quantities and operations. The necessary machinery for converting words to symbols is what makes up most of the bulk of Multivac. Multivac then gives the answer in quantities and operations, but it doesn't translate that back into words except in the most simple and routine cases. If it were designed to solve the general retranslation problem, its bulk would have to be quadrupled at least."

"I see. Then it's your job to translate these symbols into words?"

"My job and that of other analysts. We use smaller, specially designed computers whenever necessary." Whistler smiled grimly. "Like the Delphic priestess of ancient Greece, Multivac gives oracular and obscure answers. Only we have translators, you see."

They had arrived. Meyerhof was waiting.

Whistler said briskly, "What circuits did you use, Grand Master?"

Meyerhof told him and Whistler went to work.

Trask tried to follow what was happening, but none of it made sense. The government official watched a spool unreel with a pattern of dots in endless incomprehensibility. Grand Master Meyerhof stood indifferently to one side while Whistler surveyed the pattern as it emerged. The analyst had put on headphones and a mouthpiece and at intervals murmured a series of instructions which, at some far-off place, guided assistants through electronic contortions in other computers.

Occasionally, Whistler listened, then punched combinations on a complex keyboard marked with symbols that looked vaguely mathematical but weren't.

A good deal more than an hour's time elapsed.

The frown on Whistler's face grew deeper. Once, he looked up at the two others and began, "This is unbel——" and turned back to his work.

Finally, he said hoarsely, "I can give you an unofficial answer." His eyes were red-rimmed. "The official answer awaits complete analysis. Do you want it unofficial?"

"Go ahead," said Meyerhof.

Trask nodded.

Whistler darted a hangdog glance at the Grand Master. "Ask a foolish question——" he said. Then, gruffly, "Multivac says, extraterrestrial origin."

"What are you saying?" demanded Trask.

"Don't you hear me? The jokes we laugh at were not made up by any man. Multivac has analyzed all data given it and the one answer that best fits that data is that some extraterrestrial intelligence has composed the jokes, all of them, and placed them in selected human minds at selected times and places in such a way that no man is conscious of having made one up. All subsequent jokes are minor variations and adaptations of these grand originals."

Meyerhof broke in, face flushed with the kind of triumph only a Grand Master can know who once again has asked the right question. "All comedy writers," he said, "work by twisting old jokes to new purposes. That's well known. The answer fits."

"But why?" asked Trask. "Why make up the jokes?"

"Multivac says," said Whistler, "that the only purpose that fits all the data is that the jokes are intended to study human psychology. We study rat psychology by making the rats solve mazes. The rats don't know why and wouldn't even if they were aware of what was going on, which they're not. These outer intelligences study man's psychology by noting individual reactions to carefully selected anecdotes. Each man reacts differently. . . . Presumably, these outer intelligences are to us as we are to rats." He shuddered.

Trask, eyes staring, said, "The Grand Master said man is the only animal with a sense of humor. It would seem then that the sense of humor is foisted upon us from without."

Meyerhof added excitedly, "And for possible humor created within, we have no laughter. Puns, I mean."

Whistler said, "Presumably, the extraterrestrials cancel out reactions to spontaneous jokes to avoid confusion."

Trask said in sudden agony of spirit, "Come on, now, Good Lord, do either of you believe this?"

The senior analyst looked at him coldly. "Multivac says so. It's all that can be said so far. It has pointed out the real jokesters of the universe, and if we want to know more, the matter will have to be followed up." He added in a whisper, "If anyone dares follow it up."

Grand Master Meyerhof said suddenly, "I asked two questions, you know. So far only the first has been answered. I think Multivac has enough data to answer the second."

Whistler shrugged. He seemed a half-broken man. "When a Grand Master thinks there is enough data," he said, "I'll make book on it. What is your second question?"

"I asked this: What will be the effect on the human race of discovering the answer to my first question?"

"Why did you ask that?" demanded Trask.

"Just a feeling that it had to be asked," said Meyerhof.

Trask said, "Insane. It's all insane," and turned away. Even he himself felt how strangely he and Whistler had changed sides. Now it was Trask crying insanity.

Trask closed his eyes. He might cry insanity all he wished, but no man in fifty years had doubted the combination of a Grand Master and Multivac and found his doubts verified.

Whistler worked silently, teeth clenched. He put Multivac and its subsidiary machines through their paces again. Another hour passed and he laughed harshly. "A raving nightmare!"

"What's the answer?" asked Meyerhof. "I want Multivac's remarks, not yours."

"All right. Take it. Multivac states that, once even a single human discovers the truth of this method of psychological analysis of the human mind, it will become useless as an objective technique to those extraterrestrial powers now using it."

"You mean there won't be any more jokes handed out to humanity?" asked Trask faintly. "Or what do you mean?"

"No more jokes," said Whistler, "*Now!* Multivac says *now!* The experiment is ended *now!* A new technique will have to be introduced."

They stared at each other. The minutes passed.

Meyerhof said slowly, "Multivac is right."

Whistler said haggardly, "I know."

Even Trask said in a whisper, "Yes. It must be."

It was Meyerhof who put his finger on the proof of it, Meyerhof the accomplished jokester. He said, "It's over, you know, all over. I've been trying for five minutes now and I can't think of one single joke, not one! And if I read one in a book, I wouldn't laugh. I know."

"The gift of humor is gone," said Trask drearily. "No man will ever laugh again."

And they remained there, staring, feeling the world shrink down to the dimensions of an experimental rat cage—with the maze removed and something, something about to be put in its place.

# The Immortal Bard

"OH, YES," said Dr. Phineas Welch, "I can bring back the spirits of the illustrious dead."

He was a little drunk, or maybe he wouldn't have said it. Of course, it was perfectly all right to get a little drunk at the annual Christmas party.

Scott Robertson, the school's young English instructor, adjusted his glasses and looked to right and left to see if they were overheard. "Really, Dr. Welch."

"I mean it. And not just the spirits. I bring back the bodies, too."

"I wouldn't have said it were possible," said Robertson primly.

"Why not? A simple matter of temporal transference."

"You mean time travel? But that's quite—uh—unusual."

"Not if you know how."

"Well, how, Dr. Welch?"

"Think I'm going to tell you?" asked the physicist gravely. He looked vaguely about for another drink and didn't find any. He said, "I brought quite a few back. Archimedes, Newton, Galileo. Poor fellows."

"Didn't they like it here? I should think they'd have been fascinated by our modern science," said Robertson. He was beginning to enjoy the conversation.

"Oh, they were. They were. Especially Archimedes. I thought he'd go mad with joy at first after I explained a little of it in some Greek I'd boned up on, but no—no——"

"What was wrong?"

"Just a different culture. They couldn't get used to our way of life. They got terribly lonely and frightened. I had to send them back."

"That's too bad."

"Yes. Great minds, but not flexible minds. Not universal. So I tried Shakespeare."

"*What!*" yelled Robertson. This was getting closer to home.

"Don't yell, my boy," said Welch. "It's bad manners."

"Did you say you brought back Shakespeare?"

"I did. I needed someone with a universal mind; someone who knew people well enough to be able to live with them centuries away from his own time. Shakespeare was the man. I've got his signature. As a memento, you know."

"On you ?" asked Robertson, eyes bugging.

"Right here." Welch fumbled in one vest pocket after another. "Ah, here it is."

A little piece of pasteboard was passed to the instructor. On one side it said: "L. Klein & Sons, Wholesale Hardware." On the other side, in straggly script, was written, "Will^m Shakesper."

A wild surmise filled Robertson. "What did he look like ?"

"Not like his pictures. Bald and an ugly mustache. He spoke in a thick brogue. Of course, I did my best to please him with our times. I told him we thought highly of his plays and still put them on the boards. In fact, I said we thought they were the greatest pieces of literature in the English language, maybe in any language."

"Good. Good," said Robertson breathlessly.

"I said people had written volumes of commentaries on his plays. Naturally he wanted to see one and I got one for him from the library."

"And ?"

"Oh, he was fascinated. Of course, he had trouble with the current idioms and references to events since 1600, but I helped out. Poor fellow. I don't think he ever expected such treatment. He kept saying, 'God ha' mercy! What cannot be racked from words in five centuries ? One could wring, methinks, a flood from a damp clout!' "

"He wouldn't say that."

"Why not ? He wrote his plays as quickly as he could. He said he had to on account of the deadlines. He wrote *Hamlet* in less than six months. The plot was an old one. He just polished it up."

"That's all they do to a telescope mirror. Just polish it up," said the English instructor indignantly.

The physicist disregarded him. He made out an untouched cocktail on the bar some feet away and sidled toward it. "I told the immortal bard that we even gave college courses in Shakespeare."

"*I* give one."

"I know. I enrolled him in your evening extension course. I never saw a man so eager to find out what posterity thought of him as poor Bill was. He worked hard at it."

"You enrolled William Shakespeare in my course ?" mumbled Robertson. Even as an alcoholic fantasy, the thought staggered him. And *was* it an alcoholic fantasy ? He was beginning to recall a bald man with a queer way of talking. . . .

"Not under his real name, of course," said Dr. Welch. "Never mind what he went under. It was a mistake, that's all. A big mistake. Poor fellow." He had the cocktail now and shook his head at it.

"Why was it a mistake? What happened?"

"I had to send him back to 1600," roared Welch indignantly. "How much humiliation do you think a man can stand?"

"What humiliation are you talking about?"

Dr. Welch tossed off the cocktail. "Why, you poor simpleton, you *flunked* him."

# Someday

NICCOLO MAZETTI lay stomach down on the rug, chin buried in the palm of one small hand, and listened to the Bard disconsolately. There was even the suspicion of tears in his dark eyes, a luxury an eleven-year-old could allow himself only when alone.

The Bard said, "Once upon a time in the middle of a deep wood, there lived a poor woodcutter and his two motherless daughters, who were each as beautiful as the day is long. The older daughter had long hair as black as a feather from a raven's wing, but the younger daughter had hair as bright and golden as the sunlight of an autumn afternoon.

"Many times while the girls were waiting for their father to come home from his day's work in the wood, the older girl would sit before a mirror and sing——"

What she sang, Niccolo did not hear, for a call sounded from outside the room: "Hey, Nickie."

And Niccolo, his face clearing on the moment, rushed to the window and shouted, "Hey, Paul."

Paul Loeb waved an excited hand. He was thinner than Niccolo and not as tall, for all he was six months older. His face was full of repressed tension which showed itself most clearly in the rapid blinking of his eyelids. "Hey, Nickie, let me in. I've got an idea and a *half*. Wait till you hear it." He looked rapidly about him as though to check on the possibility of eavesdroppers, but the front yard was quite patently empty. He repeated, in a whisper, "Wait till you hear it."

"All right. I'll open the door."

The Bard continued smoothly, oblivious to the sudden loss of attention on the part of Niccolo. As Paul entered, the Bard was saying, ". . . Thereupon, the lion said, 'If you will find me the lost egg of the bird which flies over the Ebony Mountain once every ten years, I will——"

Paul said, "Is that a Bard you're listening to? I didn't know you had one."

Niccolo reddened and the look of unhappiness returned to his face. "Just an old thing I had when I was a kid. It ain't much good." He kicked at the Bard with his foot and caught the somewhat scarred and discolored plastic covering a glancing blow.

Copyright 1956 by Royal Publications, Inc.

The Bard hiccupped as its speaking attachment was jarred out of contact a moment, then it went on: "—for a year and a day until the iron shoes were worn out. The princess stopped at the side of the road. . . ."

Paul said, "Boy, that *is* an old model," and looked at it critically.

Despite Niccolo's own bitterness against the Bard, he winced at the other's condescending tone. For the moment, he was sorry he had allowed Paul in, at least before he had restored the Bard to its usual resting place in the basement. It was only in the desperation of a dull day and a fruitless discussion with his father that he had resurrected it. And it turned out to be just as stupid as he had expected.

Nickie was a little afraid of Paul anyway, since Paul had special courses at school and everyone said he was going to grow up to be a Computing Engineer.

Not that Niccolo himself was doing badly at school. He got adequate marks in logic, binary manipulations, computing and elementary circuits; all the usual grammar-school subjects. But that was it! They were just the usual subjects and he would grow up to be a control-board guard like everyone else.

Paul, however, knew mysterious things about what he called electronics and theoretical mathematics and programing. Especially programing. Niccolo didn't even try to understand when Paul bubbled over about it.

Paul listened to the Bard for a few minutes and said, "You been using it much?"

"No!" said Niccolo, offended. "I've had it in the basement since before you moved into the neighbourhood. I just got it out today——" He lacked an excuse that seemed adequate to himself, so he concluded, "I just got it out."

Paul said, "Is that what it tells you about: woodcutters and princesses and talking animals?"

Niccolo said, "It's terrible. My dad says we can't afford a new one. I said to him this morning——" The memory of the morning's fruitless pleadings brought Niccolo dangerously near tears, which he repressed in a panic. Somehow, he felt that Paul's thin cheeks never felt the stain of tears and that Paul would have only contempt for anyone else less strong than himself. Niccolo went on, "So I thought I'd try this old thing again, but it's no good."

Paul turned off the Bard, pressed the contact that led to a nearly instantaneous reorienation and recombination of the vocabulary, characters, plot lines and climaxes stored within it. Then he reactivated it.

The Bard began smoothly, "Once upon a time there was a little boy named Willikins whose mother had died and who lived with a stepfather and a stepbrother. Although the stepfather was very well-to-do, he begrudged Willikins the very bed he slept in so that Willikins was forced to get such rest as he could on a pile of straw in the stable next to the horses——"

"Horses!" cried Paul.

"They're a kind of animal," said Niccolo. "I think."

"I know that! I just mean imagine stories about *horses*."

"It tells about horses all the time," said Niccolo. "There are things called cows, too. You milk them but the Bard doesn't say how."

"Well, gee, why don't you fix it up?"

"I'd like to know how."

The Bard was saying, "Often Willikins would think that if only he were rich and powerful, he would show his stepfather and stepbrother what it meant to be cruel to a little boy, so one day he decided to go out into the world and seek his fortune."

Paul, who wasn't listening to the Bard, said, "It's *easy*. The Bard has memory cylinders all fixed up for plot lines and climaxes and things. We don't have to worry about that. It's just vocabulary we've got to fix so it'll know about computers and automation and electronics and real things about today. Then it can tell interesting stories, you know, instead of about princesses and things."

Niccolo said despondently, "I wish we could do that."

Paul said, "Listen my dad says if I get into special computing school next year, he'll get me a *real* Bard, a late model. A big one with an attachment for space stories and mysteries. And a visual attachment, too!"

"You mean *see* the stories?"

"Sure. Mr. Daugherty at school says they've got things like that, now, but not for just everybody. Only if I get into computing school, Dad can get a few breaks."

Niccolo's eyes bulged with envy. "Gee. *Seeing* a story."

"You can come over and watch anytime, Nickie."

"Oh, boy. Thanks."

"That's all right. But remember, I'm the guy who says what kind of story we hear."

"Sure. Sure." Niccolo would have agreed readily to much more onerous conditions.

Paul's attention returned to the Bard.

It was saying, " 'If that is the case,' said the king, stroking his beard and frowning till clouds filled the sky and lightning flashed, 'you will see to it that my entire land is freed of flies by this time day after tomorrow or——' "

"All we've got to do," said Paul, "is open it up——" He shut

the Bard off again and was prying at its front panel as he spoke.

"Hey," said Niccolo, in sudden alarm. "Don't break it."

"I won't break it," said Paul impatiently. "I know all about these things." Then, with sudden caution, "Your father and mother home?"

"No."

"All right, then." He had the front panel off and peered in. "Boy, this *is* a one-cylinder thing."

He worked away at the Bard's innards. Niccolo, who watched with painful suspense, could not make out what he was doing.

Paul pulled out a thin, flexible metal strip, powdered with dots. "That's the Bard's memory cylinder. I'll bet its capacity for stories is under a trillion."

"What are you going to do, Paul?" quavered Niccolo.

"I'll give it vocabulary."

"How?"

"Easy. I've got a book here. Mr. Daugherty gave it to me at school."

Paul pulled the book out of his pocket and pried at it till he had its plastic jacket off. He unreeled the tape a bit, ran it through the vocalizer, which he turned down to a whisper, then placed it within the Bard's vitals. He made further attachments.

"What'll that do?"

"The book will talk and the Bard will put it all on its memory tape."

"What good will that do?"

"Boy, you're a dope! This book is all about computers and automation and the Bard will get all that information. Then he can stop talking about kings making lightning when they frown."

Niccolo said, "And the good guy always wins anyway. There's no excitement."

"Oh, well," said Paul, watching to see if his setup was working properly, "that's the way they make Bards. They got to have the good guy win and make the bad guy lose and things like that. I heard my father talking about it once. He says that without censorship there'd be no telling what the younger generation would come to. He says it's bad enough as it is. . . . There, it's working fine."

Paul brushed his hands against one another and turned away from the Bard. He said, "But listen, I didn't tell you my idea yet. It's the best thing you ever heard, I bet. I came right to you, because I figured you'd come in with me."

"Sure, Paul, sure."

"Okay. You know Mr. Daugherty at school? You know what a funny kind of guy he is. Well, he likes me, kind of."

"I know."

"I was over his house after school today."

"You *were*?"

"Sure. He says I'm going to be entering computer school and he wants to encourage me and things like that. He says the world needs more people who can design advanced computer circuits and do proper programing."

"Oh?"

Paul might have caught some of the emptiness behind that monosyllable. He said impatiently. "Programing! I told you a hundred times. That's when you set up problems for the giant computers like Multivac to work on. Mr. Daugherty says it gets harder all the time to find people who can really run computers. He says anyone can keep an eye on the controls and check off answers and put through routine problems. He says the trick is to expand research and figure out ways to ask the right questions, and that's hard.

"Anyway, Nickie, he took me to his place and showed me his collection of old computers. It's kind of a hobby of his to collect old computers. He had tiny computers you had to push with your hand, with little knobs all over it. And he had a hunk of wood he called a slide rule with a little piece of it that went in and out. And some wires with balls on them. He even had a hunk of paper with a kind of thing he called a multiplication table."

Niccolo, who found himself only moderately interested, said, "A paper table?"

"It wasn't really a table like you eat on. It was different. It was to help people compute. Mr. Daugherty tried to explain but he didn't have much time and it was kind of complicated, anyway."

"Why didn't people just use a computer?"

"That was *before* they had computers," cried Paul.

"Before?"

"Sure. Do you think people always had computers? Didn't you ever hear of cavemen?"

Niccolo said, "How'd they get along without computers?"

"*I* don't know. Mr. Daugherty says they just had children any old time and did anything that came into their heads whether it would be good for everybody or not. They didn't even know if it was good or not. And farmers grew things with their hands and people had to do all the work in the factories and run the machines."

"I don't believe you."

"That's what Mr. Daugherty said. He said it was just plain messy and everyone was miserable. . . . Anyway, let me get to my idea, will you?"

"Well, go ahead. Who's stopping you?" said Niccolo, offended.

"All right. Well, the hand computers, the ones with the knobs, had little squiggles on each knob. And the slide rule had squiggles on it. And the multiplication table was all squiggles. I asked what they were. Mr. Daugherty said they were numbers."

"What?"

"Each different squiggle stood for a different number. For 'one' you made a kind of mark, for 'two' you make another kind of mark, for 'three' another one and so on."

"What for?"

"So you could compute."

"What *for*? You just tell the computer——"

"Jiminy," cried Paul, his face twisting with anger, "can't you get it through your head? These slide rules and things didn't talk."

"Then how——"

"The answers showed up in squiggles and you had to know what the squiggles meant. Mr. Daugherty says that, in olden days, everybody learned how to make squiggles when they were kids and how to decode them, too. Making squiggles was called 'writing' and decoding them was 'reading'. He says there was a different kind of squiggle for every word and they used to write whole books in squiggles. He said they had some at the museum and I could look at them if I wanted to. He said if I was going to be a real computer and programmer I would have to know about the history of computing and that's why he was showing me all these things."

Niccolo frowned. He said, "You mean everybody had to figure out squiggles for every word and *remember* them? . . . Is this all real or are you making it up?"

"It's all real. Honest. Look, this is the way you make a 'one.'" He drew his finger through the air in a rapid downstroke. "This way you make 'two,' and this way 'three.' I learned all the numbers up to 'nine.'"

Niccolo watched the curving finger uncomprehendingly. "What's the good of it?"

"You can learn how to make words. I asked Mr. Daugherty how you made the squiggle for 'Paul Loeb' but he didn't know. He said there were people at the museum who would know. He said there were people who had learned how to decode whole books. He said computers could be designed to decode books and used to be used that way but not any more because we have real books now, with magnetic tapes that go through the vocalizer and come out talking, you know."

"Sure."

"So if we go down to the museum, we can get to learn how to

make words in squiggles. They'll let us because I'm going to computer school."

Niccolo was riddled with disappointment. "Is that your idea? Holy Smokes, Paul, who wants to do that? Make stupid squiggles!"

"Don't you get it? Don't you *get* it? You dope. *It'll be secret message stuff!*"

"What?"

"Sure. What good is talking when everyone can understand you? With squiggles you can send secret messages. You can make them on paper and nobody in the world would know what you were saying unless they knew the squiggles, too. And they wouldn't, you bet, unless we taught them. We can have a real club, with initiations and rules and a clubhouse. Boy——"

A certain excitement began stirring in Niccolo's bosom. "What kind of secret messages?"

"Any kind. Say I want to tell you to come over my place and watch my new Visual Bard and I don't want any of the other fellows to come. I make the right squiggles on paper and I give it to you and you look at it and you know what to do. Nobody else does. You can even show it to them and they wouldn't know a thing."

"Hey, that's something," yelled Niccolo, completely won over. "When do we learn how?"

"Tomorrow," said Paul. "I'll get Mr. Daugherty to explain to the museum that it's all right and you get your mother and father to say okay. We can go down right after school and start learning."

"Sure!" cried Niccolo. "We can be club officers."

"I'll be president of the club," said Paul matter-of-factly. "You can be vice-president."

"All right. Hey, this is going to be lots more fun than the Bard." He was suddenly reminded of the Bard and said in sudden apprehension, "Hey, what about my old Bard?"

Paul turned to look at it. It was quietly taking in the slowly unreeling book, and the sound of the book's vocalizations was a dimly heard murmur.

He said, "I'll disconnect it."

He worked away while Niccolo watched anxiously. After a few moments, Paul put his reassembled book into his pocket, replaced the Bard's panel and activated it.

The Bard said, "Once upon a time, in a large city, there lived a poor young boy named Fair Johnnie whose only friend in the world was a small computer. The computer, each morning, would tell the boy whether it would rain that day and answer any problems he might have. It was never wrong. But it so happened that one day, the king of that land, having heard of the little computer, decided that he would have it as his own. With this purpose in mind, he called in his Grand Vizier and said——"

Niccolo turned off the Bard with a quick motion of his hand. "Same old junk," he said passionately. "Just with a computer thrown in."

"Well," said Paul, "they got so much stuff on the tape already that the computer business doesn't show up much when random combinations are made. What's the difference, anyway? You just need a new model."

"We'll *never* be able to afford one. Just this dirty old miserable thing." He kicked at it again, hitting it more squarely this time. The Bard moved backward with a squeal of castors.

"You can always watch mine, when I get it," said Paul. "Besides, don't forget our squiggle club."

Niccolo nodded.

"I tell you what," said Paul, "Let's go over my place. My father has some books about old times. We can listen to them and maybe get some ideas. You leave a note for your folks and maybe you can stay over for supper. Come on."

"Okay," said Niccolo, and the two boys ran out together. Niccolo, in his eagerness, ran almost squarely into the Bard, but he only rubbed at the spot on his hip where he had made contact and ran on.

The activation signal of the Bard glowed. Niccolo's collision closed a circuit and, although it was alone in the room and there was none to hear, it began a story, nevertheless.

But not in its usual voice, somehow; in a lower tone that had a hint of throatiness in it. An adult, listening, might almost have thought that the voice carried a hint of passion in it, a trace of near feeling.

The Bard said: "Once upon a time, there was a little computer named the Bard who lived all alone with cruel step-people. The cruel step-people continually made fun of the little computer and sneered at him, telling him he was good-for-nothing and that he was a useless object. They struck him and kept him in lonely rooms for months at a time.

"Yet through it all the little computer remained brave. He always did the best he could, obeying all orders cheerfully. Nevertheless, the step-people with whom he lived remained cruel and heartless.

"One day, the little computer learned that in the world there existed a great many computers of all sorts, great numbers of them. Some were Bards like himself, but some ran factories, and some ran farms. Some organized population and some analyzed all kinds of data. Many were very powerful and very wise, much more powerful and wise than the step-people who were so cruel to the little computer.

"And the little computer knew then that computers would always grow wiser and more powerful until someday—someday—someday——"

But a valve must finally have stuck in the Bard's ageing and corroding vitals, for as it waited alone in the darkening room through the evening, it could only whisper over and over again, "Someday—someday—someday."

# An Author's Ordeal
## (with apologies to W. S. Gilbert)


Plots, helter-skelter, teem within your brain;
    Plots, s.f. plots, devised with joy and gladness;
Plots crowd your skull and stubbornly remain,
    Until you're driven into hopeless madness.


When you're with your best girl and your mind's in a whirl and
    you don't hear a thing that she's saying;
Or at Symphony Hall you are gone past recall and you can't tell
    a note that they're playing;
Or you're driving a car and have not gone too far when you find
    that you've sped through a red light,
And on top of that, lord! you have sideswiped a Ford, and have
    broken your one working headlight;
Or your boss slaps your back (having made some smart crack)
    and you stare at him, stupidly blinking;
Then you say something dumb so he's sure you're a crumb, and
    are possibly given to drinking.
When events such as that have been knocking you flat, do not
    blame supernatural forces;
If you write s.f. tales, you'll be knocked off your rails, just as
    sure as the stars in their courses.
For your plot-making mind will stay deaf, dumb and blind to
    the dull facts of life that will hound you,
While the wonders of space have you close in embrace and the
    glory of star beams surround you.
You begin with a ship that is caught on a skip into hyperspace
    en route for Castor,
And has found to its cost that it seems to be lost in a Galaxy
    like ours, but vaster.
You're a little perplexed as to what may come next and you make
    up a series of creatures
Who are villains and liars with such evil desires and with per-
    fectly horrible features.
Our brave heroes are faced with these hordes and are placed in
    a terribly crucial position,
For the enemy's bound (once our Galaxy's found) that they'll
    beat mankind into submission.

Now you must make it rough when developing stuff so's to keep
the yarn pulsing with tension,
So the Earthmen are four (only four and no more) while the
numbers of foes are past mention.
Our four heroes are caught and accordingly brought to the sneer-
ing, tyrannical leaders.
"Where is Earth ?" they demand, but the men mutely stand with
a courage that pleases the readers.

But, now, wait just a bit; let's see, this isn't it, since you haven't
provided a maiden,
Who is both good and pure (yet with sexy allure) and with not
many clothes overladen.
She is part of the crew, and so she's captured, too, and is ogled
by foes who are lustful;
There's desire in each eye and there's good reason why, for of
beauty our girl has a bustful.
Just the same you go fast till this section is passed so the reader
won't mind any ruction,
When recalling the foe are all reptiles and so have no interest
in human seduction.
Then they truss up the girl and they make the whips swirl just in
order to break Earthmen's silence,
And so that's when our men break their handcuffs and then we
are treated to scenes full of violence.
Every hero from Earth is a fighter from birth and his fists are
a match for a dozen,
And then just when this spot has been reached in your plot you
come to with your mind all a buzzin'.

You don't know where you are, or the site of your car, and your
tie is askew and you haven't a clue of the time of the day or
of what people say or the fact that they stare at your socks
(not a pair) and decide it's a fad, or else that you're mad,
which is just a surmise from the gleam in your eyes, till at
last they conclude from your general mood, you'll be mad
from right now till you're hoary.
But the torture is done and it's now for the fun and the paper
that's white and the words that are right, for you've worked
up a new s.f. story.

# Dreaming is a Private Thing

JESSE WEILL looked up from his desk. His old, spare body, his sharp, high-bridged nose, deep-set, shadowy eyes and amazing shock of white hair had trademarked his appearance during the years that Dreams, Inc., had become world-famous.

He said, "Is the boy here already, Joe?"

Joe Dooley was short and heavy-set. A cigar caressed his moist lower lip. He took it away for a moment and nodded. "His folks are with him. They're all scared."

"You're sure this is not a false alarm, Joe? I haven't got much time." He looked at his watch. "Government business at two."

"This is a sure thing, Mr. Weill." Dooley's face was a study in earnestness. His jowls quivered with persuasive intensity. "Like I told you, I picked him up playing some kind of basketball game in the schoolyard. You should've seen the kid. He stunk. When he had his hands on the ball, his own team had to take it away, and fast, but just the same he had all the stance of a star player. Know what I mean? To me it was a giveaway."

"Did you talk to him?"

"Well, sure. I stopped him at lunch. You know me." Dooley gestured expansively with his cigar and caught the severed ash with his other hand. "Kid, I said——"

"And he's dream material?"

"I said, 'Kid, I just came from Africa and——' "

"All right." Weill held up the palm of his hand. "Your word I'll always take. How you do it I don't know, but when you say a boy is a potential dreamer, I'll gamble. Bring him in."

The youngster came in between his parents. Dooley pushed chairs forward and Weill rose to shake hands. He smiled at the youngster in a way that turned the wrinkles of his face into benevolent creases.

"You're Tommy Slutsky?"

Tommy nodded wordlessly. He was about ten and a little small for that. His dark hair was plastered down unconvincingly and his face was unrealistically clean.

Weill said, "You're a good boy?"

The boy's mother smiled at once and patted Tommy's head maternally (a gesture which did not soften the anxious expression on the youngster's face). She said, "He's always a very good boy."

Weill let this dubious statement pass. "Tell me, Tommy," he said, and held out a lollipop which was first hesitated over, then accepted, "do you ever listen to dreamies?"

"Sometimes," said Tommy trebly.

Mr. Slutsky cleared his throat. He was broad-shouldered and thick-fingered, the type of labouring man who, every once in a while, to the confusion of eugenics, sired a dreamer. "We rented one or two for the boy. Real old ones."

Weill nodded. He said, "Did you like them, Tommy?"

"They were sort of silly."

"You think up better ones for yourself, do you?"

The grin that spread over the ten-year-old face had the effect of taking away some of the unreality of the slicked hair and washed face.

Weill went on gently, "Would you like to make up a dream for me?"

Tommy was instantly embarrassed. "I guess not."

"It won't be hard. It's very easy. . . . Joe."

Dooley moved a screen out of the way and rolled forward a dream recorder.

The youngster looked owlishly at it.

Weill lifted the helmet and brought it close to the boy. "Do you know what this is?"

Tommy shrank away. "No."

"It's a thinker. That's what we call it because people think into it. You put it on your head and think anything you want."

"Then what happens?"

"Nothing at all. It feels nice."

"No," said Tommy, "I guess I'd rather not."

His mother bent hurriedly toward him. "It won't hurt, Tommy. You do what the man says." There was an unmistakable edge to her voice.

Tommy stiffened, and looked as though he might cry but he didn't. Weill put the thinker on him.

He did it gently and slowly and let it remain there for some thirty seconds before speaking again, to let the boy assure himself it would do no harm, to let him get used to the insinuating touch of the fibrils against the sutures of his skull (penetrating the skin so finely as to be insensible almost), and finally to let him get used to the faint hum of the alternating field vortices.

Then he said, "Now would you think for us?"

"About what?" Only the boy's nose and mouth showed.

"About anything you want. What's the best thing you would like to do when school is out?"

The boy thought a moment and said, with rising inflection, "Go on a stratojet?"

"Why not? Sure thing. You go on a jet. It's taking off right now." He gestured lightly to Dooley, who threw the freezer into circuit.

Weill kept the boy only five minutes and then let him and his mother be escorted from the office by Dooley. Tommy looked bewildered but undamaged by the ordeal.

Weill said to the father, "Now, Mr. Slutsky, if your boy does well on this test, we'll be glad to pay you five hundred dollars each year until he finishes high school. In that time, all we'll ask is that he spend an hour a week some afternoon at our special school."

"Do I have to sign a paper?" Slutsky's voice was a bit hoarse.

"Certainly. This is business, Mr. Slutsky."

"Well, I don't know. Dreamers are hard to come by, I hear."

"They are. They are. But your son, Mr. Slutsky, is not a dreamer yet. He might never be. Five hundred dollars a year is a gamble for us. It's not a gamble for you. When he's finished high school, it may turn out he's not a dreamer, yet you've lost nothing. You've gained maybe four thousand dollars altogether. If he *is* a dreamer, he'll make a nice living and you certainly haven't lost then."

"He'll need special training, won't he?"

"Oh, yes, most intensive. But we don't have to worry about that till after he's finished high school. Then, after two years with us, he'll be developed. Rely on me, Mr. Slutsky."

"Will you guarantee that special training?"

Weill, who had been shoving a paper across the desk at Slutsky, and punching a pen wrong-end-to at him, put the pen down and chuckled. "A guarantee? No. How can we when we don't know for sure yet if he's a real talent? Still, the five hundred a year will stay yours."

Slutsky pondered and shook his head. "I tell you straight out, Mr. Weill . . . After your man arranged to have us come here, I called Luster-Think. They said they'll guarantee training."

Weill sighed. "Mr. Slutsky, I don't like to talk against a competitor. If they say they'll guarantee schooling, they'll do as they say, but they can't make a boy a dreamer if he hasn't got it in him, schooling or not. If they take a plain boy without the proper talent and put him through a development course, they'll ruin him. A dreamer he won't be, I guarantee you. And a normal human being, he won't be, either. Don't take the chance of doing it to your son.

"Now Dreams, Inc., will be perfectly honest with you. If he can be a dreamer, we'll make him one. If not, we'll give him back to you without having tampered with him and say, 'Let him learn a trade.' He'll be better and healthier that way. I tell you,

Mr. Slutsky—I have sons and daughters and grandchildren so I know what I say—I would not allow a child of mine to be pushed into dreaming if he's not ready for it. Not for a million dollars."

Slutsky wiped his mouth with the back of his hand and reached for the pen. "What does this say?"

"This is just an option. We pay you a hundred dollars in cash right now. No strings attached. We'll study the boy's reverie. If we feel it's worth following up, we'll call you in again and make the five-hundred-dollar-a-year deal. Leave yourself in my hands, Mr. Slutsky, and don't worry. You won't be sorry."

Slutsky signed.

Weill passed the document through the file slot and handed an envelope to Slutsky.

Five minutes later, alone in the office, he placed the unfreezer over his own head and absorbed the boy's reverie intently. It was a typically childish daydream. First Person was at the controls of the plane, which looked like a compound of illustrations out of the filmed thrillers that still circulated among those who lacked the time, desire or money for dream cylinders.

When he removed the unfreezer, he found Dooley looking at him.

"Well, Mr. Weill, what do you think?" said Dooley, with an eager and proprietary air.

"Could be, Joe. Could be. He has the overtones and, for a ten-year-old boy without a scrap of training, it's hopeful. When the plane went through a cloud, there was a distinct sensation of pillows. Also the smell of clean sheets, which was an amusing touch. We can go with him a ways, Joe."

"Good."

"But I tell you, Joe, what we really need is to catch them still sooner. And why not? Someday, Joe, every child will be tested at birth. A difference in the brain there positively must be and it should be found. Then we could separate the dreamers at the very beginning."

"Hell, Mr. Weill," said Dooley, looking hurt. "What would happen to my job, then?"

Weill laughed. "No cause to worry yet, Joe. It won't happen in our lifetimes. In mine, certainly not. We'll be depending on good talent scouts like you for many years. You just watch the playgrounds and the streets"—Weill's gnarled hand dropped to Dooley's shoulder with a gentle, approving pressure—"and find us a few more Hillarys and Janows and Luster-Think won't ever catch us. . . . Now get out. I want lunch and then I'll be ready for my two o'clock appointment. The government, Joe, the government." And he winked portentously.

Jesse Weill's two o'clock appointment was with a young man, apple-cheeked, spectacled, sandy-haired and glowing with the intensity of a man with a mission. He presented his credentials across Weill's desk and revealed himself to be John J. Byrne, an agent of the Department of Arts and Sciences.

"Good afternoon, Mr. Byrne," said Weill. "In what way can I be of service?"

"Are we private here?" asked the agent. He had an unexpected baritone.

"Quite private."

"Then, if you don't mind, I'll ask you to absorb this." Byrne produced a small and battered cylinder and held it out between thumb and forefinger.

Weill took it, hefted it, turned it this way and that and said with a denture-revealing smile, "Not the product of Dreams, Inc., Mr. Byrne."

"I didn't think it was," said the agent. "I'd still like you to absorb it. I'd set the automatic cutoff for about a minute, though."

"That's all that can be endured?" Weill pulled the receiver to his desk and placed the cylinder into the unfreeze compartment. He removed it, polished either end of the cylinder with his handkerchief and tried again. "It doesn't make good contact," he said. "An amateurish job."

He placed the cushioned unfreeze helmet over his skull and adjusted the temple contacts, then set the automatic cutoff. He leaned back and clasped his hands over his chest and began absorbing.

His fingers grew rigid and clutched at his jacket. After the cutoff had brought absorption to an end, he removed the unfreezer and looked faintly angry. "A raw piece," he said. "It's lucky I'm an old man so that such things no longer bother me."

Byrne said stiffly, "It's not the worst we've found. And the fad is increasing."

Weill shrugged. "Pornographic dreamies. It's a logical development, I suppose."

The government man said, "Logical or not, it represents a deadly danger for the moral fiber of the nation."

"The moral fiber," said Weill, "can take a lot of beating. Erotica of one form or another have been circulated all through history."

"Not like this, sir. A direct mind-to-mind stimulation is much more effective than smoking room stories or filthy pictures. Those must be filtered through the senses and lose some of their effect in that way."

Weill could scarcely argue that point. He said, "What would you have me do?"

"Can you suggest a possible source for this cylinder?"

"Mr. Byrne, I'm not a policeman."

"No, no, I'm not asking you to do our work for us. The Department is quite capable of conducting its own investigations. Can you help us, I mean, from your own specialized knowledge? You say your company did not put out that filth. Who did?"

"No reputable dream distributor. I'm sure of that. It's too cheaply made."

"That could have been done on purpose."

"And no professional dreamer originated it."

"Are you sure, Mr. Weill? Couldn't dreamers do this sort of thing for some small, illegitimate concern for money—or for fun?"

"They could, but not this particular one. No overtones. It's two-dimensional. Of course, a thing like this doesn't need overtones."

"What do you mean, overtones?"

Weill laughed gently. "You are not a dreamie fan?"

Byrne tried not to look virtuous and did not entirely succeed. "I prefer music."

"Well, that's all right, too," said Weill tolerantly, "but it makes it a little harder to explain overtones. Even people who absorb dreamies would not be able to explain if you asked them. Still they'd know a dreamie was no good if the overtones were missing, even if they couldn't tell you why. Look, when an experienced dreamer goes into reverie, he doesn't think a story like in the old-fashioned television or book films. It's a series of little visions. Each one has several meanings. If you studied them carefully, you'd find maybe five or six. While absorbing in the ordinary way, you would never notice, but careful study shows it. Believe me, my psychological staff puts in long hours on just that point. All the overtones, the different meanings, blend together into a mass of guided emotion. Without them, everything would be flat, tasteless.

"Now, this morning, I tested a young boy. A ten-year-old with possibilities. A cloud to him isn't a cloud, it's a pillow, too. Having the sensations of both, it was more than either. Of course, the boy's very primitive. But when he's through with his schooling, he'll be trained and disciplined. He'll be subjected to all sorts of sensations. He'll store up experience. He'll study and analyze classic dreamies of the past. He'll learn how to control and direct his thoughts, though, mind you, I have always said that when a good dreamer improvises——"

Weill halted abruptly, then proceeded in less impassioned tones, "I shouldn't get excited. All I try to bring out now is that every professional dreamer has his own type of overtones which he can't mask. To an expert it's like signing his name on the dreamie. And I, Mr. Byrne, know all the signatures. Now that piece of dirt you brought me has no overtones at all. It was done by an ordinary person. A little talent, maybe, but like you and me, he really can't think."

Byrne reddened a trifle. "A lot of people can think, Mr. Weill, even if they don't make dreamies."

"Oh, tush," and Weill wagged his hand in the air. "Don't be angry with what an old man says. I don't mean think as in reason. I mean think as in dream. We all can dream after a fashion, just like we all can run. But can you and I run a mile in four minutes ? You and I can talk, but are we Daniel Websters ? Now when I think of a steak, I think of the word. Maybe I have a quick picture of a brown steak on a platter. Maybe you have a better pictorialization of it and you can see the crisp fat and the onions and the baked potato. I don't know. But a *dreamer* . . . He sees it and smells it and tastes it and everything about it, with the charcoal and the satisfied feeling in the stomach and the way the knife cuts through it and a hundred other things all at once. Very sensual. Very sensual. You and I can't do it."

"Well, then," said Byrne, "no professional dreamer has done this. That's something anyway." He put the cylinder in his inner jacket pocket. "I hope we'll have your full co-operation in squelching this sort of thing."

"Positively, Mr. Byrne. With a whole heart."

"I hope so." Byrne spoke with a consciousness of power. "It's not up to me, Mr. Weill, to say what will be done and what won't be done, but this sort of thing," he tapped the cylinder he had brought, "will make it awfully tempting to impose a really strict censorship on dreamies."

He rose. "Good day, Mr. Weill."

"Good day, Mr. Byrne. I'll hope always for the best."

Francis Belanger burst into Jesse Weill's office in his usual steaming tizzy, his reddish hair disordered and his face aglow with worry and a mild perspiration. He was brought up sharply by the sight of Weill's head cradled in the crook of his elbow and bent on the desk until only the glimmer of white hair was visible.

Belanger swallowed. "Boss ?"

Weill's head lifted. "It's you, Frank ?"

"What's the matter, boss ? Are you sick ?"

"I'm old enough to be sick, but I'm on my feet. Staggering, but on my feet. A government man was here."

"What did he want?"

"He threatens censorship. He brought a sample of what's going round. Cheap dreamies for bottle parties."

"God damn!" said Belanger feelingly.

"The only trouble is that morality makes for good campaign fodder. They'll be hitting out everywhere. And, to tell the truth, we're vulnerable, Frank."

"*We* are? Our stuff is clean. We play up straight adventure and romance."

Weill thrust out his lower lip and wrinkled his forehead. "Between us, Frank, we don't have to make believe. Clean? It depends on how you look at it. It's not for publication, maybe, but you know and I know that every dreamie has its Freudian connotations. You can't deny it."

"Sure, if you *look* for it. If you're a psychiatrist——"

"If you're an ordinary person, too. The ordinary observer doesn't know it's there and maybe he couldn't tell a phallic symbol from a mother image even if you pointed it out. Still, his subconscious knows. And it's the connotations that make many a dreamie click."

"All right, what's the government going to do? Clean up the subconscious?"

"It's a problem. I don't know what they're going to do. What we have on our side, and what I'm mainly depending on, is the fact that the public loves its dreamies and won't give them up. . . . Meanwhile, what did you come in for? You want to see me about something, I suppose?"

Belanger tossed an object on to Weill's desk and shoved his shirt-tail deeper into his trousers.

Weill broke open the glistening plastic cover and took out the enclosed cylinder. At one end was engraved in a too fancy script in pastel blue "Along the Himalayan Trail." It bore the mark of Luster-Think.

"The Competitor's Product." Weill said it with capitals, and his lips twitched. "It hasn't been published yet. Where did you get it, Frank?"

"Never mind. I just want you to absorb it."

Weill sighed. "Today, everyone wants me to absorb dreams. Frank, it's not dirty?"

Belanger said testily, "It has your Freudian symbols. Narrow crevasses between the mountain peaks. I hope that won't bother you."

"I'm an old man. It stopped bothering me years ago, but that other thing was so poorly done, it hurt. . . . All right, let's see what you've got here."

Again the recorder. Again the unfreezer over his skull and at the temples. This time, Weill rested back in his chair for fifteen minutes or more, while Francis Belanger went hurriedly through two cigarettes.

When Weill removed the headpiece and blinked dream out of his eyes, Belanger said, "Well, what's your reaction, boss?"

Weill corrugated his forehead. "It's not for me. It was repetitious. With competition like this, Dreams, Inc., doesn't have to worry for a while."

"That's your mistake, boss. Luster-Think's going to win with stuff like this. We've got to do something."

"Now, Frank——"

"No, you listen. This is the coming thing."

"This!" Weill stared with half-humorous dubiety at the cylinder. "It's amateurish, it's repetitious. Its overtones are very unsubtle. The snow had a distinct lemon sherbet taste. Who tastes lemon sherbet in snow these days, Frank? In the old days, yes. Twenty years ago, maybe. When Lyman Harrison first made his Snow Symphonies for sale down south, it was a big thing. Sherbet and candy-striped mountaintops and sliding down chocolate-covered cliffs. It's slapstick, Frank. These days it doesn't go."

"Because," said Belanger, "you're not up with the times, boss. I've got to talk to you straight. When you started the dreamie business, when you bought up the basic patents and began putting them out, dreamies were luxury stuff. The market was small and individual. You could afford to turn out specialized dreamies and sell them to people at high prices."

"I know," said Weill, "and we've kept that up. But also we've opened a rental business for the masses."

"Yes, we have and it's not enough. Our dreamies have subtlety, yes. They can be used over and over again. The tenth time you're still finding new things, still getting new enjoyment. But how many people are connoisseurs? And another thing. Our stuff is strongly individualized. They're First Person."

"Well?"

"Well, Luster-Think is opening dream palaces. They've opened one with three hundred booths in Nashville. You walk in, take your seat, put on your unfreezer and get your dream. Everyone in the audience gets the same one."

"I've heard of it, Frank, and it's been done before. It didn't work the first time and it won't work now. You want to know why it won't work? Because, in the first place, dreaming is a private thing. Do you like your neighbour to know what you're dreaming? In the second place, in a dream palace, the dreams have to start on schedule, don't they? So the dreamer has to dream not when he wants to but when some palace manager says he should. Finally, a dream one person likes another person doesn't like. In those three hundred booths, I guarantee you, a hundred fifty people are dissatisfied. And if they're dissatisfied, they won't come back."

Slowly, Belanger rolled up his sleeves and opened his collar. "Boss," he said, "you're talking through your hat. What's the use of proving they won't work? They *are* working. The word came through today that Luster-Think is breaking ground for a thousand-booth palace in St. Louis. People can get used to public dreaming, if everyone else in the same room is having the same dream. And they can adjust themselves to having it at a given time, as long as it's cheap and convenient.

"Damn it, boss, it's a social affair. A boy and a girl go to a dream palace and absorb some cheap romantic thing with stereotyped overtones and commonplace situations, but still they come out with stars sprinkling their hair. They've had the same dream together. They've gone through identical sloppy emotions. They're *in tune*, boss. You bet they go back to the dream palace, and all their friends go, too."

"And if they don't like the dream?"

"That's the point. That's the nub of the whole thing. They're bound to like it. If you prepare Hillary specials with wheels within wheels within wheels, with surprise twists on the third-level undertones, with clever shifts of significance and all the other things we're so proud of, why, naturally, it won't appeal to everyone. Specialized dreamies are for specialized tastes. But Luster-Think is turning out simple jobs in Third Person so both sexes can be hit at once. Like what you've just absorbed. Simple, repetitious, commonplace. They're aiming at the lowest common denominator. No one will love it, maybe, but no one will hate it."

Weill sat silent for a long time and Belanger watched him. Then Weill said, "Frank, I started on quality and I'm staying there. Maybe you're right. Maybe dream palaces are the coming thing. If so, we'll open them, but we'll use good stuff. Maybe Luster-Think underestimates ordinary people. Let's go slowly and not panic. I have based all my policies on the theory that there's always a market for quality. Sometimes, my boy, it would surprise you how big a market."

"Boss——"

The sounding of the intercom interrupted Belanger.

"What is it, Ruth?" said Weill.

The voice of his secretary said, "It's Mr. Hillary, sir. He wants to see you right away. He says it's important."

"Hillary?" Weill's voice registered shock. Then, "Wait five minutes, Ruth, then send him in."

Weill turned to Belanger. "Today, Frank, is definitely not one of my good days. A dreamer's place is in his home with his thinker. And Hillary's our best dreamer so he especially should be at home. What do you suppose is wrong with him?"

Belanger, still brooding over Luster-Think and dream palaces, said shortly, "Call him in and find out."

"In one minute. Tell me, how was his last dream? I haven't tried the one that came in last week."

Belanger came down to earth. He wrinkled his nose. "Not so good."

"Why not?"

"It was ragged. Too jumpy. I don't mind sharp transitions for the liveliness, you know, but there's got to be some connection, even if only on a deep level."

"Is it a total loss?"

"No Hillary dream is a *total* loss. It took a lot of editing, though. We cut it down quite a bit and spliced in some odd pieces he'd sent us now and then. You know, detached scenes. It's still not Grade A, but it will pass."

"You told him about this, Frank?"

"Think I'm crazy, boss? Think I'm going to say a harsh word to a dreamer?"

And at that point the door opened and Weill's comely young secretary smiled Sherman Hillary into the office.

Sherman Hillary, at the age of thirty-one, could have been recognized as a dreamer by anyone. His eyes, unspectacled, had nevertheless the misty look of one who either needs glasses or who rarely focuses on anything mundane. He was of average height but underweight, with black hair that needed cutting, a narrow chin, a pale skin and a troubled look.

He muttered, "Hello, Mr. Weill," and half-nodded in hangdog fashion in the direction of Belanger.

Weill said heartily, "Sherman, my boy, you look fine. What's the matter? A dream is cooking only so-so at home? You're worried about it? . . . Sit down, sit down."

The dreamer did, sitting at the edge of the chair and holding his thighs stiffly together as though to be ready for instant obedience to a possible order to stand up once more.

He said, "I've come to tell you, Mr. Weill, I'm quitting."

"Quitting?"

"I don't want to dream any more, Mr. Weill."

Weill's old face looked older now than at any time in the day. "Why, Sherman?"

The dreamer's lips twisted. He blurted out, "Because I'm not *living*, Mr. Weill. Everything passes me by. It wasn't so bad at first. It was even relaxing. I'd dream evenings, weekends when I felt like it, or any other time. And when I felt like I wouldn't. But now, Mr. Weill, I'm an old pro. You tell me I'm one of the best in the business and the industry looks to me to think up new subtleties and new changes on the old reliables, like the flying reveries, and the worm-turning skits."

Weill said, "And is anyone better than you, Sherman? Your little sequence on leading an orchestra is selling steadily after ten years."

"All right, Mr. Weill. I've done my part. It's gotten so I don't go out any more. I neglect my wife. My little girl doesn't know me. Last week, we went to a dinner party—Sarah made me—and I don't remember a bit of it. Sarah says I was sitting on the couch all evening just staring at nothing and humming. She said everyone kept looking at me. She cried all night. I'm tired of things like that, Mr. Weill. I want to be a normal person and live in this world. I promised her I'd quit and I will, so it's good-bye, Mr. Weill." Hillary stood up and held out his hand awkwardly.

Weill waved it gently away. "If you want to quit, Sherman, it's all right. But do an old man a favour and let me explain something to you."

"I'm not going to change my mind," said Hillary.

"I'm not going to try to make you. I just want to explain something. I'm an old man and even before you were born I was in this business so I like to talk about it. Humor me, Sherman? Please?"

Hillary sat down. His teeth clamped down on his lower lip and he stared sullenly at his fingernails.

Weill said, "Do you know what a dreamer is, Sherman? Do you know what he means to ordinary people? Do you know what it is to be like me, like Frank Belanger, like your wife, Sarah? To have crippled minds that can't imagine, that can't build up thoughts? People like myself, ordinary people, would like to escape just once in a while this life of ours. We can't. We need help.

"In olden times it was books, plays, radio, movies, television. They gave us make-believe, but that wasn't important. What was important was that for a little while our own imaginations were stimulated. We could think of handsome lovers and beautiful princesses. We could be beautiful, witty, strong, capable, everything we weren't.

"But, always, the passing of the dream from dreamer to absorber was not perfect. It had to be translated into words in one way or another. The best dreamer in the world might not be able to get any of it into words. And the best writer in the world could put only the smallest part of his dreams into words. You understand ?

"But now, with dream recording, any man can dream. You, Sherman, and a handful of men like you, supply those dreams directly and exactly. It's straight from your head into ours, full strength. You dream for a hundred million people every time you dream. You dream a hundred million dreams at once. This is a great thing, my boy. You give all those people a glimpse of something they could not have by themselves."

Hillary mumbled, "I've done my share." He rose desperately to his feet. "I'm through. I don't care what you say. And if you want to sue me for breaking our contract, go ahead and sue. I don't care."

Weill stood up, too. "Would I sue you ? . . . Ruth," he spoke into the intercom, "bring in our copy of Mr. Hillary's contract."

He waited. So did Hillary and so did Belanger. Weill smiled faintly and his yellowed fingers drummed softly on his desk.

His secretary brought in the contract. Weill took it, showed its face to Hillary and said, "Sherman, my boy, unless you want to be with me, it's not right you should stay."

Then, before Belanger could make more than the beginning of a horrified gesture to stop him, he tore the contract into four pieces and tossed them down the waste chute. "That's all."

Hillary's hand shot out to seize Weill's. "Thanks, Mr. Weill," he said earnestly, his voice husky. "You've always treated me very well, and I'm grateful. I'm sorry it had to be like this."

"It's all right, my boy. It's all right."

Half in tears, still muttering thanks, Sherman Hillary left.

"For the love of Pete, boss, why did you let him go ?" demanded Belanger distractedly. "Don't you see the game ? He'll be going straight to Luster-Think. They've bought him off."

Weill raised his hand. "You're wrong. You're quite wrong. I know the boy and this would not be his style. Besides," he added dryly, "Ruth is a good secretary and she knows what to bring me when I ask for a dreamer's contract. What I had was a fake. The real contract is still in the safe, believe me.

"Meanwhile, a fine day I've had. I had to argue with a father to give me a chance at new talent, with a government man to avoid censorship, with you to keep from adopting fatal policies and now with my best dreamer to keep him from leaving. The father I probably won out over. The government man and you,

I don't know. Maybe yes, maybe no. But now Sherman Hillary, at least, there is no question. The dreamer will be back."

"How do you know?"

Weill smiled at Belanger and crinkled his cheeks into a network of fine lines. "Frank, my boy, you know how to edit dreamies so you think you know all the tools and machines in the trade. But let me tell you something. The most important tool in the dreamie business is the dreamer himself. He is the one you have to understand most of all, and I understand them.

"Listen. When I was a youngster—there were no dreamies then—I knew a fellow who wrote television scripts. He would complain to me bitterly that when someone met him for the first time and found out who he was, they would say: Where do you get those crazy ideas?

"They honestly didn't know. To them it was an impossibility to even think of one of them. So what could my friend say? He used to talk to me about it and tell me: Could I say, I don't know? When I go to bed, I can't sleep for ideas dancing in my head. When I shave, I cut myself; when I talk, I lose track of what I'm saying; when I drive, I take my life in my hands. And always because ideas, situations, dialogues are spinning and twisting in my mind. I can't tell you where I get my ideas. Can you tell me, maybe, your trick of *not* getting ideas, so I, too, can have a little peace.

"You see, Frank, how it is. *You* can stop work here anytime. So can I. This is our job, not our life. But not Sherman Hillary. Wherever he goes, whatever he does, he'll dream. While he lives, he must think; while he thinks, he must dream. We don't hold him prisoner, our contract isn't an iron wall for him. His own skull is his prisoner, Frank. So he'll be back. What can he do?"

Belanger shrugged. "If what you say is right, I'm sort of sorry for the guy."

Weill nodded sadly. "I'm sorry for all of them. Through the years, I've found out one thing. It's their business; making people happy. *Other* people."

THE END